# Winter 2018 / 19

## SAM WANAMAKER PLAYHOUSE THEATRE SEASON

### Macbeth
William Shakespeare

### Doctor Faustus
Christopher Marlowe

### Ralegh: The Treason Trial
Dramatised by Oliver Chris

### Dark Night of the Soul:
The feminine response to the Faustian myth
Writers: Lily Bevan, Lisa Hammond and Rachael Spence,
Katie Hims, Athena Stevens and Amanda Wilkin
Director: Jude Christian

### Edward II
Christopher Marlowe

### Richard II
William Shakespeare

### After Edward
Tom Stuart

**SHAKESPEARE'S GLOBE**

# GRANTA

12 Addison Avenue, London W11 4QR | email: editorial@granta.com
To subscribe go to granta.com, or call 020 8955 7011 (free phone 0500 004 033)
in the United Kingdom, 845-267-3031 (toll-free 866-438-6150) in the United States

## ISSUE 145: AUTUMN 2018

| | |
|---|---|
| PUBLISHER AND EDITOR | Sigrid Rausing |
| DEPUTY EDITOR | Rosalind Porter |
| POETRY EDITOR | Rachael Allen |
| DIGITAL DIRECTOR | Luke Neima |
| ASSISTANT EDITOR | Francisco Vilhena |
| SENIOR DESIGNER | Daniela Silva |
| EDITORIAL ASSISTANTS | Eleanor Chandler, Josie Mitchell |
| SUBSCRIPTIONS | David Robinson |
| MARKETING MANAGER | Simon Heafield |
| PUBLICITY | Pru Rowlandson |
| TO ADVERTISE CONTACT | Charlotte Burgess, charlotteburgess@granta.com |
| FINANCE | Mercedes Forest, Josephine Perez |
| SALES MANAGER | Katie Hayward |
| IT MANAGER | Mark Williams |
| PRODUCTION ASSOCIATE | Sarah Wasley |
| PROOFS | Katherine Fry, Jessica Kelly, Lesley Levene, Jess Porte |
| CONTRIBUTING EDITORS | Daniel Alarcón, Anne Carson, Mohsin Hamid, Isabel Hilton, Michael Hofmann, A.M. Homes, Janet Malcolm, Adam Nicolson, Edmund White |

# SPEND THE NIGHT WITH A GOOD BOOK

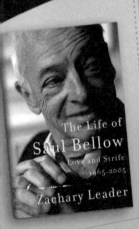

The Life of Saul Bellow
Love and Strife
1965–2005
Zachary Leader

HARUKI MURAKAMI
KILLING COMMENDATORE
A novel

WILLIAM BOYD
LOVE IS BLIND
A NOVEL

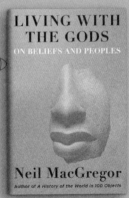

Nothing Is Lost
Selected Essays of
INGRID SISCHY
Foreword by LAURIE ANDERSON

LIVING WITH THE GODS
ON BELIEFS AND PEOPLES
Neil MacGregor
Author of A History of the World in 100 Objects

THE WILLIAM H. GASS READER

Christina Rossetti: Vision & Verse

Exhibition on 13 November to 17 March

wattsgallery.org.uk | Guildford, Surrey GU3 1DQ

WATTS
GALLERY
ARTISTS
VILLAGE

**National Art Pass**___

Harry Ingrams
Individual

Please show your card for free admission and reduced price entry to participating museums and galleries

___can
join the dots

See more art for less.
Search National Art Pass.

_with Art Fund

Art Fund is the operating name of National Art Collections Fund, a charity registered in England and Wales 209174 and Scotland SWC038331. National Art Pass is issued to Art Fund members. Subscriptions start from £67.

# HARVARD REVIEW

Fiction · Essays · Poems · Book Reviews · Art
New Translations · Conversations with Writers

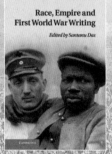
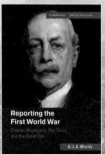

# CONTENTS

# Introduction

This issue of *Granta* is about time and about ghosts – the ghosts of our past selves, the shadows of past injuries, the ghosts of history, the ghosts in the machine.

We begin with André Aciman, who recalls a moment of desire on a crowded bus in Rome which, for all its brevity and possible lack of intention or even consciousness, was to shape an important part of his imaginary life.

We also have Amos Oz in conversation with Shira Hadad, his Israeli editor. He describes the confinement of the kibbutz that he joined aged sixteen. There were long negotiations with the kibbutz authorities about the ethics of allocating some of his hours of work duties to writing rather than to the collective labour of kibbutz life – picking fruit and milking the cows and so on. What right did Oz have to pursue creativity and individualism? What duty did he owe to the collective?

Bernard Cooper writes about sleep eating for this issue, a rare side-effect of Ambien. At a time when his partner was enduring the toxicity of an early Aids treatment, Cooper, in a twilight state of waking unconsciousness, stuffed himself with food. This is a delicate and measured piece – hunger is a known side effect of the sleeping pill, and yet Cooper's desperate hunger also reads like hunger for life, a reaction to the tragic decline of his lover and partner.

Anne Carson's short story, 'Ardor (Aghast)', sets the themes that dominate so much of contemporary discourse – sexual transgression and public scrutiny and interrogation – in the context of an academic conference in Switzerland. There has been a previous erotic encounter between a teenage boy and a female academic. The boy had become associated with other dangerous acts, probably terror-related. 'You found his murderous puberty attractive,' the interrogator says. 'Do you rekindle now a former ardor?' 'Ardor' is a word, the academic protests, that she would never use, like, she adds, the word 'aghast'. Carson's text, tersely poetic and controlled, gives little away, but something, we sense, has been lost in translation between cultures and between eras. Clean trains figure, and good muesli in bowls, but perhaps passion has been lost, captured in those very words, no longer in use? 'On leaving you will close both doors', the story ends. 'Thank you.'

We are also publishing an excerpt of Vasily Grossman's forthcoming *Stalingrad*, a newly translated novel, in this issue. It's not quite a prequel to *Life and Fate*, but rather a companion piece, returning to the same characters – and some new ones – fighting the same war and displaying the same ambiguity or ardour (that word again) about the Soviet system.

Grossman, whose mother was murdered by the Nazis, reaches a chilling understanding of the Nazi mind in this extract, conveying how easy it must have been to fall into the ready-made ideology of Nazism, to wage war and genocide, to loot and murder, and yet still be concerned with matters of ordinary life. Hannah Arendt's phrase, the banality of evil, has become controversial, but here it is: ordinary Germans lending themselves to the malevolent machinery of Nazi Germany.

Finally, we are publishing three short chapters from Turkish writer Ahmet Altan's prison diary. Altan was imprisoned in the wake of the crackdown following the attempted Turkish coup in 2016. He was charged with disseminating coded messages to Gülen supporters in a TV show – an accusation manifestly absurd, but of course he is not alone. Turkey's democracy turns out to have been more fragile than we imagined in the heady days of EU accession talks. Thousands of people are now in prison, charged with fantastical conspiracies. The EU accession track requires that countries build the institutions and incorporate the rights of democracy, including free and fair elections, an independent judiciary, a free press, religious freedom and respect for minority rights. At a time when Europe is struggling to defend democracy within its own borders, those talks and requirements feel almost forgotten. ∎

Sigrid Rausing

*Apollo Sauroktonos*, Roman copy in marble of the statue by Praxiteles (active 375–326 BC)

# IN FREUD'S SHADOW

## *André Aciman*

Freud would understand. I long for Rome, but there is always something unsettling, perhaps disturbingly unreal about Rome. Very few of my memories of Rome are happy ones, and some of the things I wanted most from Rome, Rome just never gave me. These continue to hover over the city like the ghost of unfledged desires that forgot to die and stayed alive without me, despite me. Each Rome I've known seems to drift or burrow into the next, but none goes away. There's the Rome I saw the first time, fifty years ago, the Rome I abandoned, the Rome I came looking for years later and couldn't find, because Rome hadn't waited for me and I'd lost my chance. The Rome I visited with one person, then revisited with another and couldn't begin to weigh the difference, the Rome still unvisited after so many years, the Rome I'm never quite done with, because, for all its imposing, ancient masonries, so much of it lies buried and out of sight, elusive, transient and still unfinished, read: unbuilt. Rome the eternal landfill with never a rock bottom. Rome my collection of layers and tiers. The Rome I stare at once I open my hotel window and can't believe is real. The Rome that never stops summoning me, then throws me back to wherever I've come from. *I am all yours*, it says, *but I'll never be yours.* The Rome I forgo when it becomes too real, the Rome I let go of before it lets go of me. The Rome that has more of me in it than there is of Rome itself, because it isn't really Rome I come looking for each time, but me, just me, though I can't do this unless I seek out Rome as well. The Rome I'll take others to see, provided it's mine we'll visit, not theirs. The Rome I don't want to believe could go on without me. Rome, the birthplace of a self I wished to be one day and should have been but never was and left behind and didn't do a thing to nurse back to life again. The Rome I reach out for yet seldom touch, because I don't know and may never learn how to reach out and touch.

Not a speck of me is Roman any longer, and yet once I've emptied my suitcase in Rome I know that things are in their right place, that I have a center here, and that Rome is home. I have yet to discover them but there are, so I'm told, about seven to nine ways to leave my apartment and head down the hill of the Gianicolo to Trastevere, but I am reluctant to learn shortcuts yet; I like the slight confusion that delays familiarity and lets me think I'm in a new place and that so many new things are open and possible. Perhaps what makes me happy these days is that I have no obligations, can afford to do whatever I please with my time, love spending my evenings sitting at Il Goccetto, where witty and smart Romans come to while away the hours before heading home for dinner. Some even change their minds while they're drinking, as happened to me a few times, and end up having dinner right then and there. I like this Roman way of improvising dinner when all I'd planned for was a glass of wine. After wine sometimes I'll buy a bottle and head back to Trastevere to visit friends. On certain evenings, when I wish to go home, I avoid the bus and go up the hill on foot.

On my way across the Tiber at night I love to see the illuminated Castel Sant'Angelo with its pale ocher ramparts glowing in the dark, just as I love to see St Peter's at night. I know that at some point I will reach the Fontanone and stop to stare at the city and at all of its glorious floodlit domes, which I know I will miss soon enough.

I love where I am staying. I have a balcony that overlooks the city. And when I'm lucky, a few friends will drop by and we'll drink while gazing out at the city by night like characters in a Fellini or Sorrentino film, wondering in silence perhaps what each of us still lacks in life or would want changed, or what keeps beckoning from across the other bank, though the one thing we wouldn't change is being here. To paraphrase Winckelmann, life owed me this. I've been owed this moment, this balcony, these friends, these drinks, this city for so long.

This could actually be my home. Home, says a writer I've read recently, is where you first put words to the world. Maybe. We all have ways of placing markers on our lives. The markers move sometimes; but some are anchored and stay forever. In my case, it's not words, it's where I touched another body, longed for another body, went home to my parents and, for the remainder of the evening and the rest of my life, would never banish that other body.

It was a Wednesday evening, and I was just coming back from a long walk after school. I used to like wandering about the center of the city late afternoons, arriving home just in time to do my homework. Before taking the bus, I would frequently stop at a large remainders bookstore on Piazza di San Silvestro and, after riffling through a few books, seek out the book I had come for: a thick volume by Richard von Krafft-Ebing, *Psychopathia Sexualis*. There were several large, hardbound volumes on sale in that bookstore, and by now I knew the ritual. I would pick one up, sit at a table and sink into a prewar universe that was beyond anything I could ever imagine. The book was intended for medical professionals and was, as I discovered years later, intentionally obscure, with segments rendered in Latin to discourage lay readers, to say nothing of curious adolescents eager to navigate the uncharted, troubling ocean called sex. And yet as I pored over its arcane and detailed case studies on what was called inversion and sexual deviancy, I was transfixed by its wildly pornographic scenarios that turned out to be unbearably stirring precisely because they seemed so matter-of-fact, so ordinary, so unabashedly cleansed of moral stricture. The individuals concerned could not have seemed more proper, more urbane, more serenely well behaved: the young man who loved to see his girlfriend and her sister spit in his glass of water before drinking it all up; the man who loved to watch his neighbor undress at night, knowing that the latter knew he was being watched; the timid girl who loved her father in ways she knew were wrong; the young man who stayed longer than he should in the public baths – I was each of them. Like someone who reads all twelve horoscopes in the back of a magazine, I identified with every sign of the zodiac.

After reading Krafft-Ebing's case studies, I would eventually have to take the 85 bus for the long ride home, knowing that my mother would have dinner ready by the time I was back. Lightheaded after so many case studies, I knew I'd eventually suffer from a migraine and that the incipient migraine, coupled with the long bus ride, might trigger nausea. At the station before boarding the bus there was a newspaper and magazine kiosk that also sold postcards. I'd stare at the statues, male and female, longingly, then buy one, adding some postcards of Roman vistas to conceal my purpose. The first card I bought was the *Apollo Sauroktonos*. I still have it today.

One afternoon, after leaving the bookstore, I spotted a large crowd waiting for the 85 bus. It was cold and it had been raining, so once the bus arrived we all massed into it as fast as we could, hurtling and jamming into one another, which is what one did in those days. I too pushed my way in, not realizing that the young man right behind me was being pushed forward by those behind him. His body was pressed to mine, and though every part of him was glued to me and I was completely trapped by those around us, I was almost sure that he was pushing into me so overtly and yet so seemingly unintentionally that when I felt him grab both of my upper arms with his hands, I did not struggle or move away but allowed my whole body to yield and sink into his. He could do with me whatever he wanted, and to make it easier for him, I leaned back into him, thinking at some point that perhaps all this was in my head, not his, and that mine was the guilty, unchaste soul, not his. There was nothing either of us could do. He didn't seem to mind, and perhaps he sensed that I didn't mind either, or perhaps he didn't pay it any heed, the way I too wasn't quite sure I did. What could be more natural in a crowded bus on a rainy evening in Italy? His way of holding my upper arms from behind me was a friendly gesture, the way a mountain climber might help another steady himself before moving further up. With nothing to hold on to, he had grabbed my arms. Nothing to it.

I had never known anything like this in my life.

Eventually, steadying himself a bit, he let go of me. But as the doors of the bus closed and the bus started to sway, he immediately grabbed on to me again, holding me by the waist, pushing even harder, though nobody around us could tell, and part of me was sure that he himself still couldn't tell. All I knew is that he would let go of me once he'd steadied himself and held on to one of the hand bars. I could even tell he was struggling to let go of me, which is why I pretended to stagger away from him only to lean back, as soon as the bus stopped, to prevent him from moving.

Part of me was ashamed that I'd allowed myself to do to him what I'd heard so many men did to women in crowded spaces, while another part suspected that he knew what we were both doing; but I didn't know for sure. Besides, if I couldn't really fault him, how could he fault me? But I was swooning and doing everything I could not to let him pass. Eventually he managed to slip between me and another passenger, which is when I got a good look at him. He was wearing a gray sweater and a brown pair of corduroys and looked at least seven or eight years older than I was. He was also taller, skinny and sinewy. He finally found a seat in front of me and, though I kept my eyes on him hoping he would turn to look back, he never did. In his mind, nothing had happened: crowded bus, people slithering their way between people, everyone almost lurching and holding on to someone else – it happens all the time. I saw him get off before the bridge somewhere on Via Taranto. A sudden sickness began to seize me. The headache I had feared before stepping into the bus, stirred by the gas fumes, turned to nausea. I needed to get off earlier than I meant to and walked the rest of the way home.

I didn't throw up that evening, but when I got home I knew that something genuine and undeniable had happened and that I would never live it down. All I wanted was for him to hold me, to keep his hands on me, to ask nothing and say nothing, or, if he needed to ask, to ask anything, provided I didn't have to talk, because I was too choked up to talk, because if I had to talk I might have said something right out of the cloying, bookish, *fin de siècle* universe of Krafft-Ebing, which would have made him laugh. What I wanted was for him to put an arm around me in that man-to-man way that friends do in Rome.

I returned to Piazza di San Silvestro many times afterward, always on Wednesdays, read from Krafft-Ebing for a while, stared at the statue of Apollo on display in the magazine kiosk, made sure I wore the same clothes I'd worn on the day I'd felt him lean into me, boarded the bus at the same hour. I saw one crowded bus come after the other and I know I waited and kept watching for him. But I never saw him again. Or if I did I didn't recognize him.

Time had stopped that day.

Now, whenever I come to Rome, I promise to take the 85 bus at more or less the same time in the evening to try to turn the clock back to relive that evening and see who I was and what I craved in those days. I want to run into the same disappointments, the same fears, the same hopes, come to the same admission, then spin that admission on its head and see how I'd managed in those days to make myself think that what I'd wanted on that bus was nothing more than illusion and make-believe, not real, not real.

When I reached home that evening feeling sick and with a migraine, my mother was preparing dinner with our neighbor Gina in the kitchen. Gina was my age and everyone said she had a crush on me. I did not have a crush on her. Yet, as we sat together at the kitchen table while mother cooked, we laughed and I could feel my nausea ebb. Gina smelled of incense and chamomile, of ancient wooden drawers and unwashed hair, which she said she washed on Saturdays only. I did not like her smell. But, as soon as I let my mind drift back to what had happened on the 85 bus, I knew that I wouldn't have cared what he smelled of. The thought that he too might smell of incense and chamomile and of old wooden furniture turned me on. I pictured his bedroom and his clothes strewn about the room. I was thinking of him when I went to bed that night but, as I let arousal wash over me, at the right moment, I made myself think of Gina instead, picturing how she'd first unbutton her shirt and let everything she wore slide to the floor and then walk up to me naked, smelling, like him, of incense, chamomile and wooden drawers.

Night after night I would drift from him to her, back to him and then her, each image feeding off the other. And like Roman buildings of all ages snuggling into, on top of, under and against each other, body parts stripped from his body were given over to her, and parts stripped from hers were given to him. I was like Emperor Julian, the two-time apostate who buried one faith under the other and no longer knew which was truly his. And I thought of Tiresias who was first a man, then a woman, then a man again, and of Caenis who was a woman, then a man and finally a woman again, and of the postcard of Apollo, the killer of lizards, and longed for him as well, though his unyielding and forbidding grace seemed to chide my lust, as though he had read my thoughts and knew that, if part of me wished to sully his marble-white body with what was most precious in me, another still couldn't tell whether what it longed for on Apollo's frame was the man or the woman or something both real and unreal that hovered between the two, a cross between marble and what could only be flesh.

The room upstairs where I fudged the truth each night, and dissembled it so well that, without turning into a lie, it stopped being true, was a shifting land where nothing seemed fixed, and where the surest and truest thing about me could, within seconds, lose one face and take on another, and another after that. Even the self who belonged to a Rome that seemed destined to be mine forever knew that, within moments of crossing over to a different continent, I would acquire a new identity, a new voice, a new inflection, a new way of being me. As for the girl whom I eventually drew to my bedroom one

Friday afternoon when we were alone together and found pleasure without love, if she lifted the cloud that was hovering over me ever since the 85 bus, she could not stop it from settling back less than a half-hour later.

I have frequently thought about Rome and about the long walks I used to take after school in the center of Rome on those rainy October and November afternoons in search of something I knew I longed for but wasn't too eager to find, much less give a name to. I would much rather have had it jump at me and give me a chance to say maybe, or hold me without letting go, as someone did on the bus that day, or coax me with smiles and good cheer the way men flirt when they put up a coy front with girls they know will eventually say yes.

In Rome, my itinerary on those afternoon walks was always different and the goal undefined, but wherever my legs took me, I always seemed to miss running into something essential about the city and about myself – unless what I was really doing on my walks was running away both from myself and the city. But I wasn't running away. And I wasn't seeking either. I wanted something gray, like the safe zone between the hand I only wished might touch me somewhere without asking and my hand that didn't dare stray where it longed to go.

On the bus that evening, I knew I was already trying to put together a flurry of words to understand what was happening to me. I had once heard a woman turn around and curse a man in a crowded bus for being *sfacciato*, meaning impudent, because in a typical street-urchin manner he had rubbed his body against hers. But now I didn't know which of us had been truly *sfacciato*. I loved blaming him to absolve myself, but I also reveled in my newfound courage and was thrilled by the way I'd struggled to block his passage each time he seemed about to release me to move elsewhere on the bus. I had followed my own impulse and didn't even pretend I was unaware we were touching. I even liked the arrogance with which he had taken me for granted.

All I had at home was my picture of the *Sauroktonos*. Chaste and chastening, the ultimate androgyne, obscene because he lets you cradle the filthiest thoughts but won't approve or consent to them and makes you feel dirty for even nursing them. The picture was the next best thing to the young man in the bus. I treasured it and used it as a bookmark.

In the end, I went to find the original in the Vatican Museums. But it wasn't what I'd expected. I expected a naked young man just posing as a statue; what I saw was a trapped body. I looked for flaws on his body to be done with him once and for all, but the flaw and the stains I found were the marble's, not his. In the end I couldn't take my eyes off him. I stared not only because I liked what I was staring at but because such stunning beauty makes you want to know why you keep staring.

Sometimes I'd catch something so tender and gentle on the features of the young Apollo that it verged on melancholy. Not a spot of vice or lust or of anything remotely illicit on his youthful body; the vice and lust were in me, or perhaps it was just the start of a kind of lust that I couldn't begin to fathom because it was instantly diffused by how humbled I felt each time I stared at him. *He does not approve of me, yet he smiles.* We were like two strangers in a Russian novel who, before being introduced, have already exchanged meaningful glances.

But then, I remembered, the candor would gradually dissipate from his features, and something like an incipient look of distrust, fear and admonition would settle, as though what he expected from me was remorse and shame. But it's never so simple: admonition became forgiveness, and from clemency I could almost behold a look of compassion, meaning, 'I know this isn't easy for you.' And from compassion, I was able to spot a touch of languor behind his mischievous smile, almost a willingness to surrender, which scared me, because it asked me to confront the obvious. *He's been willing all along and I wasn't seeing it.* Suddenly I was allowed to hope. I didn't want to hope.

Today, after being in Rome for a month almost, I am taking the 85 bus. I will not catch it somewhere along its long route, which might be easier for me, but I will take it where the terminal used to be fifty years ago. I will get on the bus at dusk, because this is when I used to take the 85 bus, and I will ride it all the way to my old stop, get off and walk down to where we used to live. This is my plan for the evening.

I expect that my return may not bring me much pleasure. I never liked our old neighborhood with its row of small stores that peddled overpriced merchandise to people who are almost all pensioners now, or young salesclerks who live with their parents, smoke too much and cradle large hopes on meager incomes. I remember hating the square balconies jutting out like misbegotten shoeboxes from ugly squat buildings. I'll walk down that street and ask why I always want to come back, since I know there's nothing I want here. Am I returning to prove that I've overcome this place and put it behind me? Or do I return to play with time and make-believe that nothing essential has really changed, either in me or in the city, that I am still the same young man and that an entire lifetime has yet to be lived, which also means that the years between me-then and me-now haven't really happened, or don't really matter and shouldn't count, and that, like Winckelmann, I am still owed so much?

Or perhaps I'll come back to reclaim a me-interrupted. Something was sown here, and then, because I left so soon, it never blossomed but couldn't die. Everything I've done in life suddenly pales and threatens to come undone. I have not lived my life. I've lived another.

And yet, as I walk around my old neighborhood, what I fear most is to feel nothing, touch nothing and come to grips with nothing. I'd take pain instead of nothing. I'd take sorrow and think of my mother still alive upstairs in our old building rather than just walk by, probably with some degree of haste, eager to catch the first taxi back to the center of Rome.

I get off the bus at my old stop. I walk down the familiar street and try to recall the evening when I came so close to throwing up. It must have been in the fall – same weather as today. I walk down the same street again, see my old window, pass by the old grocery store, imagine my mother miraculously still upstairs preparing dinner, though I see her now as she was most recently, old and frail, and finally, because I want to arrive at this thought last, I pass by the refurbished film theater where someone came to sit next to me once and placed a hand on my thigh while I took my time before acting shocked when all I wanted was to feel his hand glide ever so softly up my leg. 'What?' I had asked. Without wasting a second, he got up and disappeared. *What?* as if I didn't know. *What?* to say tell me more because I need to know. *What?* to mean, don't say a thing, pay no mind, don't even listen, don't stop.

The incident never went anywhere. It stayed in that movie house. It's in there now as I'm walking past it. That hand on my thigh and the young man on the 85 bus told me there was something about the real Rome that transcended my old, safe, standby collection of postcards of Greek gods and of the teasing boy-girl Apollo who'd let you stare at him for however long you pleased provided it was with shame and apprehension in your heart, because you had infringed every curve on his body. I used to think at the time that, however disturbing the impact of a real body was against mine, the weeks and months ahead might cast a balm and quell the wave that had swept over me in the bus. I thought I would eventually forget, or learn to think I'd forgotten, the hand I let linger on my bare skin for a few seconds more than others my age might allow. Within a few days, a few weeks, I was sure the whole thing would blow over or shrink like a tiny fruit that falls to the ground in the kitchen and rolls under a cabinet and is discovered many years later when someone decides to redo the floors. You look at its shriveled, dried shape and all you can say is, 'To think that I could have eaten this once.' If I didn't manage to forget, then perhaps experience might turn the whole incident into the insignificant thing it was, especially since life would eventually unload so many more gifts, better gifts that would easily overshadow these fragments of near-nothings on a crowded Roman bus or in an ugly neighborhood theater in Rome.

We remember best what never happened.

I've gone back to the Vatican Museums to see my Apollo who is about to kill a lizard. I need special permission to see the wing where he stands. The public is not allowed to see him. I always pay homage to the Laocoön, and to *Apollo Belvedere*, and to the other statues in the Pio Clementino, but it was always the *Apollo Sauroktonos* whom I longed for and whom I'd put off seeking. The best for last. It's the one statue I want to revisit each time I'm in Rome. I don't have to say a word. He knows, by now he surely must know, always knew, even back then when he'd see me come by after school, knowing what I'd done with him.

'Have you ever tired of me?' he asks.

'No, never.'

'Is it because I'm made of stone and cannot change?'

'Maybe. But I too haven't changed, not one bit.'

How he wished he could be flesh, just this once, he used to say when I was young.

'It's been so long,' he says.

'I know.'

'And you've grown old now,' he says.

'I know.' I want to change the subject. 'Are there others who've loved you as much?'

'There'll always be others.'

'Then what singles me out?' He looks at me and smiles.

'Nothing, nothing singles you out. You feel what every man feels.'

'Will you remember me, though?'

'I remember everyone.'

'But do you feel anything?' I ask.

'Of course I feel, I always feel. How could I not feel?'

'For me, I mean.'

'Of course for you.'

I do not trust him. This is the last time I see him. I still want him to say something to me, for me, about me.

I'm about to walk out of the museum when my mind suddenly

thinks of Freud, who surely must have come to the Pio Clementino with his wife or his daughter or with his good friend from Vienna then based in Rome, the curator Emanuel Löwy. Surely the two Jews must have stood there a while and spoken about the statue – how could they not? And yet Freud never mentions the *Sauroktonos*, which he must have seen both in Rome and in the Louvre during his student days. Surely he must have thought about it when writing about lizards in his commentary to Jensen's *Gradiva*. Nor does he mention Winckelmann except once, Winckelmann who, himself, surely must have seen the original bronze version of the statue every day during his tenure in Cardinal Albani's home. I know that Freud's silence on the matter is not an accident, that his silence means something peculiarly Freudian, just as I know he must have thought what I myself thought, what everyone seeing the *Sauroktonos* thinks: 'Is this a man who looks like a woman, or a woman who looks like a man, or a man who looks like a woman who looks like a man . . .' So I ask the statue, 'Do you remember a bearded Viennese doctor who'd sometimes come alone and pretend he wasn't staring?'

'A bearded Viennese doctor? Maybe.'

Apollo is being cagey again, but then so am I.

But I remember his final words. They were spoken to me once, and he repeated the exact same ones fifty years later: 'I am between life and death, between flesh and stone. I am not alive, but look at me, I'm more alive than you are. You, on the other hand, are not dead, but were you ever alive? Have you sailed to the other bank?' I have no words to argue or reply with. 'You found beauty but not truth. You must change your life.' ∎

Amos Oz and Shira Hadad in conversation at Amos's home, Tel Aviv, 2018
Courtesy of Amir Hadad

# A ROOM OF ONE'S OWN

## *Amos Oz in conversation with Shira Hadad*

TRANSLATED FROM THE HEBREW BY SONDRA SILVERSTON

**SHIRA HADAD:** I want to ask you about your family name, which you changed from Klausner to Oz when you left your father's house to go to a kibbutz at the age of fourteen and a half. You write about that only very briefly in *A Tale of Love and Darkness*. How did you choose Oz, a name that means courage or strength?

**AMOS OZ:** I don't remember exactly, but maybe when I felt I was going to leave home to go to a kibbutz, courage and strength were what I lacked the most. It was like jumping off a diving board at night without knowing whether there's water in the pool. So that name, Oz, was a bit of wishful thinking. Besides, maybe – and I'm not quite sure about what I'm about to tell you, because really, it's been more than sixty years – maybe because there was a slight similarity between the middle letters of Klausner and the word *oz*. Maybe, but I'm not sure. It's the name a fourteen-year-old boy chose, like whistling in the dark. Today, I would never choose such a resounding name for myself.

**HADAD:** What name would you choose today?

**OZ:** A much quieter one, even a bit more common: Oren. Gal. Evin.

HADAD: Amos Oren. Amos Gal. Maybe you would be a different man and a different writer if that was your name. Was it clear to you that you were going to change your name?

OZ: Yes, absolutely. When I decided to cut all ties and leave home, I didn't want to belong to them. Not to the famous, esteemed professor and not to the one who craved to be a professor. I didn't want to belong to them. The only person I felt bad about was my grandfather Alexander: I didn't want to cause him pain.

HADAD: In 1970, you wrote, 'I abandoned the Klausner name only because I thought that a young man who is beginning to write well, to walk on his own feet, should not be borne into literature on broad shoulders.' Meaning that you connected the name change to writing, to the need to make a place for yourself as a young writer. And today your explanation is a little different, maybe deeper. Do you remember how your father and your great-uncle reacted?

OZ: My father took it very badly. He suffered a great deal. He said, 'Amos Klausner, that's not a name you just throw away. You're an only son.' At the time, I was an only son. My cousin Daniel was murdered by the Nazis, my great-uncle Josef had no children and my uncle Bezalel had already changed his name to Elizedek, so who was left? 'Only you,' he told me. It wasn't easy. Not for me either. It hurt me, what he said: that no one was left to bear the name Klausner. Later, my father remarried and my sister Marganita and my brother David were born, but I changed my name even before that.

HADAD: Were you ever sorry for that?

OZ: No. But I think that while I was writing *A Tale of Love and Darkness*, I made up for it because anyone can find out what came before Oz. Half made up for it. But no, I never regretted it. When I went to the kibbutz, I said that was my name, and two days after my sixteenth birthday, I went to the Interior Ministry office in Ramla and changed it on my identity card, because according to the law, you can't legally change your name until you're sixteen.

HADAD: But on the kibbutz, they called you Oz even before you did that.

OZ: Yes.

HADAD: You just told them that was your name?

OZ: Yes. I think even the kibbutz didn't know. Except for the school principal, Ozer Huldai, who had the documents. I asked him not to tell the other boys, and they didn't know my real name. But somehow, I have no idea how, they found out that I was from a right-wing Revisionist family, and Revisionism was the ideological enemy of the labor Zionists who founded the kibbutz movement. So some of them suspected I was a kind of fifth column, maybe I'd come to spy. It really wasn't fair, because I was the most left-wing person in Kibbutz Hulda. I can tell you another secret: in Hulda, at elections, the entire kibbutz always voted for the center-left Mapai Party, and they were very proud that Mapai received one hundred percent of the votes. In the evening, right after the votes had been counted, they would post a note on the bulletin board: 'This time too, Mapai received one hundred percent of our votes.' That's how it was until the 1960 elections, when there was a huge scandal in Hulda. As the votes were being counted, they suddenly found one vote for the left-wing party, Mapam. The entire kibbutz moved heaven and Earth to find out who the traitor was. But they never did. They suspected Elyosha, suspected Honzo, but it was me. That was the first time I had the right to vote, and I simply betrayed them and voted for Mapam, and I didn't tell anyone. I was that kind of fifth column. Today they're gone, that older generation in Hulda. If they had known about it, they would have killed me. I never voted for Mapai in my life. Ever.

Shimon Peres and I were friends for almost forty years, but I never voted for him or his party. And he knew it.

HADAD: When you moved to the kibbutz as a teenager, you also decided to stop writing stories.

OZ: I started writing when I was a child. Even before I was taught how to write, I would make up stories and tell them, because that was the only thing I had to offer: I wasn't tall, or athletic, or a good student, and I didn't know how to dance or make people laugh. The only way I could impress girls was to tell them stories. I used to make up stories and tell them in installments. The children – even the girls – would gather to hear my stories because I put a lot of suspense, action and violence in them. And even sometimes, a bit of romance. So as a child in Jerusalem, I would stand in Pnina's kindergarten during recess and tell suspenseful stories in installments to the other children, boys and girls. Later, in the Tachkemoni religious elementary school, during every recess a circle of boys would gather around me, even those who, before or after the stories, used to hit me. Maybe because I expressed myself well and that annoyed them.

Later on, in Kibbutz Hulda, I started to write in the back room of the kibbutz culture hall. That distressed me very much because, after all, I had left my home in Jerusalem in order to cut all ties with the entire world of books and writing. When I left my father's house, I was done with writing. I didn't want to be a writer, didn't want to write stories, I wanted to be a tall, suntanned tractor driver. What I wanted most of all was to be very suntanned and very, very tall. So girls would finally pay attention to me too.

HADAD: And you failed at that. I don't mean at being suntanned or tall, but at not writing stories.

OZ: In the end, I did manage to get a bit tanned, but I failed miserably at being tall. And writing stories – that urge was stronger than I.

Stronger than the shame. I would walk over to the back room at night, the reading room in the culture hall at the far end of the kibbutz. The boys were out playing basketball or chasing girls, and since I had no chance at either, I sat there alone in that back room of the culture hall and wrote poems. I was fifteen or sixteen, and so ashamed. As ashamed as I was when I masturbated. What are you doing? What on Earth are you doing? What the hell are you doing? Are you crazy? Just a minute ago you promised yourself you were done with it, that you'd never do it again, so what's all this now? Again? When will you ever stop? But I couldn't stop. In fact, in that back room I stopped writing poems and began to try prose. Sherwood Anderson freed my writing hand, but I think I've already written about that in *A Tale of Love and Darkness*.

When I was in the army, I started publishing stories in the very prestigious literary magazine *Keshet*, edited by Aharon Amir. I think I sent him one story, which he rejected. Then I sent another one, and he wrote me a postcard with five words on it: 'Well done! It's being printed.'

One of my first stories published in *Keshet* was 'The Way the Wind Blows', a story about a paratrooper who lands on live electric wires. It was partially based on a disaster that happened in the fields of Kibbutz Hulda during a parachuting show on Independence Day. Maybe three or four years after that story was published, it was suddenly added to the Ministry of Education's required reading list for the literature matriculation exam. I took my matriculation exams while I was doing my compulsory army service. If I had done it a few years later, I most likely would have been tested on that story. And I probably would have failed.

I wrote a story, then another story, then another one. And I received two or three letters that were some help to me in overcoming my dread that maybe I wasn't any good at all. Although I didn't know her, the poet Dahlia Ravikovitch wrote one of her heartwarming Dahlia-esque letters that began with the words, 'I hear you're an extraordinarily young person.' I fell a little bit in love with her because of her poems and that letter, and that was even before I met her. But I remember cutting her picture out of the newspaper literary supplement and putting it between the pages of her book, *The Love of an Orange*. (In my mind, I always called Dahlia Ravikovitch 'golden apple', the original Hebrew term for orange.) But I never told her I was a little bit in love with her, and I never told her she was a golden apple.

More than fifty years ago, when my first book, *Where the Jackals Howl*, came out, I went to the kibbutz secretariat and asked for one day a week to write. A heated argument broke out, but not between good and bad people, or enlightened and ignorant people. Those who were against my request had two reasons: first, anyone can say he's an artist. And who will milk the cows? One will want to be a photographer, one a dancer, one a sculptor and one a movie maker. So who will milk the cows?

Besides, that kibbutz committee said, and justifiably so, that they weren't qualified to decide who's an artist and who isn't. 'If we give Amos time to write, we'll have to give time to everyone else who asks for it. After all, we have no way of ranking self-proclaimed artists.' That was a solid argument. I had no answer for it. I couldn't stand there like a gorilla pounding its chest and say, 'No, but I'm special. I'm not like anyone else.' There was an old man sitting there – when I say old, I mean forty, forty-five, because we all called the founders old, even they called themselves old. His name was David Ofer, and he said – I'll never forget it – 'Young Amos might be a new Tolstoy. But at the age of twenty-two, what does he know about life? Nothing. He knows nothing. Let him work in the fields with us for another twenty, twenty-five years, and then he can write *War and Peace* for us.' That was a weighty reason. To this day I'm not entirely convinced there wasn't something in what he said.

There were discussions, there were arguments, votes and appeals, and in the end, it reached the kibbutz general meeting, where I was granted one day a week, provided that on the other days I worked twice as hard. And so I was given one day a week to write and on the other days, I worked in the fields. Later on, I taught in the local high school, known on the kibbutz as 'advanced education'.

I used to go into the bathroom to write *My Michael*. At the time, we lived in a one-and-a-half-room apartment and the bathroom was the size of an airplane toilet. And I didn't sleep half the night. I would write in the bathroom and smoke until midnight, or one o'clock, for as long as I could hold out. I would sit on the toilet seat cover, a Van Gogh album we'd received as a wedding gift on my lap, a pad of letter paper on the album, a ballpoint pen in one hand, a lit cigarette in the other. That's how I wrote *My Michael*. At least most of it.

Often, when people tell me they're traveling somewhere to find inspiration for a book, a place of mountains or lakes or forests or the ocean shore, I recall that tiny bathroom of ours in Hulda.

When *My Michael* was published, I summoned the courage, went to the secretariat again and said, 'I'd like one more day a week for writing.' Again a long debate, again an argument. People said, 'It's a dangerous precedent.' Some said, 'Others will want the same thing.' But since there was already some money coming in, the members of the secretariat agreed. 'Let's say we're adding another small branch to our economy.' And now I had two days a week to write. Then I published another book and another one, increasing the kibbutz income, and in the end I was given three days to write, which was the maximum. It was a creeping annexation, not of territory, but of time: three days of writing and three days of high-school teaching, plus the regular shifts all kibbutz members had to do, night-guard duty, helping with fruit harvesting and weeding the cotton fields, and on vacations, I either drove the tractor in the fields or worked in the orchards.

HADAD: And you still wrote on the toilet?

OZ: No. Sometime around 1975, when I was already thirty-six, the secretariat of Kibbutz Hulda gave me a small place to work in. A few weeks earlier, one of the founders, a kibbutz member named

Giza who had lived alone, died. She came from Poland, actually from Galicia, had never married and never had children. Giza was an elegant, self-possessed woman with cropped, well-groomed gray hair and sharp, perceptive eyes behind her glasses. The housing committee gave me Giza's spartan furniture for my new place. Giza loved me very much. She was devoted to my Wednesday-evening literary sessions. She even knitted me a sweater once and gave me a small, original painting as a gift, a melancholy watercolor by some romantic Polish painter. She also told me some of her secrets on the condition that I swore not to tell them to anyone or write about them, and if I did eventually decide to write about them, then I had to swear I'd change all the names and details so no one would know that the story was about her. The truth is that she really hoped I would write her story one day. But camouflaged. Because on the one hand, she would be so ashamed if anyone knew that twice she'd had 'something' with a married man, and on the other, she was frightened that, in another few years, there would be no trace of her life left, no one in the world would know that she'd lived once, had suffered and loved, and had even had dreams. She was totally alone, and I, in fact, was her heir, even though the kibbutz forbade its members to leave anything to their heirs.

All my life, solitary old ladies have been very fond of me. I used to do readings one evening a week in Hulda, for example. I'd read from Agnon's *Only Yesterday* and discuss it, read and explain, and the old ladies would come. Giza was the most enthusiastic of them because the book was about Galicia, her home, and it brought back memories and emotions. Giza once told me, 'I'd agree to be your mother, and maybe I'd even agree to be your girlfriend. By that I mean in the nice sense of the word, not in the bad sense, you know what I mean.' I understood, but I didn't completely believe the last part of what she said.

When Giza died, she didn't leave a will, but it was clear that I could use her furniture. By the way, that furniture came with me to Arad and was in my study for more than thirty years, until I left

Arad. Giza's furniture: her couch and two armchairs. Furniture from austerity days. From the fifties. With MINISTRY OF RATIONING AND SUPPLY printed on the bottom of each piece. And so I already had a room where I could write.

HADAD: And with time, your books began to bring money into the kibbutz coffers.

OZ: The kibbutz financial manager, Oded Ofer, once came to see me (he was the son of David Ofer, who had said in the secretariat meeting that I might be the new Tolstoy when I was forty, but in the meantime, I was still too young to be a writer). Oded Ofer said that he'd seen the accounts, and my books were bringing in a very nice income. He asked tactfully whether my productivity would increase if he gave me two pensioners, too old for physical work, to help me out – he didn't know exactly how this production worked. I told him, 'Look, Oded, I'm still young and healthy, maybe you should have three pensioners do the writing and send me out to the fields?'

When we left Hulda, the kibbutz said, 'Amos and Nily will not receive the severance money we usually give to people who leave because Amos is taking an entire branch of our economy with him.' We went to arbitration, and the secretariat of Kibbutz Hulda claimed, 'We nurtured him, we gave him time to write, we sent him to university, we invested in him, and now he's leaving – okay, fine, we have no complaints, but they have to give up the severance money.' After thirty years of membership on the kibbutz, we would have received a substantial sum, which we really needed because we didn't have a penny. Nothing. We were both almost fifty. I said no. Because, though I had received many things from Hulda, including time for writing and a room in which to do it, and I was grateful for everything, I had not received my writing ability from Kibbutz Hulda. Besides, that branch of the economy in no way resembled other kibbutz branches because during high-pressure times, people were mobilized, members would volunteer to work overtime picking fruit, or thinning cotton, or gathering cotton, but no one was ever mobilized to my particular branch. When I was sick, no one replaced me, and when I worked overtime, no one recorded the extra hours. What's more, if writing books is a branch of the kibbutz economy, then I'm definitely prepared to spend two months showing the ropes to the person the kibbutz appoints to take my place. In the end, the arbitrator proposed a compromise: Nily would receive her money, because how was she to blame? But I would have to relinquish mine. We left Kibbutz Hulda with no bad blood. There was no argument, no discord and no legal proceedings. We left with a compromise. But on the kibbutz, there was the whole issue of artists – I know there were similar problems with sculptors and painters who practiced their art on the kibbutz. There was the concrete problem of intellectual property. I'm not sure they've solved that problem to this day. Who owns the intellectual property when the artist is a kibbutz member?

HADAD: The rights to the books you wrote there are yours?

OZ: They're mine, yes. Naturally, I could have said that I donate all the royalties to Kibbutz Hulda, but that didn't seem just to me.

HADAD: Why did you actually leave?

OZ: Because our son Daniel choked, literally choked, on the kibbutz. We had to get out of there because of what the olives and the fertilizers did to his asthma. Later, in Arad, where we moved for the mountain-desert air he needed for his recovery, Daniel adopted a cat. When we went to see the allergist there, he was horrified when he heard we had a cat in the house and it slept in bed with Daniel. Daniel was seven and that doctor thought he didn't understand English, so he said, 'You have to choose, keep the cat or the little boy.' There was silence in the room, until Daniel said, in English: 'Keep the cat.'

HADAD: That must have been frightening, leaving with almost nothing.

OZ: It was, Shira, like jumping into a pool at night without knowing whether there's water in it.

HADAD: Interesting, that's the same image you used to describe leaving your father's house at the age of fourteen.

OZ: Shira, if we had to give this piece a subtitle, we could call it 'The Story of a Serial Jumper into Empty Pools'. We took out a mortgage and loans and moved into that house in Arad, which was not an expensive city to live in, and for the first few years I worked four jobs to make money. We began at forty-seven what young people usually begin in their twenties. We were a bit like a couple of refugees from North Korea: at the age of forty-seven, I wrote a check for the first time, and was amazed when I could take real money from a wall with the help of a credit card.

HADAD: What were these four jobs?

OZ: It was like this: I was a non-faculty teacher in Ben-Gurion University in Beersheba and at Sapir College, and I wrote a weekly column, sometimes two, for the newspaper *Davar*, and in addition, I traveled to various places in the country three nights a week to give lectures and readings. One month a year, I traveled to America to give lectures, which paid well. We had a few difficult and frightening years, living on the verge of poverty. But I was only forty-seven, I was strong, and gradually we paid off the mortgage on our house in Arad. Later, without my asking, Ben-Gurion University sent me a letter, out of the blue saying that from then on I was a full professor, no longer a non-faculty teacher.

HADAD: You say you left, actually fled, because you had to. But still, were you glad to leave?

OZ: Nily was glad, I less so. She and the children weren't happy on the kibbutz. I was all right, I had a few friends there and I found it interesting. I also believed in the kibbutz ideology. Today I know the children's houses were terrible, and the truth is that I knew it then too, but suppressed the thought. If I could do it all over again, I would have left the kibbutz much sooner, even before Daniel's asthma. I would have left because my daughters were unhappy in the children's house. And also because Nily wasn't happy.

HADAD: Without getting into your children's private lives, can you say something else about that?

OZ: There's one story in my book *Between Friends* that describes it better than anything I could tell you. The story is called 'Little Boy'. The communal children's house was a Darwinistic place. The kibbutz founders, both men and women, thought, like Rousseau, that a person is born good and it's only circumstances that corrupt him. They believed, as did the Christian Church, that innocent children are actually small angels who have not yet tasted sin, and that the kibbutz children's house was a Garden of Eden filled with affection, friendship and kindness. What did they know, those founders of the kibbutz? They'd never seen children in their lives. They themselves were children. What did they know about what happens when you leave children unsupervised? It's enough to stand at the fence of a kindergarten to know once and for all that it should not be done. They developed entire theories: that if the children saw only each other, it would prevent them from imitating the negative aspects of their parents' behavior. But at night, after the adults said goodnight and left, the children's house sometimes turned into the desert island from *Lord of the Flies*. Heaven help the weak. Heaven help the sensitive. Heaven help the misfits. It was a cruel place.

I'm ashamed that I let my children, Fania and Galia, grow up in the kibbutz children's houses. Daniel was six when we left the kibbutz, and actually, when he was two, the system was reformed and all the children in Hulda moved in with their parents. And even more, I regret and am ashamed that when my daughters were bullied, I didn't have the courage to intervene and go to war to protect them. I believed that such things were not done on the kibbutz. Besides, I was terribly insecure because I had been a 'boarding child', not born and raised there. I always had to behave better than everyone.

HADAD: Even then.

OZ: Yes, I knew very well what happened in the children's houses to children who were a little weaker or a little unusual. I knew from my own experience. I can't hide behind the excuse that I didn't know what was going on because I went through all of it. Maybe for me it was even worse than for my daughters. As a 'boarding child', I was beaten every day. They beat me for being white when they were tanned, for not playing basketball, for writing poems, for speaking well, for not knowing how to dance, and also I was the victim of what they call in the Israel Defense Forces a 'preemptive counterattack', because they knew I would leave the kibbutz one day. My two roommates, who both left the kibbutz twenty-five years before me, supplied preemptive beatings because it was absolutely clear that I wouldn't stay on the kibbutz.

HADAD: That's terrible.

OZ: I can't look into my daughters' eyes and say I didn't know how horrible it was for them. Because I did know. If I could turn back the clock, I would have left the kibbutz many years earlier. Even though I was drawn to the kibbutz ideology, its people and – I've already spoken about this – what the kibbutz is for a writer: perhaps the best university in which to study human nature. But it was selfish of me to stay there. Truthfully, I was also very frightened of leaving because we had nothing, not a penny. Not from my parents, not from Nily's parents, and in fact, I had no profession: I was a high-school teacher without a teaching license because I had never studied education.

What could I have done? Perhaps Nily could have found a job as a librarian and I could have been a schoolteacher in some remote place where they might have employed me even without a teaching certificate. We were terrified. What could I do? I didn't know then that the day would come when I would earn money from writing books. I didn't know that then. I didn't even dream of it. I was afraid I would never be able to support a family. Today I think that I should have dared to leave the kibbutz much sooner.

HADAD: Yet there must have been some middle ground, some course of action you could have taken between the extremes of leaving and non-intervention?

OZ: I intervened sometimes, but it didn't help very much. And I wasn't courageous enough. I was afraid of arguments and altercations with the other parents.

HADAD: And that wasn't done then. Parents did not intervene.

OZ: Parents didn't intervene. Look, some did. There were people more resolute than Nily and me who did intervene and voiced their complaints loudly to the women working in the children's houses and to the education committee: What's going on here, They did this to my children, They did that to my children, It can't go on like this. I didn't do that. I should have, but I didn't.

HADAD: From our conversation, I'm getting a pretty gloomy picture of kibbutz ideology, especially the way it was implemented.

OZ: Several kibbutz genes have remained in the DNA of Israeliness, genes I consider good. Do you remember Stanley Fischer, who was once the governor of the Bank of Israel? On one occasion he told a story about flying to Cyprus with his wife Rhoda. At two thirty in the morning, a very tired Stanley and Rhoda Fischer were standing at the conveyor belt in Limassol waiting for their luggage. An Israeli passenger came over to them and asked politely, 'Excuse me, sir, are you the governor of the Bank of Israel?' He said yes. 'Where's the best place to change money? Here in the airport or in the bank tomorrow?' Shira, I love that so much. They ask me what I love about Israel. That. He didn't insult Stanley Fischer, he wasn't rude, but he knew that Stanley Fischer worked for him. That would never have happened in, let's say, France, or to the president of the bank of Germany. That's the gene the kibbutzim left for Israeli society, and I love it. The anarchism, the directness, the chutzpah, the argumentativeness, the absence of hierarchy. 'No one's going to tell me what to do.' That's the gift from the kibbutz of that period, the time of the first waves of immigration to Israel. I know, of course, that this is a time for slaughtering sacred cows. When I wrote *Where the Jackals Howl* and came out against Ben-Gurion in the Lavon Affair, I was filled with the joy that comes with slaughtering sacred cows: the kibbutz ethos, the myth of the 'Father of the Nation' and all that. Today, when I see a swarm of slaughterers eagerly attacking one old sacred cow, the kibbutz, I suddenly feel that I've moved slightly to the side of the cow. Not because I worship it; I remember very well how it kicked and how it stank. But at least it gave milk that wasn't half bad.

HADAD: Over the last few years, kibbutzim have fallen apart or been privatized. Do you think that the kibbutz is about to disappear?

OZ: No. Today, there are at least one hundred cooperative kibbutzim that have not been privatized or become garden communities. Most of them continue to maintain joint ownership of the means of production, and that has always been the core of the social democratic vision.

It could be that the kibbutz will have a sort of comeback sometime. They won't dance the *hora* in the dining hall and they won't make love on the threshing floor at night. That's finished. But there might be a more mature version of what those people tried to do in a childish way.

Not out in the countryside, maybe not even in Israel. Perhaps in the future there will be more urban communes that will try to establish something similar to the extended family, with security in old age, with greater mutual responsibility in raising children. Actually, they already exist today: a few of my grandchildren are members of fascinating urban communes. I don't know about you, but what I see here, and saw in Arad as well, is a huge number of people working beyond their capacity in order to make more money than they actually need, to buy things they really don't need, to impress people they don't even like. Some are fed up with that. Not the majority. The majority will remain competitive, that's human nature. But there will be some who search for an alternative. And those people might draw from the original ideas of the kibbutz the good concept of some sort of extended family, without changing human nature, without perfect equality, without peering into other people's rooms to see who has an electric kettle and who doesn't.

In any case, that was the society that succeeded in conquering the hills of social injustice only to discover on the other side of those hills were the steep precipices of existential injustice. What do I mean? In a society that eliminates the gap between a rich young woman and a poor young woman, the gap between an attractive and unattractive one becomes more prominent. What will the unattractive young woman do? Go to the equality committee and say, 'I deserve it too'? I said young woman, but I could just as easily have said young man. There is no way to resolve such things. And I hope that someday, in our next incarnation, the idea of the kibbutz returns, implemented by grown-ups and not adolescent boys and girls who don't have a clue. People who understand that if they try to change the basic elements of human nature, it won't end well. Most people will never want it, but it might be possible to offer slightly different rules of the game to a minority.

HADAD: Apart from leaving the kibbutz, what else would you do differently if you could live a second time?

OZ: Perhaps I would invest more work in political activity. Under no circumstances would I ever run for the Knesset, although left-wing groups – Moked, Sheli, Meretz – have asked me two or three times to be a candidate. But I wouldn't have gone to the Knesset. Maybe I would have engaged in more political activity during the times I still thought the scales could be tipped, maybe if I knew everything I know today. I'm not sure it would have changed anything, probably not. Here and there are things I'm sorry I said publicly. I wouldn't say them today, or I might say them in a totally different way. I won't tell you other things I'm sorry about.

HADAD: Are you prepared to talk about those things you said publicly?

OZ: Yes. I can give you an example. Several times I wrote and said that when it comes to the occupation, peace and the future of the occupied territories, the Israeli right wing thinks with its gut and the left thinks with its head. I regret that statement. It's a simplistic thought and it's wrong. Now it seems to me that both the left and the right think with their heads and also their gut, and sometimes they think about the territories and about peace with their heads and their gut at one and the same time.

HADAD: Somehow, from the funny story about your writing room, this is where we've ended up.

OZ: Yes, on the day they gave me a room of my own and I was surrounded by furniture I inherited from Giza, the world changed for me. Because until then, I had to hide in all sorts of places to write what I wrote. In the reading room behind the culture hall, at night when no one was there, or in the bathroom of our one-and-a-half-room apartment. Now I suddenly had a place where I knew I could close the door and have the space of a few hours. The world changed. Everything was different. I felt as if I had won a million dollars in the lottery. I never believed in muses, in inspiration or anything like that, but the moment I had a table and a chair and a door I could close, it was different. For example, as soon as I could take a break to write for a few hours, leave the papers on the table to wait for me and not fold them and shove them quickly into some cardboard file so no one would see them, my life changed. Completely. Perhaps poets can write in cafes, compose a poem in a kind of trance, then make changes. But prose? Writing a novel is like building all of Paris from matchsticks and glue. You can't do it in a few hours of leisure time, or in an ongoing trance. There are so many days when I sit down here at this desk before five in the morning, I sit and sit, and nothing happens.

HADAD: Do you feel guilty on days like that?

OZ: Today I know it's part of the game, but I felt guilty for many years. When the kibbutz gave me two days and then three to write, I used to get up at five, go to the room they gave me, sit there until noon, write four or five sentences, erase two. There were days when I wrote four sentences and erased six, two from the previous day. Then, at noon, I would go to the dining hall to eat lunch and I was filled with shame because sitting on my left was someone in work clothes who had already plowed five acres of land on the tractor that morning, and on my right sat another who had already milked thirty cows, and there I sat between them thanking God that no one knew I'd spent the entire morning writing six lines and erasing three of them. What right did I have to eat lunch here? I felt terribly guilty. Then gradually, I developed a mantra for myself. 'Amos,' I said, 'what you are doing is similar to what a clerk does. You go to work every morning, open the grocery store, then sit and wait for customers. If they come, it's a good day. If not, you've still done your job by sitting and waiting.' You have no idea how much that mantra calmed me down.

HADAD: With your permission, I'm going to adopt that mantra for myself.

OZ: I don't read the papers when I'm supposed to be writing, I don't play solitaire or do anything else. No chats, no tweets, no emails, no porn films – I just sit there and wait. Sometimes I listen to music. That mantra did calm me down. I don't have to tell you that guilt is a Jewish invention. Our forefathers invented it here in Israel. Then the Christians came and marketed it with colossal success throughout the world. But the patent is ours. As a Jew, I have terrible guilt feelings about our having invented guilt feelings. But at the same time, if a day goes by and I don't have guilt feelings, I feel guilty at night because an entire day has passed and I haven't had any guilt feelings. We're different from the Christians, who also have an abundance of guilt, because we Jews are apparently world champions in suffering from guilt feeling without enjoying the pleasures of the sin in the first place. I know that line should be Woody Allen's, but I just happen to be the one who said it. Sometimes guilt can be a driving force. A person who has guilt feelings suffers, but someone who doesn't have them is a monster.

HADAD: Maybe the Buddhists succeeded in ridding themselves of guilt. I don't know.

OZ: If they did, I'm terribly jealous, but only momentarily. A minute later, I'm not jealous, but almost pity them. Guilt feelings are a little like a good spice for almost everything: creativity, sex, parenting, relationships. A little bit of spice. But if we're served a plateful – help! ■

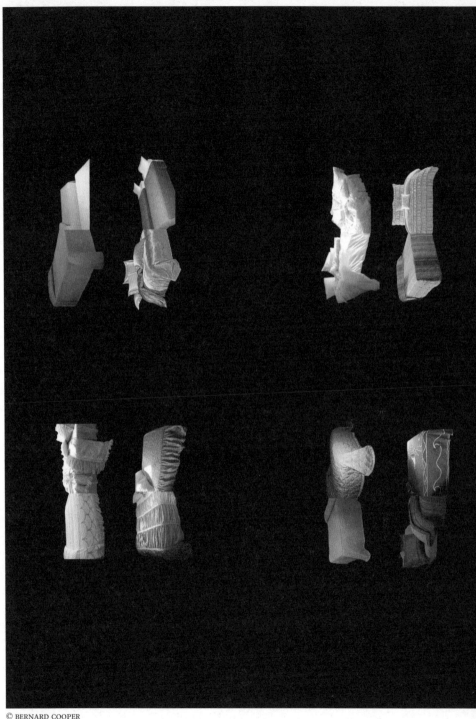

*An Insomniac's Guide to the Night*, 2015
Courtesy of the author

# GREEDY SLEEP

## *Bernard Cooper*

I knew I had a problem when I woke up in a Motel 6 in Fresno. I'd driven there from Los Angeles late the previous afternoon, barreling for hours through the Central Valley, its furrowed green farmland rippling out on either side of the interstate. Humid wind blew through the windows, heavy with the smell of fertile earth. I checked into my room after dark and went straight to bed.

Fresno State University had invited me to appear on a panel at their annual writers' conference – at least I remembered that much when I opened my eyes the next morning. Still bleary from a long night's sleep, I had a harder time recalling the panel's title – 'The Memoir: Unforgotten Recollections of the Past', or some such redundancy. In which direction was the lobby? I wondered. Where had I parked my car? Every moment of disorientation turned out to be temporary and could easily be blamed on the effects of waking up in a strange place. But the same couldn't be said of what happened next.

As I sat up in bed, I heard a faint rustling and looked down to see dozens of foil and paper wrappers cascade off my chest and land in my lap. Cookie crumbs had gathered in the folds of my T-shirt. Around me lay several half-eaten crackers and a cube or two of Cheddar cheese. Gummy bears were strewn across the blanket like colorful, rubbery carnage.

My heart started racing. It was as if someone had snuck into the room while I'd slept and smashed a piñata above the bed. I scanned the room for evidence of an intruder – the year was 1996 and 'home invasion robberies' had started making national headlines – but the door to my room was closed and bolted, and the placard requesting PRIVACY PLEASE, in both Spanish and English, dangled from the knob. My wallet lay untouched on the nightstand along with my car keys, eyeglasses, an amber vial of Ambien and the book I'd been reading. Nothing had been disturbed except for me. I considered calling the front desk, though exactly how to phrase my complaint presented a challenge: pretty much any words I chose – *I'm in room 103, covered in crumbs!* – would make me sound crazy.

As I sat there, baffled, an image slowly formed in my mind, perhaps a scene from a dream I'd had the night before.

I'm standing at the intersection of four long hallways. Before me rises a monolith that glows from within. I stare through its huge glass window at metal coils arranged in rows like the innersprings of a luminous mattress. One of the coils corkscrews toward me, pushing before it a foil-wrapped package that drops into a shallow trough near my knees and lands with a thud. The sound fills me with satisfaction; I want more thuds. I press a bunch of numbered buttons and another coil begins to turn, and still another, the bounty piling up.

The shadowy figure of a man approaches. We exchange a few words. Paper money is traded for coins. I quickly pivot back toward the machine, but my face now burns with embarrassment; I've been dressed in boxer shorts and a threadbare T-shirt this whole time. The man who gave me change is gone, but he's left me with the realization that my dream is peopled. While shoving quarters into the slot, I become dimly aware of comings and goings along the corridors. At the rounded sound of a nearby bell, several strangers walk out of the wall. Although some remote part of me realizes that the phenomenon of people emerging from the wall can be explained by the word 'elevator', the word is elusive and, once I've found it, hard to retain. Still, none of this is alarming enough to send me scurrying back to my room; that people rise and descend inside a box is a fact that belongs to the physics of my waking life, about which I seem to possess a faint knowledge. What *is* alarming is how the people who land in the hallway turn and glance at the holes in my T-shirt, at my hairy legs and bare feet. I attempt, with great effort, a nonchalant smile. I can barely keep hold of all the junk food gripped in my fists.

B ack in Los Angeles, I told myself that my raid on the vending machine was an anomaly. I didn't bother mentioning the incident to my partner, Brian, though he was a psychotherapist and no stranger to aberrations in human behavior. Before I'd left for Fresno, there'd been a precipitous drop in his T-cell count (he was HIV-positive and I was HIV-negative), edging him closer to a diagnosis of full-blown Aids, and so, in the larger scheme of things, my having gorged on Gummy bears hardly seemed worth his concern.

My tale of gluttony might also have been an unpleasant reminder to Brian that the primary symptom of his failing immune system was his growing inability to metabolize food, no matter how much he ate, no matter how rich or frequent his meals. We'd learned of the difference in our HIV status in 1986 – two years into our twenty-three-year relationship – soon after the HIV antibody test became available and national trials were being planned to determine the efficacy of a promising new drug called azidothymidine, or AZT. We'd discussed at length the risks involved in Brian's decision to try and become a participant in the trial. He had majored in psychology and minored in statistical research; he believed that his grasp of the methodology behind 'blind' scientific studies would render him a candidate able to articulate the effects of AZT in both medical and anecdotal terms, which in turn would give him a slightly better than 50/50 chance of not only being chosen for the study, but of being placed in the control group who received the drug instead of a placebo.

He was right on both counts. Waves of nausea offered him reassurance that he was ingesting the real thing, as did the neuropathy that stung his hands and feet like needles. In a world turned inside out, side effects were a harbinger of hope. Knowing that he would be called upon to describe these side effects allowed him a kind of dominion over their existence; he had to stand outside of himself and assume the observant, clinical distance he practiced when listening to his clients. This obliged Brian to find words for what might otherwise have been a kind of misery he could neither name nor escape. By 1987, the Center for Disease Control estimated that, in the United States, 50,352 Aids cases had been reported and 40,849 deaths had occurred.

What no one involved with the AZT study could have foreseen was that the high dose prescribed to Brian's cohort resulted in all sixty men developing a resistance to the drug, which the virus rapidly mutated to reject. It was learned in a subsequent trial that AZT is effective only when administered at *lower* doses and in conjunction with other drugs, the combinations of which had to be switched like shells in a shell game in order to constantly trick the virus. During the trial, the tissue lining Brian's intestinal walls had been damaged, which meant he then absorbed fewer nutrients from food. Unable to benefit from the drug cocktail or reverse the effect on his intestines, Brian's wasting became difficult to stop. The lower his T-cell count, the more weight he lost, as if the absence of the cells themselves was measurable on a bathroom scale. At five foot nine, Brian had been 135 pounds when we'd first met at a local bar, and although he'd jokingly referred to himself that night as a 'runt', I saw his remark for what it was: a ploy to elicit the compliments I was glad to offer if they paved the way to sex. I told him I'd never met a runt with such well-developed pecs and biceps. Now veins became prominent on his calves and forearms. His collars grew roomy, his belt loops too few.

I hadn't sidestepped the Fresno story solely to spare Brian's feelings. That night of snacking nagged at me with its utter surrender to impulse. I hadn't consciously made the decision to leave my room and look for food, and for the first time in my life I imagined the shock and indignity a somnambulist might feel when he wakes up and finds himself somewhere other than where he went to sleep, suddenly confronted with the understanding that his urges have a life of their own. The bout of morning amnesia had particularly unnerved me, reliant as I am on memory in my writing; the sheer amount of food I'd devoured was proof of a powerful craving I'd obeyed yet couldn't recall. Still, no matter how hungry I might have been, I'm too shy a person to walk into a public place wearing boxer shorts and a tattered T-shirt (a shirt I couldn't bring myself to throw away because its over-laundered softness held the very promise of sleep), though neither am I the kind of person who'd have to put on dress shoes before fleeing a burning house. I suspected that Ambien might have played a role in all this, but at that point I'd been taking it regularly for over a year and had enjoyed a run of predictable, restorative sleep without any episodes of nocturnal binging. In the end, the simplest explanation for what happened at the Motel 6 seemed to be this: disinhibited by a sleeping pill, I'd gone in search of something to eat, having found myself far hungrier after the long drive than I'd realized.

My doctor, after all, had instructed me not to take Ambien with food. The drug's active ingredient, zolpidem tartrate, is absorbed into the bloodstream through the stomach, so the emptier one's gut, the faster the medication works. I'd been fairly disciplined about not eating close to bedtime because I *wanted* the drug to metabolize as quickly as possible; I've experienced chronic insomnia since my late twenties, and I was never the kind of stayer-awake who could make those late hours productive by doing the laundry, say, or paying bills. Instead, I'd lie there and worry about how groggy and out of sorts I'd be the next day.

Under the influence of Ambien, however, I was knocked unconscious by what I'd come to think of as the chemical equivalent of a velvet sledgehammer. I could be turning the last, engaging pages of a novel, or watching a forensic expert on TV explain blood-spatter patterns from a double homicide, when the need to sleep abruptly trumped every reason to stay awake.

Ambien doesn't work for everyone, but for the 26 million who make it America's most prescribed sleeping aid, its effectiveness is unequivocal. It acts as a central nervous system depressant and within about twenty minutes of ingestion, it relaxes muscles and slows brain activity by increasing gamma-aminobutyric acid, a naturally occurring neurotransmitter in the brain that inhibits messages between other neurotransmitters. It allows me to turn off the whirring thought-machine – an occupational hazard for many writers – and to stop strip-mining the day's events, images and snippets of conversation for potential insights into human nature in general, or my own nature in particular, all the while wondering how I might make use of these ruminations in my work. Consciousness may be sublime, but it's also exhausting. Six hours later, Ambien's targeted molecules are flushed from the bloodstream, which is why relatively few users experience fogginess or lingering fatigue the next morning.

My raid on the vending machine was the first instance of a sleep-related eating disorder (sleep researchers refer to this phenomenon by its acronym: SRED) that has dogged me ever since. The second instance occurred several months after my trip to Fresno. On my way to the kitchen one morning to make coffee, I was stopped in my tracks by two nearly identical orange stains on the hallway carpet. I bent over for a closer look, and there, at the perimeter of each stain, lay a wooden Popsicle stick. Since I had no recollection of eating Popsicles the night before, and since I don't even like Popsicles, I wondered if Brian, still in the bedroom dressing for work, had eaten a midnight snack. I went to ask him about it, but before I could open my mouth he asked, 'What's with your T-shirt?' For the second time in my life, I looked down at my favorite threadbare T-shirt to discover indisputable evidence, writ in sticky orange, of a meal I didn't remember. 'It's time,' Brian added, cinching his tie, 'to throw that ratty thing away.'

I am an Ambien eater. I don't mean I eat the medication itself – I mean that taking Ambien causes me to feel, in the five-minute window before I conk out, a visceral and urgent hunger. Regardless of how hearty my dinner was, regardless of how unhungry I am when I turn out the light and slide beneath the covers, something shifts as I'm drifting off to sleep. First, the sharp contours of consciousness begin their predictable softening. It's not that the object of my concentration grows blurry – the printed words in a book, for example, remain typographically distinct – but the complex mental and physiological mechanisms for understanding those words and caring about what they say evaporates like water in the sun. Then, like clockwork, I'm encompassed by hunger, an emptiness swelling to the size of night itself. Next thing I know, I'm up and searching for something to eat, or more precisely, I'm asleep on my feet and hoarding provisions against what I sense is the coming of some endless dark, the Earth a lifeless chunk of ice, the firmament stripped of planets and stars. What must I eat to delay or escape it? I'm rummaging through cupboards, ransacking the refrigerator, pondering the salvageability of bruised fruit, scrutinizing use-by dates, sniffing cartons of milk and Chinese takeout. What do I want? What do I want? All I need is a slice of bread. Or two, or ten. I'll harvest the fields of wheat myself. I'll wrestle with mountains of rising dough. I'll fill a yawning, infernal oven with loaf after yeasty loaf.

For the sake of gaining weight, Brian's physician advised him to supplement his meals with cans of Ensure, a viscous nutritional drink whose artificial chocolate or vanilla flavoring barely masked an insipid chemical odor that bore so little connection to the smell of any actual foodstuff that Brian sometimes held his nose as he swigged it. (Having once taken a whiff myself, I completely bypassed the shelf of Ensure during my raids on the kitchen.)

The two of us began a campaign to stock the house with food likely to whet Brian's appetite, including his own personal manna: the peanut butter we bought by the giant jarful from a bulk-food discount store that sold juice boxes by the pallet and bags of potato chips the size of bed pillows, amounts so formidable that buying a supply of chewing gum, say, became a commitment comparable to marriage. When Brian and I paused in an aisle to deliberate over a particular purchase, I sometimes asked, 'Do we want to eat X for the rest of our lives?' The question hastened our decision – several foods seemed tempting in the moment but intolerable over the long haul – while also expressing my supposed certainty regarding his long-term survival, about which I felt anything *but* certain; the man was starving before my eyes despite continued advances in drug therapies and research. Still, voicing this question, with its implication of a future, offered me a fleeting relief from the almost continual dread of losing him, for I was the one who could better afford to contemplate for long, obsessive stretches of time – especially at night – the terrifying possibility of his death, while he permitted himself only rare, dizzying glimpses at his own demise, firmly believing that a steady diet of fear would harm his mental and physical health. 'Statistics show,' he insisted, citing a study about anxiety's detrimental effect on the immune system.

This is not to suggest Brian was fearless, but rather to say that, of the two of us, he had always been the more logical; he was professionally trained, after all, to achieve empathy and insight through the practice of detachment. A statistician at heart, he loved the data that proved the rule, whereas I argued that literature proved the exception to the rule, and I loved it when norms were thrown into doubt. What *was* inarguable was the fact that I lived with a man who, while remaining fully aware of the severity of his illness, could successfully forestall thoughts of his own mortality in the name of a greater, self-preserving calm. I marveled at his self-control because it was utterly unlike the sloshing sea of emotional flotsam I found myself constantly tossed upon. Deep within me, a superstitious reflex demanded that I imagine the worst in great detail as a way to trap catastrophe in the realm of *idea* instead of *event*. It sometimes seemed to me that by picking up the slack of Brian's worry, he would be free to fret even less, and the less he fretted – if statistics were correct – the longer he'd live.

'How do you manage to stay so optimistic?' I once asked him. I realized with a start that this question sounded like a measure of my pessimism rather than my admiration. We were in the bathroom, the mirror fogged with steam from the shower, and Brian, a towel wrapped around his waist, was applying to his shoulder the twenty-four-hour transdermal testosterone patch that was a new part of his routine, a hormonal prod to gain muscle mass and the weight that came with it.

'You're the optimist,' he said matter-of-factly, 'not me.'

I must have looked puzzled.

'You're the optimist,' he persisted, 'because you hold out hope that things will get better. That's what makes you afraid they won't.'

Brian swiped his palm across the mirror and frankly assessed his own reflection. 'Some treatment might eventually come along to break through my resistance,' he said. 'Or it might not. I'm walking a fine line between hopelessness and hope, and that's the line I'm going to stay on until there's a reason to move to either side.'

Brian and I hated it when a friend or acquaintance referred to one of us as the other's 'better half', which demoted both of us from *whole*. But standing beside him in the bathroom that day, I found myself so shaken by the prospect of his absence that I couldn't help but say, 'I know we're autonomous and all that crap, but no matter how I try to look at it, I'm afraid I'd be nothing without you.'

'*You'd* be nothing without me?' He laughed a single, propulsive laugh, then clamped the patch to his shoulder and held it there until it stuck.

E very weekday morning, Brian made three or four peanut butter and jelly sandwiches, taking them to work and forcing himself to eat one whenever he had a few extra minutes between clients. To call them snacks would be an understatement. These were the opposite of the dainty triangular tea sandwiches his mother made for her bridge club, a layer of pimento cream cheese spread as thin as tissue on crustless bread. Brian's PB&Js were glistening bricks of protein on wholewheat. They retained their shape and thickness thanks to hydrolyzed vegetable oil and artificial stabilizers. More than mere sandwiches, they were edible testaments to his will to live, cornerstones of a monument dedicated to the wonders of nut butter. They necessitated the toothbrush he kept in a desk drawer at his office in order to make sure that his mask of psychotherapeutic neutrality wouldn't be ruined by traces of Jif on his lips or teeth. He might have been especially careful in this regard after witnessing first-hand the telltale orange streaks on my now discarded T-shirt.

Although Brian told our friends that dealing with HIV was a prolonged exercise in relinquishing control, he wrested control wherever he could. With what rigor he stuck to his drug regimen, a complex, ever-changing list of pills that he and his physician had chosen as admittedly iffy substitutes for the more potent antiviral properties of the AZT cocktail. Then there were the prophylaxis against oral thrush, pneumocystis pneumonia and the purple skin lesions of Kaposi's sarcoma, just to name a few of the life-threatening assaults one's compromised immune system could fall prey to in those days. He actually read the inserts that came with every prescription, a novel's worth of fine print folded like origami into an improbably small square. He closely monitored the compartments of his translucent blue pill case, each labeled with the day of the week.

Brian was such a dedicated advocate for his own health that I had little to do but worry on his behalf and listen to his answers when I asked how he was doing. True, I performed household tasks such as doing the laundry and cooking, but they were tasks that benefited us both; I would have done these things if I were single, and so they hardly seemed like a sacrifice on my part and didn't adequately reflect the extent of my love and concern. Nor were they proportional to the impending loss that became palpable in the dark of night, a boundless void that the Ambien eater within me believed he could shrink to the size of his stomach as long as he tried to fill himself with food.

Perhaps in my frustration at not playing a more direct role in Brian's fight against the virus, of not being even more intimate with the physical particulars of his illness – in short, because I wasn't HIV-positive – I found an oblique way to know more closely what he was going through. In those days, along with Ambien, I took a common blood pressure medication called Tenormin as well as a multivitamin. To this regimen I added an amber gelcap containing ten essential minerals, as well as a chalky, almost un-swallowable chondroitin and glucosamine tablet to ease the joint pain that came from working out as often as possible in order to offset the weight I stood to gain from eating in the wee hours and then falling asleep without any activity to burn off the glut. Although I'd put on a few pounds, a strange sense of bodily decorum prevented me from gaining an amount of weight conspicuous enough to make Brian even more aware of his physical diminishment. Although Brian never suggested that I needed to be more understanding of his status – although he in fact wanted to spare me an even greater sense of identification than I already possessed – taking more pills made me a kind of compatriot and justified buying a translucent blue pill case of my own. Brian suggested that my late-night eating might also indicate the early stages of an 'exogenous' depression, i.e. a depression created by the circumstance of his deteriorating health in particular and the Aids crisis in general, and he advised me to talk to the psycho-pharmacologist who'd first given me a prescription for Ambien. On my next visit to Dr Hammond, a soft-spoken colleague of Brian's, I explained how my Ambien-eating had become a nightly occurrence.

'I start off eating at the kitchen sink,' I told him, 'but I often find food on my side of the bed when I wake up the next morning.'

The doctor waited.

'Bits of potato chips. I once woke up with a bagel on my chest. A trail of raisins . . .'

'This doesn't sound especially unhealthy.'

'I'm not eating coffee grounds or raw meat, if that's what you mean.'

'Do you stop when you're full?'

'I'm not sure I'm either hungry beforehand or full when I'm finished.'

The doctor touched his pen to his lips and thought a minute. 'You don't look like you're gaining weight.'

'I'm exercising a lot.'

'Purging?'

'Never.'

'And you sleep about how long?'

'Six hours. Seven. But I have to take an Ambien every night now. I'm afraid I'm addicted.'

'I have patients who've been taking Ambien every night for several years.'

I shifted in my chair. 'That's what I'm trying to tell you,' I said. 'I need it every night.'

'You may be dependent at present, but the drug isn't physically addictive, and I think you'd agree with me when I say that sleep is essential, especially given the stress of Brian's illness.'

'Do any of your other patients experience this eating thing?'

'Not to my knowledge.'

He told me that a ten-minute window of amnesia occurs as the medication takes effect, and the best advice he could give me was to get straight into bed once I'd swallowed the pill. I didn't have the presence of mind to tell him that getting into bed wasn't the problem. The problem was getting into bed and then, with my eyes at half-mast, lurching up for the hunt as if I'd heard a trumpet.

I returned home not only with three refills on my prescription for time-release Ambien, but with a starter pack of Effexor, a selective serotonin reuptake inhibitor. Brian assured me that my concerns about taking an antidepressant and becoming a contented but affectless zombie incapable of entertaining a creative impulse or complex thought were completely unfounded.

'Besides,' he reminded me, 'if you don't like the way it makes you feel, you can always stop taking it.'

'But what if I can't tell that I've been robbed of some essential part of my being?'

Brian rested his hand on my shoulder. 'I'll be sure to let you know if that happens.'

'Suppose you like me better when I'm drugged up?'

'Bernard,' he said.

Effexor gave a glass floor to my night terrors; it was as if I could look down and see the abyss beneath my feet, as infinite as ever, but I stayed suspended above it without the fear of falling. While gradually ramping up my dosage as per Dr Hammond's plan, my mood steadied and I became aware of what I can only describe as a kind of psychic insulation, soft as excelsior, that buffered me from the uncertainties of Brian's illness, from the vicissitudes of life itself. I remained a person susceptible to worry, but I knew, for perhaps the first time since the epidemic began, the kind of courage one associates with strength of character, and though I also knew this strength was chemical in nature – from palm to mouth to bloodstream to brain – I didn't much care where it came from.

Only three side effects were worth mentioning to the doctor in our follow-up talk, and all of them turned out to be temporary: 1) although I didn't feel sleepy, I yawned dozens of times a day; 2) while I didn't suffer the erectile dysfunction I later learned is a common side effect, I *did* experience difficulty reaching a climax; 3) Effexor, like Ambien, had a disinhibiting effect.

As far as I could tell, the increased disinhibition that came from combining Effexor with Ambien had only one serious drawback: the peanut butter we'd stocked specifically for Brian, and which I'd thus far managed to leave untouched, was now fair game. Well, not *fair*, exactly; somewhere in the greedy, twilight state that propelled my forays into our kitchen, there existed the knowledge that Jif was off limits, that to eat it was to deplete Brian's supply of the most tempting, fat-rich food in our house, and if I sleepily reamed it to the bottom, I'd have to go to the store the next morning and buy another jar. Yet the night was so immense and my sense of emptiness so distressing that ethics were muffled by existential dread. If I couldn't imagine life without Brian, wasn't his dying also mine? Wasn't his death a precipice we'd both step over?

There may have been a trace of guilt as I twisted off the lid, but it vanished when a tablespoon heaped with Jif glistened in the kitchen light. The salty-sweet glob took effort to swallow, displacing the lump of fear in my throat. For one blessed second, I believed my stomach would never be empty. For one blessed second my taste buds were eternal, the aftertaste filling my senses as an echo fills a canyon.

Not until the March 2006 issue of the *New York Times* was a link between Ambien and sleep-eating reported, when sleep researchers from both the Minnesota Regional Sleep Disorders Center and the Mayo Clinic had reason to suspect that something in the chemical composition of the drug made a subset of users confuse the urge to eat and the urge to sleep. The exact cause of the phenomenon eluded the medical community, but as far as I was concerned, the anecdotal data rang true.

One woman in the Minnesota study claimed to have gained one hundred pounds in a year without knowing why. Her nightly amnesia prevented her from believing her husband and sons' claims that she routinely masticated her way through their pantry late at night. For a while she blamed them for planting the empty wrappers and scraps of food she found scattered on the floor. Neither she nor her family had realized that Ambien was a contributing factor.

'These people are hell-bent to eat,' said one researcher, perhaps referring to the son who found his mother, a woman otherwise bedridden from back surgery and unable to walk without assistance, standing at the stove in her full-body cast, blithely frying eggs and bacon in the middle of the night. For me, though, it was Helen Carry of Dickson, Tennessee, who most memorably described the primal, dreamlike urge to eat. 'I got a package of hamburger buns and I tore it open like a grizzly bear and just stood there and ate the whole package,' the fifty-seven-year-old labor delivery nurse told researchers. Ms Carry's husband, roused from his sleep by sounds in the kitchen, watched from the doorway, his jaw gone slack. She awoke only after her husband regained his power of speech.

Not until I read the article did I have evidence that Ambien caused me to sleep-eat, a side effect that no other Ambien user I knew (and I knew several by then) had experienced. Nor would I have guessed that, across the country, others plundered the contents of their kitchens in an urgent search they'd forget by morning, a feral pack of amnesiacs foraging through the same dark woods.

I put down the *Times* and went to check on Brian. He lay beneath the covers, eyes closed, body barely forming the raised shape of a man in repose. He wore layers of sweat clothes, a woolen toque and two pairs of socks; since he hardly possessed any insulating fat, Brian shivered, cold to the bone. He weighed thirty-five pounds less than he had when he volunteered for the AZT study. There was nothing left to buffer the friction of bone against bone. His scalp gleamed through sparse hair. The virus had recently crossed the blood–brain barrier, and although he sometimes used the wrong words, or mistook the floor for a set of stairs, he was able to draw from his fund of lucidity when he needed it the most, or when I did.

'Here we are at the end,' he said one day, 'and the learning curve is steep.' On another: 'We're dismantling an entire life.' Mostly though, silence settled between us, as meaningful as speech.

In a few weeks he'd refuse food in the hope of hastening his own death. He had warned me he would do this. He needed neither my protests nor my approval. Until then, I spoon-fed him bowls of incongruous broth – incongruous because, despite his shivering, it was an unseasonably hot March in Los Angeles. The nights were as warm and sultry as the days. Sunlight and darkness grew strangely interchangeable, charged with the terrible patience of our waiting. I'd begun to take my Ambien with ice water and every night, much later in the kitchen, I'd hear ice clinking as I lifted my glass and washed down all the food I consumed, the food that couldn't sustain him. ∎

Albert Speer presents Adolf Hitler with the model of the German House for the Paris World's Fair, 1937.

# SPEER

## *Sheila Heti*

Here, among the couches, Hitler was particularly fond of drifting into endless monologues. The subjects were mostly familiar to the company, who therefore listened absently, though pretending to attention. Occasionally, Hitler himself fell asleep over one of his monologues. It was all very familiar. Once we agreed we wanted to get him a birthday present, but naturally we were given pause, confronted as we were with the problem of what present to bring a man who was incurably deranged in his mind. After eliminating a number of articles that might offend or frighten him, we chose a dainty and innocent trifle: a basket with ten different fruit jellies in ten little jars.

There were two sitting areas: one a sunken nook at the back of the room, with the red upholstered chairs grouped around a fireplace; the other, near the window, was dominated by a round table whose fine veneer was protected by a glass top. Beyond this was the movie projection cabinet, its openings concealed by a tapestry. Along the opposite wall stood a massive chest containing built-in speakers, adorned by a large bronze bust of Richard Wagner. Large oil paintings covered the walls: a picturesque reclining nude, Indians fighting Indians, a landscape with Roman ruins, a child in a jumper bathed in a bluish light. We found places on the sofas in either of the sitting areas; then the tapestry was raised and the second part of the evening began with a movie as the company gathered around the huge fireplace – some six or eight persons lined up in a row on the excessively long and uncomfortably low sofa.

According to one's taste, one had tea, coffee or chocolate, and various types of cakes and sweets, followed by liqueurs. Records were played – a few bravura selections from Wagnerian operas, promptly followed by operettas. Hitler made a point of trying to guess the names of the sopranos and was pleased when he guessed right. No one took the trouble to raise the conversation above the level of trivialities. These social occasions dragged on in monotonous, wearying emptiness for hours.

I might have been able to smuggle Aeromat into one of these gatherings, earlier in the war, but there were few newcomers brought in during the middle-war period, simply because at that point Hitler's paranoia was so extreme that he was unable to trust anybody.

Aeromat continued to want to join us, although I warned him there was not much pleasure to be had – conversations were drawn-out and Hitler's speeches were endless. Yet my friend was taken by the elegance of the gatherings, as I had described them – the chocolate, the cakes, the liqueurs, the film projections, and loafing on the upholstered couches after a rich meal. When I finally told Aeromat no, he fell upon the rug in his bare apartment and began to cry in frustration. I left. I had no time for his hysterics – not when there was so much else of greater concern on my mind.

Hitler's decision to settle in Obersalzberg was on account of his love of nature, and while he did frequently admire a beautiful view, as a rule he was more affected by the awesomeness of an abyss than the harmony of a landscape. He took little pleasure in flowers and considered them entirely as decorations. When a delegation of Berlin women's magazines visited around 1934, he was asked by the head of the organization what his favourite flower was. He telephoned round to discover what his favourite flower was, but in the end he replied, 'I haven't any.'

All winter long people plunged horribly from the mountains, young men and women, in the distance, tumbling and flipping over from front to back while on their alpine skiing and climbing vacations. Gazing out of the chalet window, as in the distance young men and women fell through the air to their deaths, Hitler's dislike for snow burst out repeatedly. 'What pleasure can there be in prolonging the horrible winter artificially by staying in the mountains?' he'd exclaim. 'If I had my way I'd forbid these sports, with all the accidents people have doing them! But of course the mountain troops draw their recruits from such fools.'

Nightly we took nature strolls along the pathways Bormann cleared. With total insensitivity to the natural surroundings, he had laid out a network of roads through this magnificent landscape. He turned forest paths, hitherto carpeted by pine needles and penetrated by roots, into paved promenades. Dormitory barracks for hundreds of construction workers clung to the slopes. Trucks loaded with building materials rumbled along the roads. At night the hills glowed with light, for work went on in two shifts, and occasionally detonations thundered through the valley.

Once, after our return from a nightly constitutional, we were seated at the round table in the teahouse and Hitler began staring at me. Instead of dropping my eyes, I took it as a challenge. Who knows what primitive instincts are involved in such staring duels. I have had others, and have frequently won, but this time I had to muster almost inhuman strength, seemingly forever, not to yield to the ever-mounting urge to look away – when Hitler suddenly closed his eyes, then opened them and looked at the woman at his side.

It snowed and snowed and snowed. Railroad and highway traffic came to a total stop. The airport runway was drifted over. We were cut off. I was taken into a hospital. For twenty days I lay on my back, my legs immovable in a plaster cast. Although the doctors prepared my wife for the worst, with the application of the morphine I fell into a remarkable euphoria. The little room expanded into a magnificent hall, and the plain wardrobe I had been staring at turned into a richly carved display piece, inlaid with rare woods. The nurses who attended me fluttered like angels, and any anxious thoughts of my situation left me as I hovered happily between living and dying. Even the angry telephone calls from Hitler failed to have any effect on my drug-addled reverie. 'Why did you have to go skiing up there!' he shouted over the telephone. 'I've always said it is madness. With those long boards on your feet! Throw those sticks into the fire!'

My return to Berlin had to be postponed. Once I had recovered, socializing with the construction workmen filled the time. Get-togethers were held, songs sung. Sepp Dietrich made speeches and was cheered. I stood by; with my awkwardness at speech-making, I did not dare say even a few words. Among the songs distributed by the army corps were some very melancholy ones, expressing a longing for home and the dreariness of the Russian steppes.

I am not at all disposed to be a hero, and since the eight days of my stay had been of no use whatsoever, and I was eating into my engineers' scarce provisions, I decided to take a train that was going to attempt to break through three snowdrifts to the west. My staff gave me a friendly – and, it seemed to me, grateful – farewell. All night we went along at six or seven miles an hour, stopped, shovelled snow, rode again. I thought we were a good deal farther to the west when, at dawn, we pulled into a deserted station.

An adjunct came in and requested I join Hitler. It was then after one o'clock in the morning. He asked me to tell him what impressions I had gathered on my visit to southern Russia, and helped me along by interjecting questions. The difficulties in restoring the railroad equipment, the social evenings with their melancholy songs – bit by bit everything came out. When I mentioned the songs, his attention sharpened and he asked about the words. I produced a handwritten text I had in my pocket. He read it over slowly and asked my opinion. My opinion was that the songs were a natural response to a grim situation. Hitler, however, decided at once that some traitor was trying to undermine morale. Later, I found out that he'd court-martialled the author of those songs.

Walking into Hitler's office, I passed an attractive young woman walking out. He said to me suspiciously, 'Imagine if on top of everything else I had a woman who interfered with my work. In my leisure time I want to have peace! I could never marry. And think of the problems if I had children! In the end they would try to make my son my successor. And the chances are slim for someone like me to have a capable son. That is almost always how it goes in such cases. Consider Goethe's son – a completely worthless person!'

Hitler had increasingly begun showing signs of distraction and overwork. At times he would be distinctly averse to making decisions, and relapse into one of his painful monologues, or else fall into a sort of muteness. He was also at all times worried about gaining weight. 'Out of the question! Imagine me going around with a pot belly. It would mean political ruin!' Then he would push aside his cake or the plate of cookies or whatever was on his desk. 'Take it away,' he would demur. 'I like it too much.'

Walking down Unter den Linden one afternoon, I noticed a former acquaintance of mine, a man of my father's age who had been a teacher in the gymnasium when I was a boy. He had been arrested ten years ago on charges of molesting some of the younger male students. But he had been the best teacher I'd ever had, casual, intelligent, so unlike the other, colourless tutors. I still felt disturbed over my visit with Aeromat, so I was in no mood to approach. I had been curious about him, however, ever since the trial. Seeing him sitting there, on a bench with a newspaper in hand, I felt something in me slacken. I remembered him young and athletic, with a distinguished posture. I turned and left the park. I hoped he hadn't seen me. Even if he had, he probably wouldn't have recognized me. I am no longer a boy of twelve. I have changed, also.

The *Observer* article of 9 April 1944 was read aloud in Hitler's chambers. Among us were Bormann, Himmler and Dorsch. I stood, and with considerable irritation, Hitler put on his glasses and began to read:

> Speer is not one of the flamboyant and picturesque Nazis, but in a sense he is more important for Germany than Hitler, Goering, Goebbels or the generals, who are mere auxiliaries to him who is the very epitome of the managerial revolution. Much less than any other German leaders does he stand for anything particularly Nazi. He rather epitomizes a type which is becoming increasingly important in this, our modern world: the pure technician; the bright, classless young man with no background, and with no more original aim than to make his way in the world with his technical and managerial abilities. It is precisely his lack of psychological and spiritual ballast, and the ease with which he handles the terrifying technical and organizational machinery of our age, which makes this slight type go so extremely far nowadays. This is their age. After the Hitlers and the Himmlers have been gotten rid of, the Speers will be long with us.

'What do you think of all this?' Hitler asked me, shouting.
I said, 'It is obviously not true.'

Back in Berlin, Aeromat telephoned me at the office. Although I was under a strict deadline for the revised plans for Unter den Linden, I told my secretary that he could come; I would see him over my dinner break, then return and finish the drawings.

Aeromat showed up shortly after seven and we left for the shop on the corner. I bought him a plate of peas, a sandwich and a beer, then ordered beef with anchovies for myself. 'And so,' I asked, 'what did you want to speak to me about?' As he sat slumped up near the window, I noticed that the hem of his jacket was coming undone at the wrists. Little threads were hanging down.

'I am getting married,' he said.

I could not imagine whom he had found to marry, but I smiled and brought my glass up in celebration. 'Good for you, Aeromat. Tell me who she is.'

'Her name is Anna. She is my landlady's daughter. She brings me meals and cleans my room.'

'Already a wife,' I chuckled.

'Anna Dieter. The celebration will be next Saturday, and I wanted you to be the witness. It would be a great honour for Anna and me.'

The following Saturday was the Führer's birthday, an occasion I could not miss. I explained that on any other day, I would gladly be a witness. Secretly, I could not believe this was happening or that it would actually come off.

'It will be a brief ceremony. In the afternoon – at my apartment. Surely the Führer's birthday party is at night?'

Admitting that it was, I saw no way out and reluctantly agreed to be there. Brightening, he began to tell me of her many lovely qualities, while I listened and cut my meat.

Hitler cried, 'How can a person be excited about such a thing? Killing animals, if it must be done, is the butcher's business. But to spend a great deal of money on it is an addiction. If only there were still some danger connected with hunting, as in the days when men used spears for killing game. But today, when anybody with a fat belly can safely shoot the animal down from a distance . . .'

Every night for three weeks, I sat with Hitler after dinner. It became my role to talk him out of his paranoid imaginings – a task at which I never succeeded. He began speaking about the possibility of using an atom bomb against England. Certainly it would have brought things to a quick and decisive end, but Professor Heisenberg had not given me a final answer to the question of whether nuclear fission could be kept under control with absolute certainty, or whether it might provoke a chain reaction.

As I spoke and explained all this, it was clear in Hitler's face that he was not delighted by the possibility that the Earth under his rule might be transformed into a glowing star.

The evening before the Führer's birthday, I sat in the black car, and decided to make a detour to the office to pick up some plans to look over the next morning. Aeromat had originially promised that the ceremony would not last more than fifteen minutes, but during our ensuing conversations, my responsibilities had stretched to two hours, and with all the work I had to complete I regretted having agreed to any of it.

Shuffling around in the dark in my office – the lights were controlled by a central lighting system – the telephone rang. I answered and it was Hitler. His demeanour had changed remarkably since the morning; he now was excited and tense.

'Can you interrupt your work at once? Come over here. It's extremely urgent! No, I can't tell you any more on the telephone.'

I returned to the car and explained to the chauffeur – an old, half-blind man named Olbricht – that I had to go to Schaedenwald, and what should I do with him? Olbricht lived in a district near mine, and had intended to drive me home, then retire for the night. 'Herr Speer, I will walk,' he said. But I could not let him walk; an old man like him could get attacked in the streets or collapse. 'It's impossible,' I said. I deliberated leaving him at the office, but it might be three in the morning before I would be able to return with the car. If I took Olbricht home first, it would be an hour before I arrived at Schaedenwald. Then I thought of Aeromat, whose apartment was close.

'Could I leave you at the apartment of my friend Aeromat? I could pick you up in the morning.'

'Ah yes, Herr Speer. Whatever is easiest for you. Whatever is best.'

We drove to the block of flats in which Aeromat was living, and leaving Olbricht in the car, I went through the courtyard to the eastern doors. It was nearly eleven at night. Hesitating, I knocked. There was no response. I knocked again, louder. There was a rattling on the other side of the wall and a terrified Aeromat answered the door, wrapped in a sheet.

'What's going on?' His eyes darted to either side of me, panicked.

I explained about Olbricht, and asked whether he could spend the night.

'Why don't you hail him a taxi!' Aeromat shrieked. 'Don't you know it is the eve of my wedding?' I had not taken that into account.

Aeromat came out into the hall, closing the door behind him. 'I have Anna inside with me. What do you think? She says she is a virgin, and yet she didn't cry out when I went into her, and there was no blood.'

'There is not always blood.'

'She is lying! I am certain of it! And where there is one lie, there are probably many more.' Aeromat was growing frantic.

I felt nervously preoccupied with Olbricht, whom I knew would be sitting there patiently, hands folded gently, like a good dog.

'Such things, little lies, do not matter much,' I said, knowing there were not many women in the world who would agree to take Aeromat for a husband. Thinking he would be better off with a woman who was a little bit immoral than no woman at all, I said, 'You must marry her tomorrow.'

'Are you sure?' he asked, searching my face.

This was all taking much longer than I had anticipated, and the Führer's excited and impatient voice was not out of my mind.

'Yes, of course! I will see you tomorrow.'

In the car, Olbricht was waiting as I'd expected, hands crossed, looking mildly ahead.

'I will have to take you with me to the Führer's.'

'Herr Speer, I will walk.'

'It will take you an hour to walk.'

'What do you worry for? I like to have a bit of exercise.' He smiled and thanked me, pressing on my hand, and left. I worried about it for another minute, then focused my mind on getting to Schaedenwald as quickly as I could. The following day, I read of how Olbricht had been murdered in the streets.

W hen I stepped into the cellar there were seven of them there. Hitler was infuriated, screaming, 'We cannot give up these areas!' Guderian retorted, 'But it's useless to sacrifice men in this senseless way. We must evacuate those soldiers at once.'

All of them were drunk.

'Speer!' Hitler cried when he saw me. His face was redder than usual, and he sounded choked up as he pointed to me. 'Do you remember that newspaper article about how long after the Hitlers of the world are gone, there will be millions of organizational men like you?'

I let them carry on like this around me, my face and words betraying nothing. I just pushed chocolates into my mouth and tried to avert my eyes.

T he ceremony was simple, and Anna was much prettier than I had expected. All the worries of the previous night seemed to have been forgotten. Aeromat introduced me to her vigorously, and during the short ceremony he tripped over his words, blushing and smiling widely at his bride. I signed my name to the marriage certificate with the same flourish with which I signed my blueprints. The girl's mother – the only other person in attendance – did not cry. She confided to me that she had never expected much from her daughter, and didn't this marriage prove it? Better that she'd had a son. 'A man like you,' she said, looking me up and down, 'with all his tools intact.'

I presented the champagne I had brought as a gift, then they invited me downstairs to the landlady's apartment for a reception, but I quietly declined, explaining that I had to return to work. The truth was, I had seen so little of my wife and children that week, I was looking forward to spending what remained of the afternoon at home with them before the Führer's birthday party.

M y wife and children were in the back garden, the girls on the swing set and the boys in the sandbox which I had built for them the previous summer. My wife was standing in the grass in her fur coat, hair in curlers, setting in preparation for our evening out.

'Has a sitter been employed?' I asked.

'Yes, she will be arriving at five thirty.'

'Will you be wearing your emerald dress?'

'Yes, of course.'

'And the necklace with the little pearls I bought you?'

'Yes.'

Satisfied, I watched my children play in the sunlight and felt my wife's warm, slender hand on the back of my neck.

When I was younger, it seemed to me a most valuable trait not to pursue delusions. But standing there then, I realized there was no period in which I was free of delusions, which during the war were in the air like a rapidly spreading contagion. During my middle years, every self-deception was multiplied as in a hall of mirrors, and in those mirrors I saw nothing but my own face, reproduced many times over. Nothing disturbed the uniformity of those hundreds of faces, all of them mine.

'Tomorrow let's go to the beach and bring the bicycles,' I said. 'It will be excellent for the children to go swimming.'

'In the snow?' she asked, bewildered.

I pretended not to hear. ■

AUTHOR'S NOTE: Many of the sentences in this story were taken from Albert Speer's autobiography, *Inside the Third Reich* (1970), translated from the German by Richard and Clara Winston. Some are reproduced here in their original form, while others have been altered, or taken out of context. I have also used some images and sentences from the opening of Vladimir Nabokov's 'Signs and Symbols' (1948).

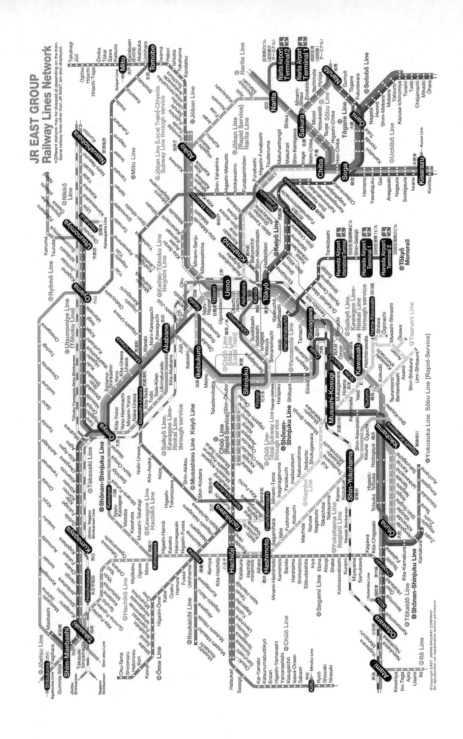

# JR EAST GROUP
## Railway Lines Network

*Different stations may be stopped at depending on the train.
Some railway lines other than JR EAST are also displayed.

© Copyright EAST JAPAN RAILWAY COMPANY
No reproduction but not regularization without permission

# YOKOSUKA BLUE LINE

## Steven Dunn

### Participation

We fly from Hawaii to Japan in order to meet the submarine. Once we get on base to check in, our Officer in Charge receives a message from the Fleet Commander that says, Due to inclement weather, the submarine will not be able to pull into port for at least one more week. He turns and says, Well, we don't have shit to do. But check in with me at least once a day. I have to physically see you, so let's say, starting tomorrow, muster with me in our hotel lobby every afternoon at 15.00.

We check into the Yokosuka Prince Hotel. What! I've never seen people smoking cigarettes while checking into a hotel! I light up too. The ash hanging from my lip falls on my receipt. Our Chief organizes a team lunch at Hard Rock Cafe. They're all excited. But this is my first time outside the States. I am not eating at Hard Rock Cafe.

No one wants to go with me anywhere else. And we're not supposed to go anywhere without at least one more person. Guess I'm going to Hard Rock. I sit for a few minutes, then tell them I have jet lag and I'm going back to the hotel. I walk across the street to the train station.

At the train station I find a color-coded railway map. Red, blue, yellow, green, black lines intersect and run parallel and figure eight and split and bunch and peak and valley. Where to go? I close my eyes and circle my finger around the map. Wherever my finger lands. Between Otsuki and Saruhashi. Otsuki.

There are too many lights and buttons on the ticket machine. Spaceship cockpit. I walk to the ticket-booth window and point to Otsuki on my map and a man gives me a ticket.

The train pulls away from Yokosuka, blue line on the map, white dots denote cities, I Pac-Man city names: Taura, Higashi-Zushi, Zushi, Yokodai, Negishi, Yamate. Transfer to green line in Yokohama. Continuing past the big Ferris wheel. Gray skyscrapers blur into bright green rice fields spotted with those old houses I've always seen in ninja movies. I wish ninjas were fighting on this train. Fuzzy green and black mountains. I'm hungry. Just a snack.

Off at Nakayama. At one of the stalls I buy a dark purple pickled radish the size of a flashlight. A lot of people are in line at another stall. Must be good. I follow. In line I see people walking from the front with paper cones filled with, crickets? An old lady tosses a few in her mouth. A young man tosses some in his. At the front and a lady is scooping crickets into oil and lightly frying them. I pay for my paper cone and toss a few into my mouth. Alternate: crickets, radish, crickets, radish. I buy a pint of beer from a vending machine.

Another hour and a half and the train pockets into a forest valley. Otsuki. I walk through a park, tree-lined path. Pink and white petals float from the gray sky. At the end of the park I walk into a wooden restaurant and sit at the bar. A woman places a rolled, warm moist towel in front of me. I want to order, but don't know how to ask. The chef starts pressing rice and placing fish on the rice and nodding when he hands it to me. I eat. I never order but the orange red white fish keeps coming. Tiny red balls piled in a crispy seaweed tub. The balls pop between my teeth and salty fish juice squirts. I point to a bottle of, sake? Gulp that shit between bites of fish. I get my bill, do the quick exchange rate, not over my $120 per diem, probably. Fuck it, pull out my government credit card. Stagger back through the dark park to the train station.

Fuck that map. I know where I'm going, goddammit: green line southeast to Yokohama, blue line south to Yokosuka. I doze off.

The train jerks me awake. Slowing. Out the window reads Shinjuku. My watch reads 23.00. I pull out the map. I got on the wrong line. Almost to Tokyo. Oh well. I don't get off the train until I'm in the heart of Tokyo, whatever that is. I can't recognize any of the shit I've seen on TV.

I turn one corner, another corner, another. Clubs everywhere. Stinky African men in black and burgundy suits urge me to come to their clubs. Tall Russian prostitutes with thick accents say they want to suck my big black dick. I try to walk into one club but three Japanese men in black suits with slicked-back hair cross their arms in an X and say, Japanese only, Japanese only. I say I'm half Japanese. They keep making an X. I scoot to the next club.

Strobe lights, bass, glow sticks swirling, pulsing rainbows, synthesizers. I push my way to the bar. Order a double Bombay Sapphire on the rocks. A blond girl next to me applauds my choice. She yells, How are you doing. I yell, Good. Where are you from, she says. Hawaii, I say, what about you. Canada. She pulls me on to the dance floor and I pretend to know how to dance to this music. We go back to the bar. She yells that I need a real drink and orders two American Girls: tall shot glass, red liquor on the bottom, clear in the middle, blue on top. I wonder why it doesn't mix before I pour it down my throat. My eyes water and snot pours out my nose, I can't close my mouth and drool drips to the floor. She's doing the same. We go back to the dance floor.

I've resigned to doing jumping jacks while shaking my head yes. She's doing a rain dance. Back to the bar. American Girl. Dance. Bar.

We stumble outside to smoke. She tells me she's teaching English in, somewhere, but comes to Tokyo to party. I tell her I'm on government business, official government business, in Yokosuka. She says, Oh, you're in the military, navy? Yeah, I'm in a hotel down there, wanna go back with me? She bursts out laughing, It's one in the morning, the trains have stopped running. You're stuck here for the night. We can get a hotel here. Sounds gooood, I say. Let's eat first, she says. I follow her down the street and around a corner to a curry house. It's the next day, new $120 per diem. I pay for both our meals. We stagger around the corner, I pay for the hotel with the good ol' government credit card. I wish she was Japanese. This is like eating at Hard Rock. In the room we strip each other's clothes, I hold in my farts from all of that curry.

When I awake she is gone. My watch reads 12.37. Good, I can make it back to muster at 15.00. Shit, I didn't use a condom. I jump in the shower and wash the white crust off my pubic hair.

I find my way back to the train station. Hop on. On the map there is a big loop around Tokyo, and I need to transfer at Shinagawa. I fall asleep, but when I awake I've missed the transfer, which means I have to ride the train around the loop. I keep falling asleep, missing my transfer, stuck on the loop three times.

I finally make it to Yokosuka. I stroll in the hotel at 15.48. My Chief is waiting in the lobby. If you hadn't showed up before 16.00 I would've reported you missing, he says. Where were you? Um . . . I went to Tokyo this morning and it took longer – I don't wanna hear it, he says. You could've been kidnapped by a terrorist and tortured for all I know. Go to your room, and stay.

I am not to be alone until we get back to Hawaii. My Chief assigns me two babysitters. Wherever they go, I am supposed to go. Which means that for the rest of the week, I eat at Hard Rock, KFC and Pizza Hut. At night I have to go with them to what they call Buy-Me-Drinkie bars, where they buy girls drinks that are really teas, but cost double what our drinks cost. My sitters brag to the girls about how they have to take care of me. The girls pretend that they think it's cute. When my sitters buy the girls enough drinks the girls give them hand jobs under the table, or the real deal in a back room. Whenever we leave, my sitters say, Yeah, this is what Japan is all about. They piss on the sidewalks and dare one of those little Japanese fuckers to say something. What are they gonna say, one of my sitters says. We bombed the shit out of their country and took all of their women, they're all pussies. Japanese women want real men. Look at these little pussy cars, they say and laugh. They squat, lift and roll the tiny car on its side. The submarine finally pulls in. I stand on the balcony in port and wonder why I volunteered for this.

steel walls steel beds steel toilets steel people. steel

here. stuff head in headphones and listen for twelve     hours just in case *ksshhk ksshhk* maximum unambiguous range for a radar is twice the speed of light ?mes the pulse repe??on frequency. pulse repe??on frequency is the mathema?cal inverse of pulse repe??on period. frequency harmonics measured from two to forty gigahertz *ksshh* keep listening. pretended listen. pretending listening *kssssssshhhhhk* Dinghai, Xiaopingdao, Jiangzhuang, Tangshan *ksssh* a radar emiHng a small pulse dura?on with high pulses per second can [possibly] detect a periscope depending on synthe?c aperture antenna over a target region to provide finer spa?al resolu?on. i wish i could look out the periscope. nothing's up there but water

*shhh*

they're following us we're following them.                     paper plates

keep sound down. don't cook in pots and pans pb & j

pb & j powdered eggs pb & j cup o' noodles instant oatmeal pb & j. can we go home?

Finally we hit port. Humidity. Back streets. Small pagodas. This is your first time here, my babysitter says, you gotta see this shit. Okay, I slur, I didn't know Thailand was so dirty. We walk around corners, through alleys, people sell meat on sticks, drowned snakes and lizards in whiskey bottles. We stumble upon a sort of house building.

We duck our heads and walk to the basement where men sit at tables and women sass around collecting money. We sit at a table toward the front of the stage and order more drinks. The deejay announces something. The other men cheer and whistle. A naked woman walks on stage. She dances, circles her nipples with long fingernails. She lies on her back with a wedge pushing her hips upward. Spreads her legs. And shoots a dart out of her vagina, pops a balloon on the other side of the stage.

Everyone cheers. Mouth open. No tricks, my sitter says, That's the real goddamn deal. The deejay places a stack of quarters on the stage. She does a split over the quarters. When she stands the quarters are gone. She walks to our table and motions me to pull her arm down like a slot machine. Out come the quarters one by one. She leaves the stage. I wonder where she lives. How does she know this stuff. We fly back to Hawaii first class. ■

Vasily Semyonovich Grossman (1905–1964)

# STALINGRAD

## *Vasily Grossman*

TRANSLATED FROM THE RUSSIAN
BY ROBERT AND ELIZABETH CHANDLER

## 1

The companies commanded by Bach and Lenard settled into the cool, spacious basement of a large building. The broken windows let in light and fresh air. The soldiers diligently carried down pieces of furniture from apartments not damaged by fire. The basement looked more like a warehouse than an army bivouac.

Each soldier had his own bed, covered with a quilt or blanket. They also carried down little tables, armchairs with fine, ornately carved legs and even a three-leaved mirror.

In one corner of the basement Stumpfe, the battalion's senior soldier and a general favourite, created a kind of model bedroom. He brought down a double bed from a top-floor apartment, spread a pale blue blanket over it and placed two pillows in embroidered pillowcases by the headboard. He stood bedside tables, covered with small towels, on each side of the bed, and laid a carpet on the stone floor. Then he found two chamber pots and two pairs of old-people's fur-trimmed slippers. And he hung ten framed family photographs, taken from different apartments, on the walls.

The photographs he chose were all rather comic. One was of an old man and an old woman, probably working class, dressed up for some important occasion. The old man wore a jacket and tie; seeming ill at ease, he was frowning severely. The old woman wore a black dress with large white buttons. She had a knitted shawl draped over her shoulders and she was sitting with her hands folded in her lap, looking meekly down at the ground.

Another, much older photograph was of the same couple (the experts were all in agreement) on the day of their wedding. She was wearing a white veil, with small bunches of wax orange blossom; pretty but sad, she looked as if she were preparing for difficult years to come. The groom stood beside her, resting one elbow on the back of a tall black chair; he was wearing patent-leather boots and a black three-piece suit, with a watch chain attached to the waistcoat.

The third photograph showed a wooden coffin lined with lace paper. Inside the coffin lay a little girl in a white dress; standing around it, their hands on the coffin's sides, were various strange-looking people: an old man in a long calico shirt with no belt; a boy with his mouth open; a man with a beard and several old women in kerchiefs, their faces fixed and solemn.

Without taking his boots off or removing the sub-machine gun hanging from his neck, Stumpfe collapsed onto the bed. His legs trembling, he called out in a high-pitched, affected voice, as if imitating a Russian woman, '*Lieber Ivan, komm zu mir!*'[1] The entire company roared with laughter.

Then he and Corporal Ledeke sat down on the chamber pots and improvised comic dialogues: first, 'Ivan and His Mother'; then, 'Rabbi Israel and His Wife Sarah'.

Very soon, soldiers from other regiments were coming to attend repeat performances. Preifi appeared too, somewhat tipsy, along with Bach and Lenard.

Stumpfe and Ledeke went through the whole programme from

---

[1] 'Dear Ivan, come to me!'

beginning to end. Preifi laughed more loudly than anyone, helplessly rubbing his hands against his huge chest and saying, 'Stop, stop! You're killing me!'

In the evening the soldiers hung blankets and shawls over the windows, lit the large pink- and green-shaded oil lamps, filled with a mixture of petrol and salt, and sat down around a large table.

Only six of them had served throughout the Russian campaign. The others were from divisions previously stationed in Germany, Poland and France. Two had been in Rommel's Africa Corps.

The company had its aristocrats and its pariahs. The Germans made fun of the Austrians, but they also often made vicious fun of one another. Those born in East Prussia were considered ignorant hawbucks. The Bavarians laughed at the Berliners, saying that Berlin was a Jewish city, a melting pot for riff-raff from Italy, Romania, Hungary, Poland, Czechoslovakia, Mexico, Brazil and any number of other countries, and that it was impossible to find a single true German there. The Prussians, the Bavarians and the Berliners all despised the Alsatians, calling them foreign swine. Men repatriated from Latvia, Lithuania and Estonia were referred to as 'quarter-German'; all the miserable weaknesses of the Slav East were thought to have entered their blood. As for *Volksdeutsche* from Central and Eastern Europe, they were not considered German at all; there were official instructions to keep an eye on them and not to entrust them with any tasks of importance.

The company's aristocrats were Stumpfe and Vogel, both former members of the SS. They were among the many thousands of SS who, on the Führer's orders, had been transferred to the Wehrmacht to boost morale.

Stumpfe was generally seen as the company's life and soul, as its moral backbone. He was tall and – unlike most corporals and rank-and-file soldiers – round and plump in the face. He was bold, smart and lucky, and he had an unrivalled ability to go round a half-destroyed Russian village and conjure up enough good foodstuffs for a parcel to send back home. He only had to look at an 'Easterner' for honey and fatback to appear. All this, naturally, impressed and delighted his fellow soldiers.

He loved his wife, his children and his brother. He was constantly writing letters to them and the food parcels he sent them were as rich and nutritious as those sent by officers. His wallet was full of photographs, which he had shown more than once to everyone in the company.

There were photos of his rather thin wife – clearing a dining table piled with dishes; leaning against the fireplace, wearing pyjamas; sitting in a boat, her hands on the oars; holding a doll and smiling; and going for a walk round the village. There were also photographs of his two children: a tall boy and a pretty little six-year-old girl with blonde hair down to her shoulders.

The other soldiers sighed as they looked at these photographs. And before returning a photograph to his wallet, Stumpfe would gaze at a dear face long and intently; he could have been contemplating an icon.

He had a gift for telling stories about his children; Lenard once said to him that, with his talents, he should be performing on stage. One of his best stories, about preparing the family Christmas tree, was full of sweet, funny invented words, sudden cries and gestures, childish hypocrisy, childish cunning and childish envy of other children's presents. The story's effect on its audience was often unexpected. While Stumpfe was speaking, people would be laughing out loud, but when he came to the end they were often moved to tears.

But it was not only Stumpfe's stories that were paradoxical. He himself combined qualities one might have thought irreconcilable. This lover of his wife and children was capable of extraordinary, devil-may-care violence. On the rampage, he truly did become a devil; it was impossible to restrain him.

In Kharkov, dead drunk, he once climbed out of a fourth-floor window and walked right round the building on a narrow ledge, pistol in hand, firing at anything that caught his attention.

On another occasion, he set fire to a house, got up onto the roof and, as if in charge of an orchestra, began to conduct the flames and smoke and the wails of the women and children.

Stumpfe ran amok a third time on a moonlit May night in a Ukrainian village. He threw a hand grenade into the middle of some trees in blossom. The grenade got caught in the branches and exploded four metres away from Stumpfe. Leaves and white petals rained down on him, while one piece of shrapnel ripped open the top of one of his boots and a second punctured a shoulder board. Stumpfe suffered only mild concussion, but it was two days before he recovered his hearing.

There was something about his face, about the sudden glassy glitter in the depths of his large, calm eyes, that terrified the 'Easterners' he so despised. When he entered a hut, sniffed disdainfully as he looked slowly around him, pointed to a stool and ordered an astonished child or dazed old woman to wipe it clean with a white towel, they understood at once that it was best to do as he said.

Stumpfe's understanding of the psychology of Russian peasants was astonishing. After observing a woman for five minutes, he could win bets as to the quantity of honey, eggs and butter in the hut and whether or not there were treasures hidden beneath the floorboards: new boots, cloth or woollen dresses.

He was intelligent and quicker than any of his comrades to learn words of Russian. He soon knew enough to be able to organise all he needed without recourse to a phrase book or dictionary. 'I've simplified the Russian language,' he used to say. 'In my grammar there is only one mood: the imperative.'

His fellow soldiers loved hearing him talk about his past; he had witnessed a great deal.

As a young man, he had worked in a sports shop. After losing his job, he spent two summers working on farms, in charge of a threshing machine. In 1926 he worked for three months in the Ruhr, in the Kronprinz coal mine. Then, after obtaining his licence, he became a professional driver. First, he delivered truckloads of milk, and next he worked as a chauffeur for a well-known dentist in Gelsenkirchen. A year later he became a taxi driver in Berlin. Then he worked for a year as an assistant concierge in the hotel 'Europe' and then as a kitchen supervisor in a small restaurant frequented by lawyers and industrialists.

He was happy to see his hands becoming soft and white and he took good care of them, wanting to erase any last trace of the harm done to his skin by some of his former jobs.

In the restaurant Stumpfe had his first real encounter with a world that had always intrigued him. On one occasion he calculated that a single deal – buying a portfolio of shares just before they shot up in value after a long slump – enabled a customer to make a profit equivalent to what he himself, in his previous job, would have earned over a period of one hundred and twenty years – or one thousand and four hundred and forty months, or forty thousand days, or three hundred thousand hours, or nineteen million minutes. The customer had made this deal between two sips of coffee, using the restaurant telephone; it had taken him less than two minutes.

Some miraculous power was at work here – and this power intrigued Stumpfe.

Breathing the atmosphere of wealth, hearing omniscient waiters talk about which of their customers had bought a new Hispano-Suiza,[2] which had just built a villa and which had bought a pendant for a well-known actress – all this was a source of both pain and pleasure.

Stumpfe's comrades enjoyed his sense of humour. He had nicknames for almost everyone in the company; he was quick to notice people's peculiarities and he could mimic them to perfection. He had a whole repertoire of campaign sketches and anecdotes: 'Sommer Four-Eyes receives a dressing-down from the battalion commander'; 'Vogel puts together a modest breakfast – twenty fried eggs and a small chicken'; 'In front of her small children Ledeke the determined womaniser wins the love of a Russian peasant woman'; 'Meierhof enables a Jew to understand that it is in his interests to leave this world sooner than the god of the Jews had decreed'.

---

[2] A Spanish company, founded in 1904, that produced luxury cars.

2

Stumpfe, Vogel and Ledeke were sitting together at a round table, lit by a lamp with a pink shade.

Bound by the ties of difficult work, shared danger and shared merriment, the three friends had few secrets from one another.

Vogel, a tall, lean youth, still a schoolboy when the war began, looked at Stumpfe and Ledeke, who were almost dozing, and asked, 'And where is our friend Schmidt?'

'On sentry duty,' replied Ledeke.

'It seems the war will soon be over,' said Vogel. 'But this really is a huge city. I got lost on my way to the regimental command post.'

'Yes,' said Ledeke. 'I've become a coward now. The closer we are to the end of the war, the more terrible it would be to get killed.'

Vogel nodded. 'Yes, we've buried a lot of men. It really would be stupid to die now.'

'I find it hard to believe I'll soon be back home,' said Ledeke.

'You'll have plenty to tell people, especially if you catch a certain illness,' said Vogel, who disapproved of womanisers. He slowly ran his hand over the ribbons attached to his medals. 'As for me, I may not have as many of these as some of our heroes at HQ, but at least I can say that I earned them honourably.'

Stumpfe had not spoken until then. Smiling wryly, he said, 'There's no writing on your medals, and the ones earned in combat look no different from the ones given out at HQ.'

'*Unexpectedly, Stumpfe falls into despondency*,' said Ledeke.

'Stumpfe's like me. He doesn't want to take risks just before the end.'

'Is something the matter?' asked Vogel. 'I don't understand.'

'Why would you?' said Stumpfe. 'You'll return to your father's razor-blade factory and you'll live like a god.'

'But you'll be doing all right for yourself too,' Ledeke replied irritably.

'Because of a few parcels?' Stumpfe asked angrily, thumping his hand down on the table. 'I don't think one or two parcels will get me very far!'

'And that little purse you wear on a chain?'

'Think I've got some great treasure in it? It's only now, at the end of the war, that I can see what a damned fool I've been. Dancing on the roof of a burning hut while others were making themselves rich!'

'It's all a matter of luck,' said Vogel. 'I know someone who was posted to Paris. Somehow he ended up with a diamond pendant. When he was back home on leave, he showed it to a jeweller. The jeweller just asked, "How old are you?" "Thirty-six," he replied. "Well, then," said the jeweller, "even if you live to a hundred and have many children and grandchildren, none of your family need ever know want." And the pendant just fell into my friend's hands.'

'Your friend was a lucky man,' said Ledeke. 'Stumpfe's right – you don't find diamond pendants in the hut of a Russian peasant. We'd have been better off on the Western Front. Or if we'd been tank men. They can take what they like – quality cloth, fine furs. We're on the wrong front and in the wrong branch of service.'

'And we're the wrong rank,' added Vogel. 'If Stumpfe were a general, he'd be looking a lot happier. They send truck after truck back home. I used to chat to their orderlies when I was on guard duty at Army HQ. You wouldn't believe it. They used to argue about which of their bosses had sent back the most furs.'

'*Pelze . . . Pelze . . .*'[3] said Ledeke. 'It's the only word you ever hear at HQ. When we get to Persia and India, it'll be carpets.'

'You're a pair of fools,' said Stumpfe. 'Unfortunately, I've realised today that I've been a fool too. Fur coats and carpets are neither here nor there.' He looked around, then went on in a whisper, 'It's a matter of my children's future. I once took part in a special action in some miserable little shtetl. That's where I obtained these little bits and pieces – this gold coin, this watch, this little ring. Well, imagine what

---

[3] 'Furs . . . Furs . . .'

treasures come the way of *Einsatzgruppen* carrying out liquidations in Odessa, Kiev or Warsaw! Do you follow me?'

'I'm not so sure about these special actions,' said Vogel. 'My nerves aren't strong enough.'

'A pfennig from every Jew who's stopped breathing,' said Stumpfe. 'That's all.'

'Then you won't do too badly,' said Ledeke. 'The Führer's fully behind these special actions. It'll be whole wagonloads of pfennigs.'

They laughed, but Stumpfe, usually only too ready to laugh and joke, was in a serious mood.

'I'm not an idealist like you are,' he said to Vogel, 'and I fully admit it. You're like Lieutenant Bach – a man of the nineteenth century.'

'That's true,' said Ledeke. 'Not everyone has a rich family. It's easy enough to say fine words if your father owns a whole factory.'

'I've made up my mind,' said Stumpfe. 'I'm going to have a word with First Lieutenant Lenard. Maybe he can get me transferred – and I can make up for lost time before it's too late. I'll tell him I can hear a call, that it's my inner voice. He's a poet and he likes things like that.'

Then Stumpfe took out another of his photographs. It showed a huge column of women, children and old men walking between rows of armed soldiers. Some were looking towards the photographer; most were looking down at the ground. In the foreground stood an open-top car. The young woman inside was wearing a black fox stole, which brought out the paleness of her skin and the gold of her hair. Some officers standing nearby were watching the column of people on foot. The woman had plump white hands and she was holding up a small dog with a big head and shaggy black hair, apparently wanting it too to look at the column of people. She could have been a mother showing some unusual sight to a small boy in order that, years later, she could tell him what he had once witnessed.

Vogel studied the photograph for a long time. 'It's a Scottish terrier,' he said. 'We've got one very like it at home. Every time she writes, my mother passes on his greetings.'

'Quite a woman!' Ledeke sighed.

'My sister-in-law,' said Stumpfe. 'And the man leaning against the car door is my brother.'

'He looks very like you,' said Ledeke. 'At first I thought it was you. But he's got SS lapels and he's a higher rank.'

'The photo was taken in Kiev, in September 1941. Near a cemetery, but I've forgotten the name of the place.[4] My brother did well out of that Purim.[5] If your dad ever wants to expand his factory, my brother can certainly lend him a few pfennigs.'

'Let me have another look at her,' said Ledeke. 'There's something of the ancient world about her, especially with this procession of death in the background. A Roman lady in the Colosseum.'

'Before the war,' Stumpfe continued, 'my brother was an actor in an operetta company and his wife was a ticket seller. If you'd come across her then, you'd hardly have noticed her. Eighty per cent of a woman's beauty comes from her clothes, the way she does her hair, the elegance of her surroundings. When the war's over, I want my own wife to be able to look like this too. My brother's in the General Government now. Reading between the lines, I understand from his letters that they've established something remarkable there – a real factory for processing Jews. What happened on the outskirts of Kiev was mere child's play. He's told me that, if I can get a transfer, he'll find me work at his factory. And don't worry – I've got nerves of steel!'[6]

---

[4] Stumpfe's brother evidently took part in the massacre at Babi Yar, a ravine just outside Kiev. There were two cemeteries nearby: a Russian Orthodox cemetery and a Jewish cemetery. The latter was closed in 1937.

[5] The Jewish festival of Purim is recorded in the Bible, in the Book of Esther. Haman, vizier to King Ahasuerus, ruler of Persia, was plotting to destroy the Jewish people. Queen Esther, a Jew herself, manages to foil this plot. The festival commemorates her success.

[6] The 'factory' in question is Treblinka. In 'The Hell of Treblinka' (an article first published in 1944), Grossman writes, 'We know about a huge young man named Stumpfe who broke out into uncontrollable laughter every time he murdered a prisoner or when one was executed in his presence. He was known as "Laughing Death".'

'But what about comradeship?' Vogel burst out. 'Apart from anything else, there does exist such a thing as comradeship. Soldierly comradeship, the comradeship of the front line. Wanting to bugger off on your own after fourteen months that have bound us closer than brothers! I call it vile!'

Ledeke, always easily influenced, joined in with Vogel. 'Yes, we've been through a lot together. And I'm not sure your plan will work anyway. There's no guarantee they'll accept you. Somewhere like that, they won't just be taking whoever shows up. Whereas if you stay here in Stalingrad, you're sure to be decorated. When the war comes to an end, there'll be no Germans further east than we are. And there'll be a special gold medal – for Stalingrad and the Volga. A medal that will bring us more than mere honour.'

'Will it buy us a castle in Prussia?' Stumpfe retorted. He blew his nose.

'Ledeke, you're missing the point!' said Vogel. 'I'm talking about feelings – and you're like a peasant selling beets in the market. These things should be kept separate.'

And suddenly the three friends were quarrelling viciously.

'Fuck you and your fucking feelings!' Stumpfe yelled at Vogel. 'You're a rich bourgeois. *I'm* afraid of having nothing to eat when the war's over.'

Shocked by the look of hate on his comrade's face, Vogel said, 'It's not quite like that, you know. The inspectors from the Ministry of Industry have been giving my father hell. He looks more like a frightened worker than a wealthy capitalist.'

'I hope they really do give him hell! You too! You're all parasites and you should be flayed alive. The Führer will show you what's what!'

Stumpfe then looked at Ledeke. But Ledeke, instead of agreeing in his usual way with one of the others, said, 'To be honest with you – now that the war's almost over – all this talk about the unity of the German nation is bullshit. The bourgeoisie will go on stuffing themselves. Nazis and SS, like Stumpfe and his dear brother, are sure to do all right for themselves too. If anyone gets flayed alive, it'll be stupid workers like me and my peasant father. So much for German unity! When the war's over, our roads will part.'

'Comrades, what's come over you?' said Vogel. 'What's happened? You've become different men.'

Stumpfe looked at Vogel intently. 'All right, all right,' he said in a conciliatory tone. 'Enough of all this. And I want you to know that if I don't go through with this plan of mine, it'll be because I care about my friends.'

A soldier came in. He'd just been relieved from sentry duty at the entrance to the company's basement.

'What was that shooting just now?' came a sleepy voice from the half-dark.

The soldier put down his sub-machine gun with a loud clatter, stretched and said, 'The duty lieutenant told me that some Russian unit has captured the railway station. But it's not in our sector.'

One of the soldiers laughed. 'They're probably so scared they lost their way. They meant to go east but ended up going west by mistake.'

'You're probably right,' said Ledeke. 'East and west mean nothing to them.'

The soldier sat down on his bed, brushed some muck off the blanket and said crossly, 'Listen. I've had to say this twice already. Before I go on duty tomorrow, I'll be putting a grenade under this blanket. I can't believe how little respect anyone has for other people's belongings. I want to take this blanket home with me – and someone's marched all over it without even taking their boots off.'

Calming down at the thought that he would soon be able to have a good rest, he pulled off his own boots and said, 'There may be shooting going on round the station, but Lenard's having a party. They've found a gramophone, they've got guests, and they've dragged in some weeping maidens. Even our Bach's joining in – seems he's decided to lose his innocence before the end of the war. Shooting in one sector – and song and dance in another!'

'They'll capitulate any day now,' said a voice from the darkness. 'I can feel it in the air. Home! The mere thought of it makes my heart miss a beat.' ■

# THE HAZARA

## Monika Bulaj

## Introduction by Janine di Giovanni

It was 2009. We had left early that rain-soaked morning, long before daybreak, loading our jeep in Kabul with plastic containers of water and petrol, spare tyres and food. I brought a sleeping bag in case we broke down on the twelve-hour journey; my driver had a gun to ward off bandits and kidnappers. We were going to Bamiyan, where Genghis Khan had tried to destroy every living thing and which is the ancient home of the Hazara Shias, the third largest ethnic group in Afghanistan.

The road was bumpy, uncomfortable, endless. Mile after mile of vast earth and sky, mud houses; women in burkas working the fields in the rain. Part of the sense of remoteness and isolation is deliberate: Bamiyan lies between the immensity of the Koh-i-Baba mountains and the Hindu Kush, making the Hazara less vulnerable to enemies.

Throughout history, the Hazara have been persecuted, scorned, outlawed, forced from their lands and religiously and ethnically cleansed. In the 1990s, the Taliban committed atrocities against them in the central and northern parts of Afghanistan, and killed their leader, Abdul Ali Mazari. Then in March 2001, they destroyed the Hazara's vast and ancient Buddhas to world protest. But the Hazara survived and the people I met once I reached Bamiyan were not victims. They were proud, resourceful, fierce in their own way.

When I was introduced to the then governor of Bamiyan Province, Dr Habiba Sarabi, a former minister of women's affairs in Afghanistan, she told me that even though she was the daughter of an illiterate mother, she was encouraged to read and write. She was mocked as she walked to school alone, her books tucked under her arm. But she fought for her education, and she fought for her daughter to have an education, which was denied during the Taliban years. Later, she introduced me to other Hazara activists who were fighting for their rights and their place in Afghanistan.

To document the Hazara in these photographs, Monika Bulaj travelled through places like Herat, Mazar-e-Sharif, Bamiyan, Jalalabad, Faisalabad, Balkha and Kunduz in 2009 and 2010, capturing the Hazara's daily life. She photographed them against the stark and sometimes terrifying beauty that surrounds them: mountains and forests; bleak landscapes and trash-filled cities. There are women praying in Shia mosques; Hazara men with their beloved birds; the ancient Shia rituals performed during holy days. There is Hazara family life and the sorrow of the refugee camps; the blank, closed faces of the opium-addicted Hazara men near Herat; the ancient ceremonies of the dead. She follows the children at school; the families in shared taxis; the Hazara quarters of Kabul.

Her work reminds me of the late Eve Arnold, the first woman to join Magnum Photos in 1957, who also travelled alone into challenging territories. Arnold spent years tracing China, then a closed country, in the 1960s, going deep into remote areas by train and bus, solo except for her cameras. Bulaj's granular depiction of the Hazara is as important as Arnold's images of the forgotten people in Mongolia.

Bulaj chronicles the Hazara ancestors, their heroes, but also gets to the heart of their dilemma: they are still frequently targeted by those who wish to destroy the building of democracy in Afghanistan. On 22 April 2018, an Islamic State terrorist blew up a voting registration centre in a western Kabul neighbourhood predominantly occupied by Hazara. About fifty-seven people, including children, were killed and more than a hundred were injured.

The Hazara are trying to become important forces in local elections and produce new leaders who can develop the practices of democracy and overcome the traditions of ethnic and tribal competition. Through Bulaj's work, we see the Hazara – ancient, battered, but strong – emerging. ∎

Two Hazara women walking close to the ruins of Darul Aman Palace, which was built by order of King Amanullah Khan in the 1920s. Khan introduced the first modern constitution to Afghanistan in 1923, which guaranteed equal rights for men and women, and promoted the education of women as well as compulsory elementary education for all. This constitution was abolished after Khan's forced abdication and the palace has since been through several cycles of damage, destruction and reconstruction.

Ziarat-e-Sakhi, Kabul. Shia Muslims (Hazara and Pashtun) beat themselves with metal chains on one of the holiest days the Shia year, Ashura, observed on the tenth day of Muharram.

Hazara women pray, Kabul.

Women entering a Shia mosque, Kabul. Shia mosques are frequently the target of terrorist attacks, especially during the month of Muharram and during Nowruz.

Charahi Qambar, a refugee camp on the outskirts of Kabul. More than 7,000 internally displaced Afghans live here, originatin from provinces such as Helmand, Kandahar and Ghazni.

Boys playing with kites close to Sultan Mohammed Khan Telai Mausoleum, Kabul.

Street view, Kabul.

The sepulchre believed to be of Ali ibn Abi Talib, Blue Mosque, Mazar-i-Sharif.

Hazara neighbourhood, Kabul.

Fatima Ahmadi, a Hazara university student, 2009. A year after this photograph was taken Ahmadi started working as journalist for Afghan TV. She now lives in Europe.

madrasa (Islamic school) for Hazara children, Kabul.

At dawn in Kabul, women and children await the nocturnal procession of thousands of Sunni men mourning Husayn ibn Ali, the grandson of the Prophet Muhammad, killed at the Battle of Karbala in the year 61 AH (AD 680).

Hazara children look out over a Shia neighbourhood, Kabul.

Bird market, Kabul.

The nocturnal procession of thousands of Sunni men in mourning during Ashura, Kabul.

Hazara women during the celebration of Ashura, Kabul.

The nocturnal procession and ecstatic prayers of thousands of Sunni men in mourning during Ashura, Kabul. The suffering of Husayn ibn Ali and his family inspires piety among both Shiites and Sunnis; the Shiites practise self-flagellation, the Sunni practise *dhikr*, a series of devotional acts in which short phrases or prayers are repeated in remembrance of Allah.

Hazara walking through the Bamiyan valley, close to where the largest of the two statues of the Buddha once stood. The statue dated from the sixth century AD, and were destroyed by the Taliban in 2001.

Boys playing near the Sultan Mohammed Khan Telai Mausoleum, Kabul.

A Hazara patient at the International Committee of the Red Cross Orthopaedic Centre, Kabul.

A Hazara man embraces a sacred pole raised during Nowruz. Ziarat-e-Sakhi, Kabul.

Boys playing by the Sultan Mohammed Khan Telai Mausoleum, Kabul.

Chindawol Heights, a Hazara neighbourhood. During Ashura, Shiite children beat their chests while wearing green tunics.

28 April 2009, Chindawol, Kabul. For the first time in sixteen years, the public celebration of Mujahideen Victory Day was cancelled and a curfew was imposed by President Hamid Karzai in response to an attempt on his life during the previous year's celebrations. Mujahideen Victory Day pays tribute to the mujahideen rebel forces who overthrew Mohammad Najibullah's socialist government in 1992. The holiday evokes a sense of heroic patriotism in some Afghans and memories of the devastation of civil war in others.

Women and children walk long distances to fetch water, Kabul.

Ziarat-e-Sakhi, Kabul.

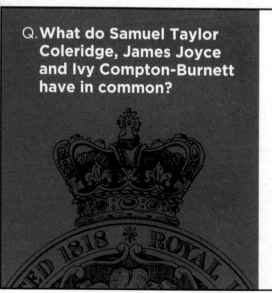

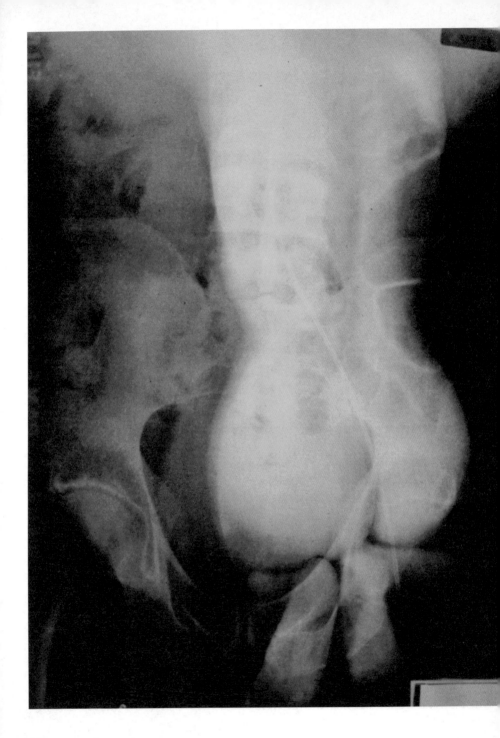

# ALL HAIL THE HOLY BONE

## Maggie O'Farrell

It is one of those static, chill days you get in Edinburgh towards the end of winter. Ice sheets the pavements and roads; no wind stirs the blackened branches of the trees; the fallen foliage from the now distant autumn is frost-gilded and crisp underfoot.

I am swathed in multiple layers of merino wool, a scarf covering half my face, and I am holding myself stiffly upright on the very edge of a stool in a small and glaringly lit room. Despite the wool, despite my mittens and sheepskin-lined boots, I am unremittingly, unavoidably cold. Chronic pain, I am discovering, is tiring, draining, domineering: it absorbs all your energy and focus; it drives other thoughts from your head. My body seems unable to keep itself at a liveable temperature, so preoccupied is it with the extreme discomfort of my back.

In the room with me is a doctor from Australia and I am wondering to myself how can he be wearing just a shirt under that white coat? Doesn't he feel the cold? How can he be unaffected by this temperature?

I have just explained to him that, three days ago, I leaned sideways to move a counter in a game I was playing with my children and I felt a crunch, followed by a rip, and then a horrible shifting sensation as something slid out of place in my lower back. Pain spread like a stain, outwards and upwards, and I have, ever since then, been unable to move, sit, walk or stand without unbelievable agony.

We are, he and I, gazing at an X-ray sheet on a lightbox. I've always had a deep fascination for X-rays: what a gift, what an unaccountable power, to be presented with the shaded, layered images of your inner workings, to be granted an oddly prescient glimpse of what you'll look like in your grave.

Other X-rays have shown me my cranium, with its recognisably ridged nose, my chaos of teeth, pitted with the stark geometry of fillings; I've seen the spread bones of my hands, the linear metatarsals of my toes, the neat socket of my ankle. But never this, before now: the astonishing twinned halves of the sacroiliac region.

The Antipodean doctor points out bones, joints, nerves, to help me get my bearings on this strange map of grey and white and black. He says my left sacroiliac joint has slipped out of alignment, causing my current state.

'And when did you break your sacrum?' he says, leaning closer to peer at something.

'What?' I say, from behind my scarf.

He repeats the question, turning around.

I tilt my head to look up at him and an invisible, answering knife slices through my side. 'I haven't broken my sacrum,' I mutter, wincing, tightening my hold on myself. 'Or at least . . . I don't think I have. Have I?'

The doctor raises his eyebrows. 'You don't remember?' he says.

The lower back is a lesson in symmetry, with the curved wings of the pelvis flaring out from the sacrum, which is cupped like an open palm and pierced with a line of paired holes. The coccyx curves up, beneath, a vestigial reminder of our simian origins. On an X-ray, the area resembles a butterfly or silver moth, pinned to a dark velvet board. There are parts of the body which, taken in magnified isolation, look strange or spindly or peculiar or unidentifiable, but the sacral area is unmistakable and unusually beautiful. It is part angel, part lepidopteran, part Rorschach inkblot.

The sacrum, the triangular, pitted central bone, is a complex, multifaceted cog, performing numerous functions. It is crucial for load-bearing, supporting the entire spine above it, and for accommodating the spinal nerves; it articulates with the hip bones, connects with the final lumbar vertebrae, above, and the tail bone, below. Strong ligaments connect it to the ilium bones of the pelvis: these joints are L-shaped and capable of a small amount of movement.

In children, the sacrum is formed of five separate vertebrae, which start to fuse into a single bone at around the age of eighteen. Women's sacrums tend to be shorter than men's, with more breadth and curvature, to allow greater capacity in the pelvis.

The term 'sacrum', which was coined by eighteenth-century anatomists, comes from the Latin name *os sacrum*, which means 'sacred bone'. Before the anatomists came along, the sacrum was also known in English as 'the holy bone'.

All this anatomical and linguistic information is unknown to me as I perch gingerly in the doctor's office, as I watch him point to a tiny grey line, like a river seen from a plane, on one side of the sacrum on the lightbox.

I can see what he means. There is evidence of fracture on the bone. I am able to see it. I also know that the X-ray is mine: I can see my name, reversed so that the surname precedes my initial, in the corner. But can I really have broken it and not known? How is that possible?

I look down at my hands, a minuscule movement which causes a shiver of discomfort from my shoulder blades, down to the base of my spine, exactly where the line of fracture must be.

'I fell,' I say to the doctor, 'on a marble floor.'

What I don't tell him is that we were on holiday, in Italy. That one of my children had been very sick. That it was early spring, Easter time, and my job that week, as the mum, was to get the family back on track, to show them that we were going to have a great time, despite illness and stress and dashes to hospital. I wasn't exactly wearing a jester's hat but I might as well have been. I had an assignment from a newspaper to write about a garden of stone monsters, built by a grieving duke for his dead wife. Monsters or no monsters, we were going to enjoy ourselves: I would make sure of it.

One morning, I was with my children beside a pond outside the villa; my son was beside me and my two daughters were chasing emerald-backed lizards in and out of the rosemary bushes. I had drawn up my feet and I was sitting cross-legged in a rickety garden chair. My son said something – I forget what – and I laughed, throwing back my head.

Balance has never been my strong point. I am forever falling sideways, lurching into bookcases or banisters or doorjambs. Turning my head can cause me to topple over. I often trip over things that aren't actually there.

So I laughed, cross-legged in my chair, and what happened next seemed to occur in slow motion. I saw the median line of the pond edge, the box hedge, the eaves of the villa tilt. The scene of the water, my children, the tiles dropped away from me and I saw instead a flash of treetops, the arrowing path of a bird. I heard the noise before I was aware of the impact: a crashing thud inside the border of my body, travelling upwards in a great sonic wave towards my ear canals.

The next moment, I was supine, in a different place entirely, as if I had dropped through a trapdoor. Here I was on a level with marble flagstones, with feet, with the lip of the pond. It seemed suddenly hard to breathe, to inflate my lungs. I tried to roll sideways, to right myself, but there was a pain so enormous, so severe, at the base of my back that I couldn't move. It was a large presence, this pain, with tentacles and claws: it gripped me tightly in its clutches, it drove an iron fist into my spine.

My children were crowding round me. I could see their sandalled feet, the hems of their clothes. The youngest was patting me on the arm, saying, Mama, Mama. Tears were streaming from my eyes and I could hear strange, hoarse, gasping sounds.

'Get your dad,' I managed to say.

It was hard to get up, to move: this I remember, more than anything else. My husband tried to help me up, but each time he touched me, I screamed. The flagstones around the pond, the instruments of my destruction, suddenly seemed like the best place to be, to remain. I would just lie here, curled like a prawn, on my side for the rest of the week. That would work, wouldn't it?

Somehow they got me into the house, my husband and my eleven-year-old boy. I recall spending some hours lying on my front on a bed, allowing tears to leak, in a drivelly and directionless fashion, into some pillows. My children came in and out, awed and silent. My husband's worried face hove into view, coming nearer and nearer. Do we need to go to hospital? he asked.

No, I muttered. The idea of going anywhere, of raising myself from this position, of – good grief – folding myself into some kind of vehicle, made me want to vomit. It hurt to move my leg, to curl my toes, to turn my head, to brush a hair off my forehead. It hurt to blink.

What I learned that day, before I had linguistic confirmation that the bone I had injured was in some way 'sacred' and 'holy', before I had pored over pictures of it, occupying the very middle of our bodies, holding up the spine, forming the basis for the nerves to our brains, the movement of our legs, was that the sacrum is central to us. It lies at our middle. If we are wheels, the sacrum is our hub. All roads lead to it; everything flows from it. Without it, that small, hand-sized bone, we can't move.

In Italy, however, I was moving the very next day. I had no choice. I had three children to look after, one of whom was still unwell, a holiday to undertake, an article to research and write. So I did what parents have always done. I took painkillers, I got myself out of bed, I stood upright, I hobbled on.

I went to the garden, because I had no choice: the stone monsters had to be seen, the article had to be written. I recall a certain amount of difficulty getting myself out of the car. I clung for a moment to the hot metal of the roof, gulping back a sob, and then stuffed bags of ice down my clothes. I was past caring what the chic Italians around me might think.

I leaned on the buggy for support as we processed around the pathways, the seat of my trousers filled with a rubble of ice cubes. I peered up at the lichenous faces of the monsters who weren't so very monstrous after all, but inscrutable, mired in weeds and soil, their gazes directed above the heads of those who had come to look at them. Are you all right? my husband kept asking me, and because I didn't want to alarm the children, I said: I'm fine.

In the cold room in Edinburgh, I condense this story to its bare essentials. I tell the doctor that I fell, on holiday, several years ago, and that ever since then I am prone to sudden and acute injuries from strangely little cause.

'Any problem with my back,' I tell him, 'seems to go straight there.'

The doctor nods. 'Well, it would,' he said, tapping the X-ray. 'Injuries like that can be life-changing.'

In my mid-twenties, I lived in London, where I worked for a newspaper. It was a job that required me to sit for long hours in front of a monitor, clicking again and again on a mouse, scrolling up, scrolling down, zooming in, zooming out, over and over again, five days a week, sometimes until midnight. It wasn't long before my back seized up: I had pins and needles between my shoulder blades and a numbness down my right arm. My boss, nervous about RSI absenteeism, sent me two floors up to see the company physiotherapist.

She was the first in a long line of practitioners, on whose couches I would lie, face down, while they prodded and measured and tested my back.

'My God,' was what she said as she pummelled me with an electric massager. 'You have the back of an eighty-year-old. Of course,' she shouted, over the noise of the hellish machine, 'the problem's all coming from down here.' I felt her hand descend on my lower back.

'Something's really not right in your lumbar. Your SI joints move around too much – they're hypermobile. And your tail bone seems kind of crooked.'

As with the Australian doctor who would X-ray me, years later, there was a lot I could have said in reply, but didn't. At the time, I got up off the couch, my back feeling kneaded and almost bruised, and went back to work.

I made phone calls, I chased copy, I discussed layouts, as if it was a normal day, but all with the sensation that there was something behind me, something only I could see, nebulous and malevolent, something I thought I had outrun, a long time ago, but here it was, back to haunt me, placing its clammy hand on my shoulder and saying, you didn't think you'd get away that easily, did you?

The uneven curvature of my coccyx was caused by spending upwards of a year lying on my back, in bed, as a child. My spine grew, of course, as would that of any eight-year-old, but it grew crooked, from the pressure of the mattress beneath. I'd contracted encephalitis and the virus was eating away at my brain, a maggot through an apple, making lacework of the neural pathways. Most of the lasting neurological damage was done to my cerebellum, that part of the brain involved in movement and coordination, but the virus also dismantled many of the neuromuscular junctions in my spine and pelvis. Muscles in my back and upper legs were left much weakened and foreshortened.

Don't get me wrong: I consider myself to be an extremely lucky person. The doctors first said that I would die; when I didn't, they said I wouldn't walk again. To have recovered, to have found a loophole out of one of these destinies, let alone both, strikes me as the very best fortune a person could ever have.

As as twenty-something journalist, however, it came as a shock to realise that I hadn't – couldn't – leave all this behind me. At that age, you believe yourself invincible. You think the world will always be like this, that a life of working long hours and staying out late and barely eating and flitting from one rental flat to another is a permanent state.

Your teens, your childhood, seem indistinct and distant, in contrast to the speedy Technicolor of the present. What happened to that child, that teenager, might well have happened to somebody else.

What I hadn't realised then is that parts of life come in and out of focus as you get older. Events that might at the time have seemed to pass without consequence may return with great import; something you thought you might have shrugged off or come through can always rear its head again, very much the way a virus can lie dormant in your system.

The truth is that my sacroiliac region is a part of me that could tell a long story, should anyone wish to hear it. It is my synecdoche and also my equivalent of Achilles' famed heel, which didn't make it into the magic waters of the Styx. I had avoided an early death, I managed to find a way out of a life of incapacity and dependency. In my teens and twenties, I fled from this knowledge; I wanted to put as much distance as possible between myself and that ailing, immobile child in a hospital bed. I ran away from her, as fast and as far as I could, but my sacroiliac area, my lower back, was always there to remind me that I could do no such thing, that she is me and I am her. There will be no escape.

It is of course a very, very small price to pay. So what if my coccyx curves too much to the right? So what if my pelvic ligaments are too loose and the muscles connected to them too tight or too weak or atrophied or whatever it is they are? So what if I had to wear what the obstetricians called a 'truss' throughout my pregnancies, to hold the bones of my pelvis together? So what if I broke my sacrum and didn't realise? I can walk, I can grip a pen, I can lead an independent life, and that's more than the neurologists expected for me.

As I sit staring at the healed fracture on my X-ray, as the doctor guides my hand to the corresponding place on my lower back and I feel, yes, a tiny calcified lump, a frozen pea beneath the skin, I am struck by the strangeness of it all. We think we know our bodies, these shells of blood and muscle and tissue and bone, but they lead lives of their own, they keep secrets from us. We inhabit them but they remain unknowable, elusive, brave, carrying on with the business of living, despite our accidents and choices and incursions and foolishnesses.

I leave the hospital walking slowly and carefully, with shortened, hesitant steps, the gait of a woman wearing leg irons. Crossing the car park, I am filled with an unfamiliar and absurd desire to apologise to my back. I had no idea, I want to say, I didn't realise, I didn't know. I edge my way over wet tarmac, navigating the banks of cleared snow, and think, for the first time: we can't go on like this.

This is what I have learned about living with pain: you need to be careful that your baseline for what's acceptable doesn't sink too low. There were days, after my fall in Italy, when I found myself thinking, well, I can't turn my head to the left but it's fine because I can still turn it to the right. It's too painful for me to sit down but if I just balance my laptop on a desk, a cardboard box and three dictionaries, and if I stand in front of this wobbly ziggurat, then I can keep working. I can't bend down to tie my laces but, hey, I'll just find some slip-on shoes.

Some injuries are life-changing, the doctor said, and so I have duly changed my life.

These days, a year or so on from my X-ray, my sacrum and I have reached an equilibrium of a very tentative and hesitant nature. Our relationship is unambiguously uneven: the sacrum is in charge and I am the willing, reverential supplicant.

I am filled at all times with a dutiful respect for the holy bone and pay regular obeisance to it. I do whatever I can to keep it happy. I rub scented ointment into it, I appease it with hot packs. I have special cushions to ease its comfort, all over the house; I take one with me when I travel, for hard and unforgiving surfaces in trains or planes or airports. In the manner of a cat meeting a dog for the first time, I will eye up a chair before I will commit to sitting in it. I avoid any that are too soft or too hard, or ones that recline too much or are shaped like a bucket. Anything that might tip backwards doesn't even get a second glance.

I don't cross my legs, I don't lift anything heavier than a bag of flour, I don't row boats, I have to tell my daughter that no, I can't carry her, no matter how tired her legs are. I even forgo the pleasure of sledging.

Like a religious fanatic, a medieval mystic, I prostrate myself for my sacrum, on a mat, at least three times a day. I have a series of twelve exercises, 'for sacral stability', the sheet says. I move through them, always in the same order, with mute, pious regularity, once in the morning, once at midday and once in the evening. I never miss a single one of these physical novenas.

As I do them, moving my legs one way, my arms the other, bending and supplicating my spine, I can hear my sacral joints clicking, realigning, settling themselves, speaking to me. It is a wordless language, almost as old as I am, and I am happy to hear it. ■

# Cortney Lamar Charleston

## Turn the River

'Our Negro problem, therefore, is not of the Negro's making. No group in our population is less responsible for its existence. But every group is responsible for its continuance . . .'
– Chicago Commission on Race Relations, *The Negro in Chicago*

Segregation now, tomorrow, forever if there they stayed
in living form, after life: violence the cash crop of soil
otherwise known for cotton or clay, indigenous hue swayed
ever more toward blood that runs with its own current and boils

on printing presses, under spotlights, changes color once dried
but denotes a passion in broad daylight dripping off moonless
nightsticks. Time to believe in God or gunpowder, somehow stride
for the promised but still owed since civil war rippled time. Yes,

let frustration flood every street. Dare capitalism to keep
keeping on without coloreds' consent; govern empty pockets
then ask what a governor is worth compared to those who reap
wrath, effuse mercy and confine sparrows to their eye sockets.

Tides turn against the against. A river's mouth is too clean to
say *nigger*; they wade into water and emerge something new.

Say *nigger*: they wade into water and emerge something new.
One black boy bobs up from the belly of flow a made symbol
for the struggle, reverse migration a chest pain relieved due
to a magazine spread. O, how the light itself did tremble

at the sight of his face, Chicago fruit estranged from the dream
like a bird tilting toward frost when it's time to rove for heat.
Brown liquor drinkers would take the shorter path to heaven, gleam
in the dull burn and yet still have enough sense of mind to beat

back the notion this place is colder than that one was. *A job
is a job*, they say. One family has multiple guts and
only one throat to stuff greenbacks down like collards, mustards, cobs
of corn, like coins, easier to come by in a pinch, one hand

washing the other. A neighbor has to count for something, right?
As soon as the caravan arrived, the whole block went pitch night.

As soon as the caravan arrived, the whole block went pitch night.
One house contracted the disease of a black body and spread
it to the next and the next like God's tenth plague. Whites took fast flight,
defining blight as their absence and leaving whole wards for dead,

to generations of darknesses: there are many ways to
inform people they are unwanted without slitting the throat
of a word over an offering stone, truancy the true
test of one's spite for another kind of sameness. The black vote

was for forgiveness, not forgetting, but neither is a route
out of the proverbial desert that had not before been
tried and trapped them in roles of servitude, shackled by their roots.
If the North provides nothing else, it provides clarity, thin

consciousness like silk so easily ruined when wet. And yet,
this is not the purpose of water; water pays off a debt.

*This* is not the purpose of water; water pays off a debt.
Down south one could own nil and owe. O, to mortgage a future
with a past, pigmentation as poverty, but please don't fret!
Lay down the burden before feet of brass. For all wounds, suture,

as surely as a ray of sunlight breaks over a lashed back—
sweating, sharecropping. Go, head on down to the river, offspring
of the bolls and blues! Bring the ghosts. Shake the shadows off. Backtrack
to the bones of the matter, which are the bones themselves. And sing.

And swing, from the branch of a good feeling. Evidently there
is a coming back to glory, however gory the road.
What pushes a shiver down the trunk of a tree has the air
of the familiar finding home with us again, so live. Odes

to the stolen ones, live! Prosper under the pressure. Cut rough
when necessary as a means to endure. Be new. Rebuff.

When necessary as a means to endure: be new, rebuff.
An answer for hounds is an answer for hoodlums, slips neatly
into a shoe. Here jazz means living creatively enough
to avoid notice, horns blaring in one's head, walking fleetly

from corner to corner, or coroner as it could be. Shame:
it has always been this way, wild men, boys even, dipping skulls
in the dust like ministers of massacre, all a rigged game
with moving thrones as in chess, something to distract, destroy, cull

the angry from the righteousness of their anger, this a brief
history of money, power and isolation. Set up
to get got, imagine that: the great urban plan. Thug or thief,
hustler or con artist, a way of getting by, winding up

paid more than pennies—or jailed, writing letters, begging pictures.
What is heaven-sent: an innocent face, clippings of scripture.

What is heaven-sent: an innocent face, clippings of scripture.
Things to tuck in a wallet, affix to a routine mirror.
Love is a labor from the beginning till the end, fixture
like something that holds light, and black people do. Never clearer

is one's work than this, no less humble than sweeping the sidewalk
in front of the store with a broom that has seen better days, gray-
flecked bristles bent under the weight of everything work means. Talk
sacrifice, being spit on so much the world owes gold as pay.

Alas, still waiting on the acres. Still waiting on the mule.
Traced the Mississippi northward and still, nothing. Not much at
all, but not least like before, through depression, through war, played fool
on film so they could laugh away their pain, provide more grief that,

if anything, became a magnet for grace going about
city living: money, black mayor, the impression of clout.

City living? Money. Black mayor. The impression of clout:
novelists and poets and playwrights; shiny new Cadillacs;
chicken shacks, rib tips; kitchenettes, bungalows and two-flats; bouts
in boxing; baseball games; blues houses; Curtis Mayfield 8-tracks;

*Ebony, Jet,* all things jet black—like the Panthers, the Nation.
Black like the P. Stones, Lords and Disciples; black like the projects,
jails and graveyards; black like the river at night, as a Haitian
once saw it, losing his face in the water. O, to reflect

and return, in some sense, like a phantom, to where one came from
and see that distance measured by memory means *never too
far.* And far too close to home this home is at times, though it hums
how midnight crickets can't, with bustle, to which bidding adieu

would be hustling backwards. Of the forward path, be not afraid.
*Segregation now, tomorrow, forever if there they stayed.*

# THE HEAVENS

## Sandra Newman

B en met Kate at a rich girl's party. He didn't know the rich girl
personally; it was one of those parties where no one knew the
hostess. He'd come with the rich girl's cousin's co-worker, whom he
instantly lost in the crowd. It had started out as a dinner party, but
the invitations proliferated, spreading epidemically through friends of
friends until it turned into a hundred people. So the rich girl opened
up both floors, made punch instead of risotto, and ordered a thousand
dumplings from a Chinese restaurant. It was August and you had to
let things happen the way they wanted to happen. Everyone was in
their twenties then, anyway, so that was how they thought.

It turned out to be a mostly francophone party, conversational
and quiet; a party with the windows open to the night, a party where
people sat talking on the floor. Most of the illumination was from
solar-powered tea lights, which the rich girl had hung on the fire
escapes all day to charge, then pasted along the walls. That light
reflected softly from the heavy glass tumblers into which wine was
poured. There wasn't even music playing. The rich girl said it gave her
bad dreams. New York City, so everyone was interning at a Condé
Nast publication or a television program or the UN. Everyone a little
in love with each other; the year 2000 in the affluent West.

Ben talked to a dozen girls that night. He wasn't seriously looking for a girlfriend. He was working and doing his PhD then, so there wasn't time for emotional investment. Still, it was pleasant to flirt with just anyone, to feel the power of being attractive and six feet tall. A night of receptive postures and parted lips; such an easy blessedness, like ascending a staircase into the air.

At 1 a.m. he went down in the elevator to buy cigarettes. Kate was outside on 68th Street with the rich girl's dog, which had needed to pee. She wore a loose dress that didn't look like party attire; at first he wasn't sure she was from the party. Then he recognized the dog, a terrier mutt with a soupçon of dachshund, elongated and shaggy. Cute. Ben stopped to pat the dog.

He went and bought his cigarettes. When he came back, Kate was still there. He paused to smoke. They talked desultorily for five minutes, then something shifted. The traffic fell quiet. They were smiling at each other and not saying anything. Already it felt strange.

Kate said, 'What's your name?'

'Pedro,' Ben said.

She laughed. 'No, I already asked you, didn't I? You said you were something else.'

'No.' He was smiling foolishly. 'I don't think you asked me.'

'I did, but I don't remember what you said.' She nodded at the dog. 'I've forgotten her name too. So if we left town now and went someplace where nobody knows us, you two wouldn't have names.'

'I could be Pedro.'

'No, I know you aren't Pedro.'

'I could be Rumpelstiltskin.'

'Done.'

He laughed, but she didn't. She just stood there, smiling her liking at him. He finished his cigarette. Then he should have gone back to the party, but he couldn't. It was strange.

And they talked for a while about taking the dog and running off to a town in South America, about the boat they would live on and the smugglers they would meet and the sunsets over the turquoise sea, where blue crabs would scuttle over the beach, and it felt as if they were even younger than they were, as if they didn't yet have jobs.

K ate was Hungarian-Turkish-Persian: three romantic, impractical strains, three peoples who had thrown away their empires. Her ancestors wore jewels in their beards; they galloped on horses, waving swords. With them, it was opium dens or Stalinism, no middle ground; so Kate said, laughing at herself. She was talking obliquely about herself.

Ben was half Bengali, half Jewish. That could be interesting, but it was sedate. He came from a line of rabbis, shopkeepers, lawyers; there was a feeling that he might be uncool by comparison, a feeling Ben had to consciously suppress. He said, 'My family didn't wave swords, but I'm always willing to try.'

Both Ben and Kate were tawny, black-eyed and aquiline; they looked like members of the same indeterminate race. They commented on this likeness, using self-deprecating terms like 'beige' and 'beaky', and became so happy at this – at nothing – that they started to walk the dog downtown. The dog was beige, too, Ben pointed out, and they paused and crouched to compare their arms to the dog's coat; that was how they first touched. The dog was licking their hands and confusing the issue. Still there was a definite spark.

Walking back toward the apartment, they traded the information that goes in dating profiles, with the feeling of belatedly completing the paperwork for something they'd already done under the table. Then up in the elevator, where they were alone, and in which he suffered and wanted to kiss her. She smiled forward at the doors, unkissable, glowing with the idea of sex. They came out, and she unleashed the dog and slung the leash onto a branch of the coatrack. Without discussion, they headed to the balcony.

There was someone already there, the rich girl's house guest, an older New Zealander whom Kate knew and who would later figure prominently in their lives. Ben didn't think much about him then. All he meant was that Ben wasn't alone with Kate. The New Zealander talked about a garden he was working on; he was a garden designer, in New York to create a rich person's garden. Ben listened to his accent and mainly considered him a useful pause, a device that would ease them more gently to the next stage.

So it was the windy balcony, the lights of New York a nether starscape. The actual stars were dull and few. From this perspective, the city was brighter and more complex than the cosmos; the cosmos in fact seemed rote, like a framed print hung on a wall solely because the wall would look wrong without pictures. There have to be pictures and there has to be a cosmos, even if no one looks at them. And Ben looked at Kate surreptitiously, wishing he could tell her this, convinced that she would understand.

She had a long nose and long black humorous eyes, a full, red-lipsticked mouth. Persian, his mind said besottedly, Persian. In heels, she was as tall as he was. Full and rounded, like a cat with a lot of fur. She stood uncannily straight, as if she'd never ever slouched, never hunched over work. She didn't even lean on the balcony's railing but stood with her arms loose at her sides. Weightless. A queenly bearing. Persian.

Outside, she'd told him she was an artist – 'works on paper' – who'd given up on her BFA at Pratt. She had suddenly not seen the point. 'If it were something like geology, maybe,' she'd said (because he'd told her he had a degree in geology, although he was also a poet – published, he had hastily added. She'd volunteered, in a helpful tone: 'Well, I read poetry.' He'd said, 'Really?' She'd said, 'I'm on Apollinaire right now,' and quoted some Apollinaire in French, as if that were a normal ability for a failed art student. She'd added, 'My French is awful, sorry,' and he'd said stupidly, 'Me neither,' because he was powerfully distracted; he was suddenly thinking in terms of love. Then she'd said, 'We should get back to the party,' and the world turned cold. How had he got to that point so quickly?).

Now the windy balcony, the obsolete stars, the city a mystery of glittering towers. Kate and the New Zealander were talking about the Great Man theory of history, according to which human progress was driven by superlative people like Socrates or Muhammad, who single-handedly changed the world. Kate defended this idea, while the New Zealander pooh-poohed it and refused to believe she was serious. He said, 'How could anyone be that much better? We all have such similar biologies.'

'They wouldn't have to be that much better,' said Kate. 'It would be all the circumstances lining up, like with any unusual event, like a supervolcano or a major earthquake.' She looked at Ben.

Ben said, 'Major earthquakes aren't that unusual.'

'Ben's a geologist,' Kate told the New Zealander.

'But is he a great geologist?' the New Zealander said.

Kate laughed. Ben laughed, too, although he also wondered if this was a slight that might diminish him in Kate's eyes. The New Zealander said he was going to get another drink and left. Ben's heart was suddenly racing. Scraps from the Apollinaire she'd quoted surfaced in his mind: *mon beau membre asinin . . . le sacré bordel entre tes cuisses* (my stupid beautiful dick . . . the sacred bordello between your thighs). When she'd said it, it had certainly seemed like flirting. But it might have just been the only Apollinaire she could call to mind.

Now Kate smiled at him vaguely and looked back at the French doors. Her face caught the light and her smooth cheek shone. Some new intention appeared in her eyes – a bad moment, where he thought she was about to ditch him. But she turned to him again, smiling wonderfully, and said, 'I've got the key to the roof deck. I'm sleeping on the roof, if that sounds like something you might want to do.'

He was nodding, breathless, while she explained that Sabine (the rich girl) was her good friend. Kate often slept on the roof. She had an inflatable bed up there. 'It blows up with a mechanism,' Kate said, making a mechanism gesture in the air.

He laughed, he was lightheaded. He made the mechanism gesture back, and Kate took him by the sleeve, just like that, and led him back to the party. She said, 'I'd better ask Sabine, but she'll say yes.'

It was breezy and wonderful in the apartment, which had two floors and twelve rooms and belonged to the rich girl's uncle; it hosted his collection of African drums, and for this reason (somehow this knowledge had filtered through to everyone) the air conditioning was meant to be always on and the windows closed. The drum skins would perish in humidity. Presumably they were from a dry part of Africa or were meant to be reskinned periodically by a caste of craftsmen who had died out, whose descendants had become engineers and postal workers. In any case, the windows were open, the air conditioning was off, and everyone kept looking at the drums, discussing them, aware that this party was subtracting from the drums' life span. Likewise, Ben now imagined the drums as sacrifices to whatever this was.

They found Sabine, the rich girl, talking to three men, who were all much taller than she was, so she appeared to be standing in a grove of men. They were speaking French and making what Ben thought of as French gesticulations. Sabine was very blond and as heavy as Kate, though on her it was not provocative but pudgy. She didn't look rich. She looked unhappy and intelligent. When Kate made her request, Sabine frowned, displeased, as if this were only the most recent in a series of Kate's unreasonable demands, and said, 'Fine. Do whatever.'

'It's not whatever,' Kate said, but didn't pursue it. She just smiled at Sabine, at Ben, at the three tall men who smiled back conspiratorially.

'I don't want to cause problems,' Ben said.

At this, Sabine suddenly changed. She grinned and tousled Kate's hair, saying to Ben, 'You won't need to cause problems if you're sleeping with this one. She'll take care of that.'

Kate laughed delightedly and looked at Ben as if she were being complimented. The three men were all looking at Kate, looking wistfully at three different parts of Kate's body. Sabine said, 'Enjoy,' and turned back to the men in a peremptory manner, mustering them to their earlier conversation. They took their eyes off Kate reluctantly.

So Ben bore her away like a prize he had won by defeating those three men or – looked at another way – he followed her obediently up the stairs, in her absolute and permanent thrall.

The roof had a deck of solid blond wood, with a plain iron railing around the edge. There was a grill, a picnic table, Adirondack chairs. To Ben's eye, there were no apparent signs of wealth, though he wasn't sure what he'd expected. Fountains? There were gardening implements but no garden, only a row of potted plants along the railing – or really several of the same plant, a shaggy blond grass with overtones of purple. The inflatable mattress, a green canvas rectangle with no sheets or blanket, had been set beside these plants. It had already been inflated, and Kate went to it without hesitation and sat, looking back at Ben seriously, as if she were inviting him to something of great moment.

He came and sat. His immediate lust was gone. He was expecting thirty minutes of conversation, anyway, before anything could happen. And in fact, Kate began to talk about the potted grass – it was an endangered species, which was why the roof hadn't been opened up for the party and possibly why Sabine had chafed at letting Ben on the roof, because the grass was illegal. It had been smuggled in by a friend of the New Zealander, a mining executive, in his corporate jet. You weren't supposed to take the grass out of its homeland, although in this case it was intended to preserve the grass from becoming extinct, which it soon would be in the part of Argentina where it was native, an area now devastated by mining. The dirt in the pots was Argentine too. It was the sort of thing that happened to Sabine, that she ended up harboring smuggled grasses.

Ben looked dutifully at the grasses, which – he now noticed – were in two different kinds of pots. Some were standard clay pots; some were green celluloid pots that had been molded to imitate the shape of standard clay pots. He pointed this out to Kate, and she immediately frowned and expressed concern for the grasses in the celluloid pots.

'I don't think the grass cares,' Ben said. 'Grass isn't that sensitive to aesthetics.'

'No, it must affect the soil.'

'It would be such a tiny difference it wouldn't matter,' Ben said with the air of a man with a degree in science.

'Even tiny differences matter. There could be a butterfly effect.'

'Oh, no, not the butterfly effect,' said Ben teasingly.

But she insisted that a plant is a complex system, just like weather; there could easily be a butterfly effect. He objected that a plant isn't very complex; a grass would have thousands of cells, not millions, and most of those cells would be exactly alike. She objected to exactly – they couldn't be exactly alike. He said, 'Well, if you're going to be like that.' They laughed. Then she reached out suddenly and took his hand, which sent a particular shock through him. He was tamed. He was impressed.

She said, 'I wasn't inviting you up here to have sex. I hope you didn't get the wrong idea.'

'Oh, no,' he lied. 'I didn't expect anything.'

'Maybe we could have sex next time, though.'

'Okay.'

'I mean, I'm not rejecting you.'

'Yes,' he said, a little hoarse. 'Don't reject me.'

'I won't,' she said. 'I don't.'

They were silent for a minute. He was wondering what the parameters of no sex were. He was thinking about the butterfly effect in the case of falling for people, the small differences between one girl and another creating a cascade of results that changed your life. He looked at the grasses and decided he shouldn't tell her this.

Then she said, sounding nervous for the first time, 'Do you remember your dreams?'

That was the last important thing before he was kissing her. He stroked her cheek, her skin soft as powder, so wonderful it was bizarre. The whole world had gone to his head, with its purple-tinted grass and its black hair, in both of which the wind moved gracefully and smelled of sky. And when they lay down together, their bodies fit in an uncanny way, interlocked; however they moved, they fit together again, plugged in, and electricity flowed between them. Then he stayed awake for hours while Kate slept easily, naturally, in his arms. For the rest of his life, he would remember it: that intoxicated moment not only of first love but of universal hope, that summer when Chen swept the presidential primaries on a wave of utopian fervor, when carbon emissions had radically declined and the Jerusalem peace accords had been signed and the United Nations surpassed its millennium goals for eradicating poverty, when it felt as if everything might work out. He could conjure it all by harking back to that inflatable mattress with no sheets, the endangered grasses fluttering and springing above their heads, the stars like dusty candy. Without sheets, the wind blew directly on his body, on his bare arms. Far below was the sound of traffic, as quiet as a thought. Occasionally a siren rose, like a frail red line that scrolled across the sky and faded again. Kate muttered and kicked in her sleep. Every time, it was adorable and he was amazed. He fell asleep at dawn, still plotting how he would make her stay.

B en breakfasted with Sabine. Kate had vanished while he was asleep, although she was expected back any minute since the dog had likewise vanished, and presumably Kate was out walking, not stealing, the dog. The breakfast was made by a servant, a middle-aged woman with jet-black hair, to whom Sabine spoke companionably in French. When Ben listened in, the conversation was about the extinction of the [word he didn't understand] in the Mediterranean, which was being killed by pollution. The pollution caused algal blooms that suffocated the [word he didn't understand]. Agricultural runoff had been cut back, but it was too late for the [word he didn't understand]. It's horrible, the servant said, and Sabine repeated in the same aggrieved tone, It's horrible. Then Sabine said that her uncle – here she gestured vaguely around at the uncle's apartment – didn't believe in pollution. He thinks all chemicals are the same, said Sabine. He says the air is made of chemicals.

At this point, Sabine and the servant noticed Ben listening and smiled at him. He said in his careful French, We are all made of chemicals too.

They laughed in a friendly way, as if they wanted to make him feel good. Then the servant brought him a plate of scrambled eggs, said, 'Bon appétit,' and left.

Sabine said to Ben, 'Kate shouldn't be long.' Then she opened a *New York Times* and started to read. It was startling, both for its rudeness and because Ben hadn't noticed the *Times* there. Also the naked feeling of being left to eat without reading material while someone else was reading. It made him feel leaden and ridiculous, while at the same time he accepted it as part of this new world, the world with Kate. There were secrets to which he would not be privy. He would have to feel stupid because he cared too much.

Then just as suddenly, Sabine put down the *Times*. 'Fuck. I just realized Kate could be a while.'

Ben made an intelligent face, chewing eggs.

'I mean, I'm not throwing you out,' said Sabine. 'You can wait. But I'm thinking she took the dog to Nick's.'

Ben swallowed awkwardly. 'Nick's?'

'Nick's her ex. She didn't say about Nick?'

'No.'

'I mean, don't worry. It's over with Nick. Nick left Kate for a mail-order bride. Somebody else's mail-order bride. I think she's Thai. But Kate brings the dog there because Nick's depressed and she thinks it cheers him up.'

Ben smiled with forced casualness. 'Nick stole someone's mail-order bride?'

'No, she'd already left her husband. She was a runaway mail-order bride. I know it sounds weird, but it's not that weird. We've got a lot of mail-order brides around, because a friend of ours started an organization to rescue them. I've got three living here now.'

At that moment, a toilet flushed upstairs. Ben immediately pictured a mail-order bride, wan and homesick, turning away from a glugging toilet and straightening her traditional Thai garb.

'Well,' he said. 'That's got to be weird.'

'Not really.' Sabine shrugged. 'Everyone stays here. Right now, I've got a congresswoman from Maine, plus two environmental activists, plus the mail-order brides and Martin and a couple other people. I'm the only person in left-wing politics who has spare rooms. I'm like the red hotel.'

'You're in politics?'

Sabine made a stupid-question face, then suddenly got up and went to the sink. She fetched a large metal pitcher from a shelf and started to fill it at the faucet. For a moment, Ben imagined she was preparing to pour cold water over his head. But when it was full, she carried the pitcher, ponderous and sloshing, to the windowsill, where Ben now noticed a gathering of elegant plants. They appeared to wait expectantly, bracing themselves to receive the water.

Sabine started to pour and said, 'I shouldn't have mentioned Nick. That sucks. I can't stand people who gossip, but then I go and do it myself.'

'It wasn't gossiping, exactly.'

'Dude, please. It was gossiping. I mean, I'm not out to poison your mind against Kate. But I have to start in about Nick or some fucking –'

Then, as if to prove her point, she launched into another story about Kate, often forgetting to water the plants and simply standing there talking with the heavy pitcher trembling in her small hands. The story began with Sabine meeting Kate when they were twelve, at the American International School in Budapest. At that time, the thing about Kate was that she believed, or said she believed, she was from another world. Kate fashioned odd headdresses from towels and said it was what the women wore there; she once made a castle from bread that was supposed to be like the castles in her world. She called it Albion. The Albionites sang beautifully; they liked to sing in four-part harmony, standing in courtyards full of otherworldly peacocks and flowering trees. Kate was a sleeping princess there, like Sleeping Beauty, only more serious. She'd been asleep for years and therefore knew little of her Albion life, except that in Albion she had a horse (as Sabine did in earthly Budapest).

Kate's fear was that our world was actually just Kate's dream, an

enchanted dream she was having in Albion. This was what Sabine
and Kate used to talk about in their sleepovers at the ambassador's
residence (Sabine's father had been the American ambassador to
Hungary). They lay in the dark and scintillatingly pondered: If Kate
woke up in Albion, would our world disappear, and everyone in it?
Was it Kate's fault when Earth people died, because she'd dreamed
their dying? Could Kate direct her dream and thereby bring about
heaven on Earth?

Soon other girls (the popular girls at school) were inducted into
the secret, and they would gather conspiratorially to discuss their
intuitions about the crisis, to draw pictures of Albion and to speculate
about whether they might also have sleeping Albion counterparts. On
this point Kate was generous; when someone claimed to have had an
Albion dream, Kate never pooh-poohed but listened intently. She
wanted to believe. Still, Kate was the official dreamer, and they would
lock themselves in Sabine's bedroom, sit in a circle around Kate and
chant 'inspirations' to help her dream a better world. Kate lay in the
middle with her palms pressed to her eyes. She wished so hard her
toes curled. A typical inspiration was: Dream no cancer, dream no
cancer – Albion! There were other chants to end poverty, infidelity
and hurricanes. At the time, they found proof of their benevolent
influence in the nightly news, though in retrospect the news had
mostly been terrible.

Then a difficult girl (the granddaughter of a Hungarian movie
star) rebelled and told Kate she was lying. She pointed out that
'Albion' was just an old word for England; Kate hadn't even made up
a new name! That girl was exiled from the group, but told the story of
Albion far and wide. Then other kids (the unpopular kids at school)
began to snigger – this was what Sabine remembered most: being
laughed at, the topsy-turvy of popular/unpopular, and how it made
her suddenly realize she'd never believed in Albion. It was just a game,
a game of make-believe, like little kids played.

Next came an ugly scene where Sabine and the popular girls
cornered Kate and hounded her to admit she'd been lying. When

she resisted, they called her names and one of them began to tear up a sandwich she was eating and threw the fragments into Kate's long hair. Kate wept but refused to change her story. The panic mounted; it made the girls vicious. One girl threatened Kate with a lit cigarette. Another told Kate she was going to call an ambulance to take Kate to a mental hospital, where Kate would be kept tied to a bed. Sabine herself walked out instead of defending Kate – ran out, although they were at her house. She ran to her boyfriend's place and got drunk there for the first time, though that was another story.

Sabine had never really believed in Albion. Still, she felt the loss of it no less. It was as if they'd almost made it real; they had almost been the gods who determined history. Now the world was magicless, a dull, inanimate thing, and they were insignificant children.

Here Sabine stopped. By now, she'd set the watering pitcher down and was sitting on the windowsill. She said, 'That's Kate.'

'Okay,' Ben said (and sickeningly wanted to protect Kate, tear-stained preteen Kate; the story had made it ten times worse), 'but what do you mean by that? What's Kate?'

Sabine paused, possibly biting her tongue. There was a gathering din upstairs, of footsteps and slamming doors and voices. A shower was running somewhere and a hair dryer somewhere else. Ben was trying to guess Sabine's point, but was distracted by images of mail-order brides in showers, of congresswomen drying their hair.

At last Sabine said slowly, deliberately, 'I guess I'm saying Kate doesn't live in the real world, and ultimately people can't deal with it and then they end up hurting her? Like, Nick was crazy in love with Kate, but then he couldn't take it and he left her for Phuong. Now Nick's depressed, and Kate goes over there and comforts him like she ruined his life. And okay, she kind of ruined his life. Nick's fucked up. But.'

'So you're warning me away from her?' Ben said, giving it an incredulous note.

'No,' Sabine said. 'I didn't mean to. Is that what I'm doing? Jesus Christ, I'm such an asshole.'

That was the last real thing Sabine said, because the door banged open and the kitchen started to precipitously fill with house guests. There was the garden designer from last night, the congresswoman from Maine, a Nigerian mail-order bride who was missing a tooth in front, and a diminutive, hirsute guy who looked like a little glum hamster and was never identified. Then more people. Most wore identical cashmere bathrobes, which Sabine presumably kept for guests, and they exuded a frowsy *bonheur*; they were pleased to be here. When the table filled, people sat on the floor or perched on the kitchen counters. The servant reappeared, a little flustered, and the egg routine began again, while the house guests made a lot of noise and laughed. They argued about labor policy and baseball and whether the Antarctic was going to melt. They quoted nineteenth-century economists and added, 'Which is horseshit straight from the horse.' They told stories about President Chen's transition team and the fight for the universal basic income and how one staffer had threatened not just to quit, but to burn himself alive on the convention floor if the UBI wasn't in the party platform. One environmental activist demonstrated how she'd set a right-wing candidate's stump speech to the tune of 'O Sole Mio', in a harsh histrionic soprano, and the Nigerian mail-order bride laughed so hard she snorted egg out of her nose. Meanwhile, others had side conversations about another right-winger's mistress's chlamydia; tickled each other and shouted, 'Revisionist!'; got up to interfere with the cooking, were threatened with a spatula and slunk back to the table with comically chastened expressions.

And Ben was taken, buoyed, caught in a widening circle of infatuation. These were Kate's people, better than people, just as Kate was better than women. Even when they discussed the congresswoman's haircut, the haircut chitchat was markedly superior: they made botanical allusions, called the haircut anti-intellectual and laughed very happily, enjoying each other. The glum hamster summed up, 'It's a bit shag carpet,' and the congresswoman said, 'Well, let's be honest, my base is a bit shag carpet.' Ben laughed and ate cold toast and imagined himself in this jovial world – with Kate – and his suspicion that she was his answer, his escape, became a conviction.

Then more footsteps came from the hallway, and Ben was caught grinning as he looked back at the door, expecting more mail-order brides. But when the door opened, it was Kate.

She was still in her rumpled dress from last night, but because she'd come from outside and was entering a room of bathrobes and bare feet, she seemed very poised and competent, as if she'd stolen a march on everyone and taken possession of the day. The dog was trotting alongside, looking up to her face with a worshipful air. Her hair was wild and windblown. She was beautiful as she hadn't quite been last night, conventionally beautiful in a way that made Ben feel wrong-footed.

She saw him there and balked. There was a pause of social embarrassment. It occurred to him for the first time that Kate had expected him to leave. She'd ditched him. Her vanishing was a hint, not even a particularly subtle hint. Sabine must have known, and that was why she'd been trying to warn Ben off. He was an idiot.

There was a sickening moment of exile. He wanted to catch all the things, to catch the morning and the careless laughter, Kate's windblown hair that had been in his hands, that belonged to him, the halcyon night where he had belonged. Even the dog, who was now looking open-mouthed at Ben, as if trying to place him.

Then Kate said, 'Ben! Are you free today?'

For a moment, he was still preparing his exit. Then the penny dropped, clangorously, thrillingly. Ben stood up from his chair. The room fell silent as Kate came toward him, dropping the dog's leash on the floor. She put a hand familiarly on his chest and said, 'I was thinking we could go to the movies.'

'Movies,' he said. 'Yes, I suddenly really want to do that.'

'Or we could do pretty much anything else.'

'Yes, I really want to do that too.'

Then they felt their audience and looked around at the table of house guests, prepared to bask in implicit congratulations.

'Sweet,' said Sabine behind them. 'But Kate? You shouldn't just take my dog.' ∎

Canvas bag given to Daisy Thomas in 1942.
Courtesy of the author

# THE CANVAS BAG

## Inigo Thomas

I was looking for something else, a ceremonial sash to decorate my father's coffin at his funeral. On top of a tall chest of drawers in his bedroom was a flat, dark blue box, which I took down and placed on his bed. What I found inside was not ceremonial: it was a canvas bag with purple piping around its edges. Embroidered onto it were various female figures looking like Girl Guides going about chores, and a cooking pot above a flame. Next to one of the figures are the words ONE OF US and CHANGI JAIL, SPRING 1942. Stamped on a piece of cotton sewn inside is CELL 001.

The canvas bag belonged to my father's aunt by marriage, Daisy Thomas. It was given to her by her Japanese captors after the Fall of Singapore on 15 February 1942 to pack the few possessions she was allowed to take with her to prison. Her husband, Shenton Thomas, was governor of what was then called the Straits Settlements, which included Singapore, the port once so central to the British Empire's Asian interests. Daisy and Shenton were separated immediately after the surrender, and Shenton was marched through the streets of the city to Changi Prison by the Japanese in an attempt to humiliate him. The two saw each other again briefly in May. Then Shenton was sent to a prison camp in Taiwan: two years later he was transferred to the Japanese camp at Hsian, Manchuria, where he was for the rest of the war. Daisy remained in Singapore at Changi, a prison designed for 600 inmates. The Japanese packed 3,000 prisoners of war into the building, soldiers and civilians, men and women; 800 of them died while incarcerated.

Two days after the Fall of Singapore, Daisy and Shenton's daughter Bridget received a letter from the Colonial Office. She kept it in a scrapbook, which she must have given to my father. 'I am afraid that you have been going through a very anxious time during the last few weeks and I do hope you have found some reassurance from the report which has appeared in the Press of the safety of Sir Shenton and Lady Thomas,' the letter began. Neither Shenton nor Daisy ever spoke about their prison years, but you wonder whether 'safe' would have been the word they would have reached for to describe their internment. Cambridge University Library has amassed an enormous archive about the people held at Changi Prison during the war; it includes the newspaper that the prisoners made for themselves. Conditions were hard, but the adversity brought out an *esprit de corps*.

'We did everything for ourselves,' said W.F.N. Churchill, a colonial official who wrote extensively about Changi after the war. 'With the poor materials and resources at our command, we made a good show of it. We produced cooks, electricians, water engineers, plumbers, tailors, roof repairers, carpenters, laundry workers, health workers, doctors, chemists and opticians. Fortunately we had a cross section of the whole community. The Japanese would never have admitted it, but I think we did, in considerable measure, earn their respect.'

As I realised after my father's death, he was meticulous about archives and papers. Inside the bag, he had placed an explanatory note as well as a book, *Shenton of Singapore*, written by Brian Montgomery in the early 1980s. The author was Daisy's cousin, and the brother of Field Marshal Bernard Montgomery. The fear at the War Office in London was that if the Japanese had known they had a Montgomery cousin in their hands, they would have tortured her. The fears were misplaced because the Japanese treated all prisoners atrociously; 30,000 POWs died in Japanese prisons, of starvation, disease and torture.

Brian Montgomery quotes from a telegram the king sent to the governor on 6 December 1941, soon after the Japanese commenced their attacks around the Pacific:

> THE STORM OF JAPAN'S WANTON ATTACK HAS BROKEN
> IN THE EAST AND MALAYA BEARS THE FIRST ASSAULTS OF
> THE ENEMY STOP AT THIS FATEFUL MOMENT ASSURE YOU
> MY HIGH CONFIDENCE IN YOUR LEADERSHIP STOP I AM
> AT ONE WITH YOU AND THEIR HIGHNESSES THE RULERS
> AND PEOPLES OF MALAYA IN THE TRIALS WHICH YOU ARE
> SUSTAINING STOP

The king was referring to the leaders of Malaya's principalities over whom the empire ruled. The telegram continued:

> I KNOW THE EMPIRE'S RELIANCE ON YOUR FEARLESS
> DETERMINATION TO CRUSH THIS ONSLAUGHT WILL BE
> FULLY JUSTIFIED AND WITH GOD'S HELP THE DEVOTED
> SERVICE OF EVERY MAN AND WOMAN IN MALAYA SHALL
> CONTRIBUTE TO OUR VICTORY ENDS

Two months later Singapore fell.

Montgomery's book was the first to make use of Shenton's diaries. (There was the war diary he wrote, and which he had sent to the Colonial Office in London before the Fall of Singapore, and there was a second day-to-day diary that he was allowed to have during his captivity.) Each page is dated, and divided into five. The diary covers the years 1941 to 1945. None of the entries are long. For example, the day Singapore fell, Shenton wrote: 'Very heavy shelling by both sides. Fraser and Newbigging' – two army officers – 'went out for the armistice. General Percival sent for. Air raid close to Singapore Club. Ceasefire for 8.30 p.m. Fine.' The matter-of-fact way Shenton concluded his entry says something about him. The situation of course was anything but fine, but in his laconic way he was implying that things weren't as bad as he thought they might have turned out. That tone is a feature of the diary. 'We have apparently arrived unannounced, and nobody knows what to do with us,' he writes after being brought to Hsian.

Below the entry detailing the Fall of Singapore is the one for the same date the following year. 'High wind, but not cold. We all had our fingerprints taken. Cold rather better. Bit of meat and gristle in evening soup.' A year later: 'Showery a.m. then overcast and cooler.' Meteorology came naturally to Shenton – my father, who saw a lot of him in the 1950s, would say that weather was always a topic of conversation.

'All oranges in the compound now picked but still more outside. Issue of seven bananas. Solid dish of beans for supper instead of soup. Saw a few swallows.' The 1945 entry for 15 February hints at his phlegmatic attitude to his surroundings. 'Lovely,' he says to begin with. 'Hot bath. Pigeons beginning to think about nesting. But the temperature at night still goes well below 0°C.'

While he was imprisoned, Shenton drew a picture of Father Christmas, and wrote a cryptic note beside it. 'I thought Christmas was Yesterday.' Was he saying that he considered every day he was held prisoner Boxing Day? I don't know, but perhaps the image was one way he kept his spirits up. Almost no news about the war reached Shenton during his imprisonment, and maybe because there was little news there were few fears about what he committed to his diary. There's no evidence of censorship within it. Beating back the boredom of prison-camp life was a central preoccupation; gardening and playing bridge helped. While in Taiwan, Shenton was briefly held with the governors of Hong Kong and Borneo, the military commander of Malaya and other high-ranking officials; they asked themselves why Singapore had fallen, as others would do once the war was over. But the gathering was short-lived; the men went to different camps.

On 29 August 1945, Bridget, who spent her war years in Kent, received a telegram from her father: ALL WELL STOP AM GOING COLLECT MUMMIE AND BRING HER HOME STOP LOVE DADDY

On 6 September 1945, she received a telegram from the governor general of Calcutta: SHENTON WITH US THIN BUT EXTREMELY WELL LADY THOMAS WELL IN SINGAPORE

A week later, there was another: HEAVENLY TO BE FREE AND TOGETHER AGAIN AT LAST. EVERYONE OVERWHELMINGLY KIND STOP REVELLING IN LUXURY AND LONGING TO SEE YOU THREE DARLINGS (Bridget and her husband Jack Lotinga had one son, Michael). RETURNING BY SEA SHORTLY STOP KISSES TO ALL AND LOVE TO EVERYONE, MUMMY AND DADDY THOMAS STOP

For staying on in Singapore, rather than fleeing from the Japanese before they captured the city, Shenton had a major street named after him in Singapore: Shenton Way. Daisy acknowledged the help she had had from a woman who smuggled medicine to her while she was imprisoned – Elizabeth Choy, who is recognised in Singapore as one of their war heroes. Daisy gave her a gold necklace, which Elizabeth later gave to Bridget. That necklace is now in the National Museum of Singapore.

Years later, when I was living in New York, I met a young man from Singapore called Marcel. He worked at the restaurant in Greenwich Village that my then wife ran. One evening, we spoke about Singapore. He told me his story and I told him mine. When I next saw him he said he had extraordinary news: Elizabeth Choy was his great-aunt. Marcel had always known his great-aunt had acted heroically during the war, but he hadn't known about the necklace. I hadn't known about Elizabeth Choy or the necklace. You can make too much of coincidence; chance and fate can be confused. What is unlikely isn't always extraordinary. When I heard this coincidence at a dark saloon bar off Sixth Avenue twenty years ago, there seemed only one way to describe it – remarkable. ■

**POST OFFICE**

**TELEGRAM**

No.

OFFICE STAMP

ASHFORD
6 SEP 1945
KENT
8-30

11   CONFIRMATION

From        111   C CW VWL 789/1 CTTA  21 4 =   21/4 SEP

GLT MRS LOTTINGA BRABOURNE LEES ASHFORDKENT =

*Pound House*      (CR)

SIR SHENTON WITH US THIN BUT EXTEMELY WELL LADY

THOMAS WELL IN SINGAPORE = MAIE CASEY +

*Governor General of Calcutta.*

---

**POST OFFICE**

**TELEGRAM**

No.

OFFICE STAMP

ASHFORD
1
29 AUG 1945
KENT

147      20   CONFIRMATION

From      20   CB 147 SSS CHUNGKING 2028/8/ 2030 BG ETAT

LOTTINGA BRABOURNE LEES ASHFORD-ENGLAND

ALL WELL STOP AM GOING COLLECT MUMMIE AND BRING HER

HOME STOP LOVE DADDY = SHENTON THOMAS +

Ahmet Altan, *c.*2009
Courtesy of the author

# I WILL NEVER SEE THE
·       WORLD AGAIN

## *Ahmet Altan*

TRANSLATED FROM THE TURKISH BY YASEMIN ÇONGAR

### 1

I woke up. The doorbell was ringing. I looked at the digital clock by my side, the numbers were blinking 05:42.

'It's the police,' I said.

Like all dissidents in this country, I go to bed expecting the ring of the doorbell at dawn.

I knew one day they would come for me. Now they had.

I had even prepared a bag and a set of clothes, so I would be ready for the police raid and what would follow.

A pair of loose black pants in linen, tied with a band inside the waist so there would be no need for a belt, black ankle socks, comfortable, soft sneakers, a light cotton T-shirt and a dark-color shirt to be worn over it.

I put on my 'raid uniform' and went to the door.

Through the peephole I could see six policemen on the landing, sporting the vests worn by counterterrorism teams during house raids, the acronym 'TEM' stamped in large letters on their chests.

I opened the door.

'These are search and arrest orders,' they said as they entered, leaving the door open.

They told me there was a second arrest order for my brother Mehmet Altan, who lived in the same building. A team had waited at his door, but no one answered.

When I asked which number apartment they had gone to, it turned out they had rung the wrong bell.

I phoned Mehmet.

'We have guests,' I said. 'Open the door.'

As I hung up, one of the policemen reached for my phone. 'I'll have that,' he said, and took it.

The six spread out into the apartment and began their search.

Dawn arrived. The sun rose behind the hills with its rays spreading purple, scarlet and lavender waves across the sky, resembling a white rose opening.

A peaceful September morning was stirring, unaffected by what was happening inside my home.

While the policemen searched the apartment, I put the kettle on.

'Would you like some tea?' I asked.

They said they would not.

'It is not a bribe,' I said, imitating my late father. 'You can drink some.'

Exactly forty-five years ago, on a morning just like this one, they had raided our house and arrested my father.

My father had asked the police if they would like some coffee. When they declined he laughed and said, 'It is not a bribe, you can drink some.'

What I was experiencing was not déjà vu. Reality was repeating itself. This country moves through history too slowly for time to go forward, so it folds back on itself instead.

Forty-five years had passed and time had returned to the same morning.

During a morning, which lasted forty-five years, my father had died and I had grown old, but the dawn and the raid were unchanged.

Mehmet appeared at the open door with the smile on his face

I always find reassuring. He was surrounded by policemen.

We said farewell. The police took Mehmet away.

I poured myself tea. I put muesli in a bowl and poured milk over it. I sat in an armchair to drink my tea, eat my muesli and wait for the police to complete their search.

The apartment was quiet.

No sound could be heard other than the police as they moved things around.

They filled thick plastic bags with the two decades-old laptops I had written some of my novels on and therefore could not bring myself to throw away, old-fashioned diskettes that had accumulated over the years and my current laptop.

'Let's go,' they said.

I took the bag, to which I had added a change of underwear and a couple of books.

We left the building. We got into the police car that was waiting at the gate.

I sat there with my bag on my lap. The doors closed on me.

It is said that the dead do not know that they are dead. According to Islamic mythology, once the corpse is placed in the grave and covered with dirt and the funeral crowd has begun to disperse, the dead also tries to get up and go home, only to realize when he hits his head on the coffin lid that he has died.

When the doors closed, my head hit the coffin's lid.

I could not open the door of that car and get out.

I could not return home.

Never again would I be able to kiss the woman I love, to embrace my kids, to meet with my friends, to walk the streets. I would not have my room to write in, my machine to write with, my library to reach for. I would not be able to listen to a violin concerto or go on a trip or browse in bookstores or buy bread from a bakery or gaze on the sea or an orange tree or smell the scent of flowers, the grass, the rain, the earth. I would not be able to go to a movie theater. I would not be able to eat eggs with sausage or drink a glass of wine or go to a restaurant and order fish. I would not be able to watch the sunrise. I would not be able to call anyone on the phone. No one would be able to call me on the phone. I would not be able to open a door by myself. I would not wake up again in a room with curtains.

Even my name was about to change.

Ahmet Altan would be erased and replaced with the name on the official certificate, Ahmet Hüsrev Altan.

When they asked for my name I would say 'Ahmet Hüsrev Altan'. When they asked where I lived I would give them the number of a cell.

From now on others would decide what I did, where I stood, where I slept, what time I got up, what my name was.

I would always be receiving orders: 'stop', 'walk', 'enter', 'raise your arms', 'take off your shoes', 'don't talk'.

The police car was speeding along.

It was the first day of a twelve-day religious holiday. Most people in the city, including the prosecutor who had ordered my arrest, had left on vacation.

The streets were deserted.

The policeman next to me lit a cigarette, then held the pack out to me.

I shook my head no, smiling.

'I only smoke,' I said, 'when I am nervous.'

Who knows where this sentence came from. Nowhere in my mind had I chosen to make such a declaration. It was a sentence that put an unbridgeable distance between itself and reality. It ignored reality, ridiculed it, even as I was being transformed into a pitiful bug who could not even open the door of the car he was in, who had lost his right to decide his own future, whose very name was being changed; a bug entangled in the web of a poisonous spider.

It was as if someone inside me, a person whom I could not exactly call 'I' but nevertheless spoke with my voice, through my mouth, and was therefore a part of me, said, as he was being transported in a police car to an iron cage, that he only smoked when he was 'nervous'.

That single sentence suddenly changed everything.

It divided reality in two, like a samurai sword that in a single movement cuts through a silk scarf thrown up in the air.

On one side of this reality was a body made of flesh, bone, blood, muscle and nerve that was trapped. On the other side was a mind that did not care about and made fun of what would happen to that body, a mind that looked from above at what was happening and what was yet to happen, that believed itself untouchable and was, therefore, untouchable.

I was like Julius Caesar, who, as soon as he was informed that a large Gallic army was on its way to relieve the siege at Alesia, had two high walls built: one around the hill fort to prevent those inside from leaving and one around his troops to prevent those outside from entering.

My two high walls were built with a single sentence to prevent the mortal threats from entering, and the worries accumulating in the deep corners of my mind from exiting, so that the two could not unite to crush me with fear and terror.

I realized once more that when you are faced with a reality that can turn your life upside down, that same sorry reality will sweep you away like a wild flood only if you submit and act as it expects.

As someone who has been thrown into the dirty, swelling waves of reality, I can comfortably say that the victims of reality are those so-called smart people who believe that you have to act in accordance with it.

There are certain actions and words that are demanded by the events, dangers and realities that surround you. Once you refuse to play the assigned role, instead doing and saying the unexpected, reality itself is taken aback; it hits against the rebellious jetties of your mind and breaks into pieces. You then gain the power to collect the fragments and to create from them a new reality in the mind's safe harbors.

The trick is to do the unexpected, to say the unexpected. Once you can make light of the lance of destiny pointing at your body, you can cheerfully eat the cherries you had filled your hat with, like the unforgettable lieutenant in Pushkin's story 'The Shot', who does exactly that with a gun pointing at his heart.

Like Borges, you can answer the mugger who asks, 'Your money or your life?' with, 'My life.'

The power you will gain is limitless.

I still don't know how I came to utter the sentence that transformed everything that was happening to me and my perception of it, nor what its mystical source might be. What I know is that someone in the police car, who was able to say he smoked only when he was nervous, is hidden inside me.

He is made of many voices, laughs, paragraphs, sentences and pain.

Had I not seen my father smile as he was taken away in a police car forty-five years ago; had I not heard from him that the envoy of Carthage, when threatened with torture, put his hand in the embers; had I not known that Seneca consoled his friends as he sat in a bathtub of hot water and slit his wrists on Nero's orders; had I not read that on the eve of the day he was to be guillotined, Saint-Just had written in a letter, 'The conditions were difficult only for those who resisted entering the grave,' and that Epictetus had said, 'When our bodies are enslaved our minds can remain free'; had I not learned that Boethius wrote his famous book in a cell awaiting death, I would have been afraid of the reality that surrounded me in that police car. I would not have found the strength to ridicule and shred it into pieces. Nor would I have been able to utter the sentence with a secret laughter that rose from my lungs to my lips. No, I would have cowered with worry.

But someone, whom I reckon to be made from the illuminated shadows of those magnificent dead reflected in me, spoke and thus managed to change all that was happening.

Reality could not conquer me.

Instead, I conquered reality.

In that police car, speeding down the sunlit streets, I set the bag that was on my lap onto the floor with a sense of ease and leaned back.

When we arrived at the Security Department, the car drove through a very large gate into the building and started down a winding road. As we descended there was less and less light and the darkness deepened.

At a turn in the road, the car stopped and we got out. We walked through a door into a large underground hall.

This was an underworld completely unknown to the people circulating above. It reeked of stone, sweat and damp. It tore from the world all those who passed through its dirty yellow walls, which resembled a forest of sulfur.

In the drab raw light of the naked lamps, every face bore the wax dullness of death.

Plain-clothes policemen waited to greet us creatures torn away from the world. Past them, a hallway led deeper inside. Piled at the base of the walls were plastic bags that looked like the shapeless belongings of the shipwrecked swept ashore.

The policemen removed the tie from around the waist of my trousers, my watch and my ID.

Here in the depths without light, the police, with each of their gestures and words, carved us out of life like a rotten, maggot-laced piece from a pear and severed us from the world of 'the living'.

I followed a policeman into the hallway, dragging my feet in my laceless shoes. He opened an iron door and we entered a narrow corridor where an oppressive heat grasped you like the claws of a wild beast.

A row of cells with iron bars ran along the corridor. Each cell was congested with people. They lay on the floor. With their beards growing long, their eyes tired, their feet bare and their bodies coated in sweat, they had melted the boundaries of their existence and become a moving mass of flesh.

They stared with curiosity and unease.

The policeman put me in a cell and locked the door behind me.

I took off my shoes and lay down like the others. In that small cell filled with people lying down, there was no room to stand.

In a matter of hours I had traveled across five centuries to arrive at the dungeons of the Inquisition.

I smiled at the policeman who was standing outside my cell, watching me.

Viewed from outside I was one old, white-bearded Ahmet Hüsrev Altan lying down in an airless, lightless iron cage.

But this was only the reality of those who locked me up. I had changed it.

I was the lieutenant happily eating cherries with a gun pointing at his heart. I was Borges telling the mugger to take his life. I was Caesar building walls around Alesia.

I only smoke when I'm nervous.

## 2

I nodded off for a moment. When I opened my eyes I saw that the staff colonel on the cot across from me and the submarine colonel curled up on a sheet of plastic on the floor were both asleep.

The young village teacher who had been told to sell out his friends laid his prayer rug between two cots and began his devotions.

In the dim light of the cell I could see his figure – a dark shadow – prostrating himself on the rug.

I had not slept for nearly twenty-four hours and I was exhausted. My bones ached.

The long black shadows of the iron bars cut through our chests, our faces, our legs and divided us into pieces.

The bare feet of the colonels shone in the cold light seeping in from the corridor, like pieces of white rock.

The colonel across from me groaned in his sleep.

I was in a cage.

In the damp dimness, in the shadows of the iron bars that cut into this dimness, in the young schoolteacher's murmurs of prayer, in the shiny stone-like feet of the colonels, in the moans that came from across the cell, in all of these, there was something more startling than death, something that resembled the empty space between life and death, a no-man's-hollow which reached neither state.

We were lost in that hollow.

No one could hear our voices. Nobody could help us.

I looked at the walls. It was as if they were coming closer.

Suddenly, I had this feeling that the walls would close in on us, crush and swallow us like carnivorous plants.

I swallowed and heard a groaning noise escape from my throat.

Something was happening.

I felt an army of ghosts stir within me. It was as if that famous army of terracotta warriors, which the Chinese emperor had built to guard his body after death, was coming alive inside me. Each carried with him a different fear, a different horror.

I sat up and leaned my back against the wall.

The heat was brushing my face like a furry animal. My forehead was sweating. I was having difficulty breathing.

This place was so narrow, airless. I wouldn't be able to stay here.

For a moment, I had an irresistible urge to get up, hold the iron bars and shout, 'Let me out of here. Let me out of here, I am suffocating.'

With horror I realized I was lurching forward.

I clenched my fists as if to stop myself.

I knew that with a single scream I would lose my past and my future, everything I had, but the urge to get myself out of that cage with its walls closing in on me was irresistible.

The terrifying urge to shout and the pressure of knowing that this shout would destroy my whole life were like two mountains colliding and crushing me in between.

My insides were cracking.

The young teacher stood up and put his hands together on his belly; the colonel across from me groaned and turned over to his other side.

I tucked in my legs and put my arms around my knees.

My vision was getting blurry, the walls were moving.

I wanted to get out of here, I wanted to get out right away and knowing this was impossible made my brain feel like it had pins and needles, as if thousands of ants were crawling in its folds.

The realization that I was about to embarrass myself intensified my fear even more.

I saw two eyes. Two eyes with a cold, cruel, almost hostile look in them, shiny as glass, like the eyes of a wolf chasing his prey in a rustling forest. Those eyes were inside me, keeping watch on my every move.

I had survived such moments in my youth, moments when one wanders to the edge of madness. I knew I had to turn back. If I took another step, I would cross the line of no return.

My lungs were rising up to my throat, blocking my windpipe.

The young teacher had again prostrated himself on the prayer rug.

He was muttering a prayer.

He, too, was begging to be saved.

The colonel lying on the floor groaned in his sleep.

I took a deep breath to push my lungs back down. I took a gulp of warm water from the plastic bottle I had by my side.

I thought of death.

Instinctively, I was trying to hold on to the idea of death. The eternity of death has the power to trivialize even the most terrifying moments of life.

Thinking that I would die had a calming effect on me. A person who is going to die does not need to fear the things that life presents.

Like everyone else, I was insignificant, what I had been living through was insignificant, this cage, too, was insignificant, the distress that suffocated me was insignificant and so too was the evil I had met.

I clung firmly to my own death. It calmed me.

The teacher saluted the angels, turning his head first to the right, then to the left, and finished praying.

He turned around and looked at me.

Our eyes met.

A shy smile appeared on his face as if he was embarrassed –
although about what I don't know.

Moving with difficulty between the two cots, he turned to lie down
beside the colonel on the plastic-covered rubber that lay on the floor.

His bare feet now shone alongside those of the colonel.

The shadow of an iron bar cut through his ankles like a black
razor. I saw two feet attached to nothing.

I was going to die one day.

What I was living through was insignificant.

The eyes inside me were shut. The wolf was gone.

I wasn't going to lose my mind.

During a scorching heat, when crops catch fire, a circle is drawn
around the blaze and the grain along that circle is set alight before the
flames can reach it. Once the fire arrives at the circle it stops, as there
is nothing left there to burn. They use fire to put out fire.

I had surrounded and extinguished the fire of terror, which life
had lit in a cage, with the fire of death.

I knew that my life from now on would be a series of opposing
fires. I would surround those started by my jailers with the fires of
my mind.

Sometimes death will be the source; sometimes the stories I write
in my mind; sometimes the pride that won't let me leave behind a
name stained by cowardice; sometimes it will be the desires of the
flesh releasing the wildest fantasies; sometimes peaceful reveries;
sometimes the schizophrenia unique to writers who twist and tweak
the truth in their red-hot hands to create new truths; sometimes it
will be hope.

My life will pass fighting invisible battles between two walls; I will
survive by hanging on to the branches of my own mind, at the very
edge of the abyss, and not by giving in to the disorienting inebriety of
weakness, even for a moment.

I had seen the monstrous face of reality.

From now on I would live like a man clinging to a single branch.

I didn't have the right to be scared or depressed or terrified for a single moment; nor to give in to the desire to be saved, to have a moment of madness, nor to surrender to any of these all-too-human weaknesses.

A momentary weakness would destroy my entire past and future – my very being.

If I were to tire and let go of the branch I was holding, it would be fatal; I would fall to the bottom of the abyss and become a mess of blood and bones.

Would I be able to endure the days, weeks, months and years of swinging in the air, unable to let go of the branch for even an instant?

If I were to let go and break into pieces in the abyss of weakness, I would lose not only my past and future but also the strength that enables me to write.

Because the prospect of being cut off from the precious lode of writing scared me more than anything, that fear would suppress all other fears and give me the ability to endure. Courage would be born of fear.

Now that the fear of losing my mind, which had momentarily licked my insides, and the heavy feeling of suffocation distress had passed, a tense fatigue took hold of my body.

The teacher, too, was fast asleep. The restless movements of those feet cut off from the ankles had stopped.

Though tired enough to pass out, I couldn't sleep. It was as if even sleep itself was too exhausted to come and take me.

When the police took me from my apartment, I threw in my bag a book I had recently ordered on medieval Christian philosophers, thinking it would have entertaining and diverting stories about their lives.

To escape what I was living through, to rest and relax a little, I would take refuge in what they had endured.

These philosophers struggled to resolve the secrets of their personal lives while still daring to unravel the mysteries of the universe. They experienced an innocent helplessness before the question 'What is life?', even though they had written thousands of pages on the subject. This, it had always seemed to me, was an amusing summary of the human condition.

In that dim light, as my cage-mates moaned and groaned, I opened the book.

I had hoped reading would calm me and put me to sleep. I was wrong.

The book did not consist of entertaining biographies. Instead, it recounted the philosophers' rather compelling views.

And St Augustine, of course, was the first one to greet me.

This bear of a man prays sincerely to be rid of the burden of sexuality, yet begs God not to do it quickly because he is having a good time. He persists in trying to find a reasonable explanation for why God, being 'absolutely good', would create such grave evil. Augustine wakens in me a sense of tenderness that contrasts with his stature and significance.

I began to read.

That a man locked in a cage would find himself with no alternative other than to read about why God created evil seems part of life's unfathomable facetiousness.

This time, reading Augustine angered me. He says that God had reason to create torture, persecution, sorrow, murder and the cage they locked me up in along with the men who locked me up in it: all this evil, says Augustine, was the result of Adam acting with 'free will' and eating the apple.

I was in a cage because a man had eaten an apple. The man who ate the apple was God's own Adam, made by his own hands; the man who was locked in the cage was me.

And Augustine was asking me to be thankful for this?

I grumbled as if he stood before me, shoddily dressed, with his big balding head, long beard and charming smile.

'Tell me,' I said, 'what is the bigger sin – a man eating an apple or punishing all of humanity with torture because a man ate an apple?'

I added furiously, 'Your God is a sinner.'

The colonel across from me turned to his side, groaning; the shadow of the bar cut off half his face.

'I am paying for your God's sins.'

My eyes were burning from fatigue, from lack of sleep. A stupor-like slumber was dragging me down.

The colonel across the room moaned.

I looked up and saw that he was awake and crying.

While he was in jail, his three-year-old child was in the hospital, grappling with death.

I turned and faced the wall so he wouldn't know I had seen him cry.

I was never going to let the branch go. Not even for a moment.

As I fell asleep I thought of that little girl, grappling with death.

'Is an apple worth all of this?' I thought.

## 3

Each cell in the prison has a stone courtyard in front of it that is six steps long and four steps wide, with an iron drain in the middle for rainwater.

The high walls of the courtyard have barbed wire on them. A steel cage covers the top.

To use the title of the novel my father wrote in prison, 'a handful of sky' is what you see when you look up, but even that is divided into the small squares of the steel cage above.

When spring arrives, migratory birds fly in through the cage and make nests on the barbed wire.

The inmates pacing in their adjacent courtyards don't see each other but they can talk by shouting. We recognize one another from our voices.

On occasion, my young cellmate Selman chats with our neighbors we have never seen.

What they talk about doesn't matter.

What matters is knowing there are people present beyond your cell walls and letting them know of your existence.

For us, the world is the neighboring courtyards that our voices can reach. Shouting is our way of communicating with the world.

One spring day, Selman was talking to the voice in the courtyard next to ours.

'The birds have started migrating here,' Selman said.

'I am looking after a parakeet,' the voice answered. 'He was born in the prison, then his mama died. I raised him.'

'I never saw your parakeet flying about,' said Selman. 'I guess I am never there at the right time.'

'He doesn't fly,' said the voice in the next courtyard.

Then, with the compassion of a father feeling sorrow for a child, the voice added: 'He is afraid of the sky.' ■

# NO MACHINE COULD DO IT

## *Eugene Lim*

I'd become friends with a Public Intellectual. He handled everything: scandal, sex, politics, political sex scandals, racism, weather, the racism of weather, Japanese cartoons. Everything was under his purview, but his specialty was the Future. He was a much more successful colleague at the university where I would occasionally adjunct. Several years ago entirely by accident, when collecting some papers from our department's office, not knowing who he was, I saw him standing next to the faculty mailboxes with a copy of a book I'd just read. I was younger and new to the place and excitable – and so I started up a brief conversation about the book. I think because I wasn't awestruck, because I'd no idea who he was, the conversation went smoothly. And a few days afterward we continued the conversation, which was rather pleasant, and soon after we more or less became friends. We had some important interests in common but these did not overlap so much that there was any real sense of competition between us. In other ways, we were a good match: he was about a decade older; we were both divorced and had daughters about the same age.

After that first meeting I googled him and realized who he was and that he was famous. Academic famous not TV famous but still. I was embarrassed that I hadn't known who he was, or anything even about his work, but I also was emboldened by my ignorance. It gave the situation a kind of ease, which somehow, especially at the beginning, was necessary and also gave things momentum. We had to play-act a little, if this makes sense. Both of us had to continue the idea of my ignorance even if it had become a fiction, to maintain our enthusiasm.

But, also, just after I found out who he was and the fact that he specialized in, and was renowned for, a sharp-eyed, bullshitless analysis of the future, a question started to shift the gravity in my mind. Though this is difficult to admit in mixed company, perhaps this is because I am the daughter of quote striver immigrant parents. And so slowly, while maintaining an attitude of nonchalance and casual good humor, I found myself yearning to ask him something. This was a question that had long been on my mind but to which I didn't think I'd ever find an answer. It was similar to when you by chance meet an orthopedic surgeon at a party and try delicately to bring the conversation around to your chronic and exquisite lower back pain – that kind of egotistical, obvious yet helpless maneuvering. My burning question was this:

Will there be any jobs in the future? What are the good jobs of the future? And what kind of jobs do you think our *children* might have in the future?

I know that this is three questions but it really is just one question disguised as three questions.

When I finally gathered the gumption to ask, the Public Intellectual was kind. He struggled in only a barely perceptible way to hide his contempt for such a crude and banal and selfish question. In addition he was, it should be said, quite practiced, as would become evident, in answering such questions and so had made a career of answering them as warm-up or filler to or, most often, as comedic relief from, the more refined, profound questions which he intensely wrestled with during his more solitary hours.

So to my question, the Public Intellectual said, 'Here's what I say to people when they ask. This is what I say.'

'Yes?' I prompted.

'I say, "You know how our pets are to us?"'

'Our pets?' I said.

'Yes, you know. Our cats and our dogs.'

'Our dogs.'

'Yes,' he said, 'and our cats.'

'What about them?' I asked.

He said, 'We keep our pets because they are *interesting* to us.'

'I see,' I said, not seeing.

'In the future . . .' the Public Intellectual continued.

'Yes?' I said.

'In the future we have to be as *interesting* to the AI as our pets are to us.'

'The AI?' I said.

'The AI,' he said.

I looked bewildered so he dumbed it down for me. 'The robots. The machines.'

'Oh,' I said, 'I see.'

'The AI,' he said. 'We have to be as interesting to them as our pets are to us.'

'Hmm,' I said.

My name is Joan Jessica Jingleheimer Schmidt. It doesn't matter what my name is. I'm a recently divorced and perennially underemployed adjunct. When I'm lucky enough to be asked, I work at a public university, teaching the children of immigrants to imagine a better life for themselves while they live out their days in the service industry. I do this by making them write five-paragraph essays. But right now, I'm out of work – and so have become a kind of low-level servant to the economic betters of my cultural class. That is, I've become a house- and dog-sitter. I'm currently on my thirty-first dog-sitting job. It's disgraceful that a middle-aged woman with a doctorate is employed as a house-sitter so I have to be a little dissembling. I tell people I'm working on a book and that the house-sitting job is a kind of ongoing writer's residency. A *staycation*, I tell them.

I'm currently in the home of Angela and Jerome, two corporate lawyers who knew a friend of a friend of a friend of mine. Over the phone I pretended I was a little more normal than I am and, since they knew someone who knew someone who knew someone who knew me – and, more importantly, because I think they'd waited until the last minute and had become a little desperate – they gave me the job. No money, as per usual, but I feed myself from whatever's left in their kitchens, which is usually enough to last months.

When I got to Angela and Jerome's I put their dog in the basement. I've brought into the house a small PA system consisting of a speaker the size of a shoebox, a 200-foot coil of wire I stole from a previous job and a handheld microphone. I go down into the basement and place the speaker in front of the dog. And then I uncoil the wire so that it goes up the basement stairs, around through the kitchen, then up through another set of stairs, until I get to a bedroom facing the back of the house. I know the dog can't come up from the basement because there's a gate at the bottom of the stairs.

When I get to the bedroom I attach the microphone to the end of the wire and I click it on.

I say, 'Hello? Hello? Is this the suicide prevention hotline?'

I pause and I hear a faint and muffled bark from the dog, two stories down in the basement.

'Hello? Is this you?' I say. 'Is this the right place? Well I hope so because I feel pretty awful. I'm right on the edge of giving it all up. I don't think I'm very good at anything. I don't enjoy anything. Everything tastes gray and I'm alone and all I do is eat butter pecan ice cream.'

I pause and listen but the dog doesn't make any sounds.

'Hello, hello? Hello dog?' I say into the microphone. 'Dear dog,' I say. 'Dear dog, hallowed be thy name,' I say into the microphone. 'Dear dog, hallowed be thy name, your kingdom come, your will be done.'

The room I was in overlooked a patio outside the basement door, and the dog could go out there through a plastic flap to shit and pee. I was watching to see if he'd go out onto the patio. I'd set the speaker volume just loud enough that you could hear it in the basement but not if you went out on the patio. I'd wanted to see if my voice would bore the dog.

I say into the microphone, 'Hello, is this returns? Well, it's defective. All of it. Also it's not what I ordered or expected. Also, I found a better price elsewhere. Also, I wanted it in a different color.'

The patio is still empty so I know the dog is still hearing my words. He's a mix but mostly a Labrador I think. His fur is black with some interesting brown underneath. The dog's name is Maurice. I agree. It's an awful name for a dog.

I say into the microphone, 'Hello, is this the collection agency? I'm finally returning your phone call, you motherfuckers.' (I say 'motherfuckers' as sweetly as I can because I want to curse but I also don't want to scare the dog with anger as this would discredit any results from my so-called experiment.) 'Hello,' I say into the microphone. 'Hello collection agency shitball-eaters,' I say, 'I'm finally getting back to you after avoiding you all these years, but I don't have any money and I don't want to set up a payment plan but I'd like to talk to an operator. Sure I'll hold. I want to talk to someone about the early death of my father and about my mother's rages and about being into new wave electronic music in junior high and about how all that might explain things.'

I give up looking out the window and go lie down on the kid's bed. This is Angela and Jerome's kid. I guess she's about eight or nine from the pictures in the house and from the room's decor. The bed is shaped like a cartoon character I don't recognize. For a moment I think I could maybe use this cartoon character instead of the dog. That is, it occurs to me I might as well just start talking to the cartoon character (who is also a bed – that part is a nice detail), but then I decide I might as well stick it out and finish what I'd started with the dog.

Who knows, I think, maybe if I give up now, the dog's feelings will be hurt. Part of me is moved by this idea because, maybe if it were true, and most of me thinks it can't possibly be true, but if it *were* true, if the dog were to actually be hurt if I happened to stop talking into the microphone, well, this would mean, of course, on some level, the dog was *interested* in what I was saying. This was enough for me to abandon the idea of just talking to the cartoon character even if the cartoon character was a bed. I say into the microphone, 'Hello, Betty. Hold all my calls. I've a big meeting with Mr Money.'

I say into the microphone, 'Okay, no more games. Or,' I say into the microphone so Maurice can hear my voice in the basement, I say, 'maybe only a few more games. Here's something I keep thinking about since my friend the Public Intellectual told me this hint about the future. I have something I like to do, Maurice. I have something I like to do and I've never shared this information with anyone else. You'll be the first I ever told, got it? Aren't you interested? Aren't you on the edge of your seat?

'Maurice, what I like to do is smoke a bowl and go to the aquarium and watch the jellyfish.

'Did you hear that, Maurice? Did you hear my great admission? I mean to say, what I like to do is, there's a bus that you can pick up not too far from here. And it goes all the way to the aquarium. It takes about an hour but you can always get a seat. I smoke some high-grade medical marijuana, a bowl of it, right before I leave. I get very high. I take the bus to the aquarium. Then, just outside the aquarium I smoke a little more and then I go into the aquarium and watch the jellyfish for an hour or so. And what's more, Maurice, while I watch the jellyfish I put on my headphones and listen to Scandinavian death metal. I listen to a Norwegian heavy-metal band called Kvelertak. I've no idea what Kvelertak means and I've no idea what they're singing about but the drummer is perfect – and when you're stoned and watching the jellyfish and listening to Kvelertak, well, it's just so fucking sublime I can't explain it.

'So, Maurice, you see, what I'm trying to tell you about is how I met Sofia. I was at the aquarium, pretty stoned, watching the jellyfish, listening to Nordic heavy metal – and I happened to look to my right . . .

'And there's another woman with headphones on. She's maybe ten feet away. And I swear I could tell she was doing the exact same thing I was doing. I *swear* it. Somehow I just knew she was also high as a kite and listening to Norwegian death metal and just watching the jellyfish bloom their translucent selves into folding and unfolding umbrellas over and over again.

'I sat there for about a half-hour and then looked to my right again. The woman was still there. I was a strange combination of paranoid and religious feeling. I felt both suspicious and also like fate was laying its hand upon me. I spent some time thinking about this, and then I thought, fuck it, I'll just go ask her. So I go over and introduce myself. She takes off her headphones and looks at me. I say, Hello, my name is Joan Jessica Jingleheimer Schmidt. Except I don't. I say my regular unimportant name. She looks at me, then she says, Hello, my name is Sofia. And then we sort of look at each other for a while.

'Then I sat down right next to her and then we both put our headphones back on and we went back to watching the jellyfish for another half-hour. I thought such behavior could only possibly make sense if we were both high, so I felt confident about my theory.

'As it happened, after half an hour she got up. And so I took this as a signal, and I got up and I followed her. We walked to the bus stop together.

'It turned out I was only partially right. Sofia indeed also had the habit of watching the jellyfish for hours at a time, but – she did it completely sober. Furthermore she didn't listen to Scandinavian death metal. Sofia preferred nineties R&B.

'Maurice, have I told you I'm the product of stereotypically quote striver immigrant parents? Well, it's true despite it being hard to admit in mixed company. But because this is true the first narrative line I'm interested in when learning about a person's life is their labor history.

So I ask Sofia about this, indirectly of course, but eventually I piece it together. Here it is. Maurice, here is Sofia's labor history. She'd grown up in Ecuador and immigrated here when she was seventeen. She passed as a man in order to pick tobacco in North Carolina where they sprayed pesticides on the leaves such that the workers made homemade hazmat suits out of garbage bags and rags, which still didn't stop them from coughing blood after a few days and such attire certainly acted as a cruel instrument of self-administered sticky torture when worn during the blistering heat of hundred-degree days. After several seasons of this she came up north and worked for many years cleaning homes. And then one day she had a revelation. On that day a delivery truck brought to their small apartment a wing-backed armchair of voluptuous deep-pile mauve velvet. She argues with the delivery people that there must be some kind of mistake, but they show her the name and address on the papers and she has no choice so accepts delivery.

'Her boyfriend at the time came home and explained it. He said, I bought it but didn't want to tell you about it because it was too expensive. How much was it? she asked. He said, It's an old chair but it was in good condition and I got it for nothing but then I had it reupholstered. You got it what? I got it reupholstered. How much? she said. Twelve hundred, he said.

'Fucking shit, she said and they had a huge fight about it and then they made up and then they had sex.

'It was after, while she was lying in bed, that she had her revelation. Her revelation was this. She was going to learn to reupholster furniture.

'And that was what she did. It turned out to be incredibly lucrative. She'd always been clever with her hands. No machine could do it. And it turned out that the very rich in the city would spend obscene amounts of money to reupholster their sofas and their love seats and their chaise longues and their armchairs and their couches. Obscene amounts.

'And now, Sofia told me, she runs a small company with three employees, but it's actually a tremendous amount of work and she's beginning to feel her age, she says, and she's not sure how long she can keep it all up. Because others are catching on and there's more and more competition. And so she's stressed out and the only thing that relaxes her is watching the jellyfish for hours at a time, she says.

'And Maurice, don't you see? I finally get it. This is what he meant. This is what it'll mean to be as interesting to the AI as our pets are to us. It'll be like Sofia reupholstering sofas for the very wealthy. Maurice, what do you think of that?'

I put down the microphone. I get up off the bed to look out the window down at the patio.

I wave at Maurice.

He barks back. ■

# LETTER OF APOLOGY

## Maria Reva

*Don't think.*
*If you think, don't speak.*
*If you think and speak, don't write.*
*If you think, speak and write, don't sign.*
*If you think, speak, write and sign, don't be surprised.*

News of Konstantyn Illych Boyko's transgression came to us by way of an anonymous note deposited in a suggestion box at the Kozlov Cultural Club. According to the note, after giving a poetry reading, Konstantyn Illych disseminated a political joke as he loosened his tie backstage. Following Directive No. 97 to Eliminate Dissemination of Untruths among Party Cadres and the KGB, my superior could not repeat the joke, but assured me it was grave enough to warrant our attention.

One can only argue with an intellectual like Konstantyn Illych if one speaks to him on his level. I was among the few in the Kozlov branch of the agency with a higher education, so the task of re-educating Konstantyn Illych fell to me.

Since Konstantyn Illych was a celebrated poet in Ukraine and the matter a sensitive one, I was to approach him in private rather than at his workplace, in case the joke had to be repeated. Public rebuke would only be used if a civil one-on-one failed. According to

Konstantyn Illych's personal file (aged forty-five, married, employed by the Cultural Club), the poet spent his Sundays alone or with his wife at their dacha in Uhly, a miserable swampland thirty kilometers south of town.

Judgment of the quality of the swampland is my own and was not indicated in the file.

The following Sunday I drove to Uhly, or as close as I could get to Uhly; after the spring snowmelt, the dachas were submerged by a meter of turbid water and people were moving between and around the dachas in rowboats.

I had not secured a rowboat for the task as the need for one was not mentioned in Konstantyn Illych's file, nor in the orders I was given.

I parked at the flood line, where five rowboats were moored: two green, two blue, one white, none black. Our usual mode of transportation was black. I leaned on the warm hood of my car (black) and plucked clean a cattail as I deliberated what to do next. I decided on the innocuous white; anyway I did not want to frighten Konstantyn Illych and cause him to flee by appearing in a black one.

The dachas were poorly numbered and I had to ask for directions, which was not ideal. One man was half deaf and, after nodding through my question, launched into an account of his cystectomy; another elderly man, who clearly understood what I was saying, rudely responded in Ukrainian; one woman, after inquiring what in hell I was doing in her brother's rowboat, tried to set her German shepherd on me (thankfully, the beast was afraid of water). I was about to head back to the car when an aluminum kayak slid out of the reeds beside me, carrying two knobble-kneed girls. They told me to turn right at the electric transformer and row to the third house after the one crushed by a poplar.

A few minutes later I floated across the fence of a small dacha, toward a shack sagging on stilts. On the windowsill stood a rusted trophy of a fencer in fighting stance, and from its rapier hung a rag and sponge. When no response came from an oared knock on the door, I rowed to the back of the shack. There sat Konstantyn Illych and, presumably, his wife Milena Markivna, both of them cross-legged atop a wooden table, playing cards. The tabletop rose just above water level, giving the impression that the couple was stranded on a raft at sea. The poet's arms and shoulders were small, boyish, but his head was disproportionately large, blockish. I found it difficult to imagine the head strapped into a fencing mask, but that is beside the point.

'Konstantyn Illych?' I called out.

'Who's asking?' He kept his eyes on the fan of cards in his hands.

I rowed closer. The wood of my boat tapped the wood of the table. 'I'm Mikhail Igorovich. Pleased to meet you.'

Konstantyn Illych did not return my politesse, did not even take the toothpick out of his mouth to say, 'You here for electric? We paid up last week.'

His wife placed a four of spades on the table. Her thick dark hair hung over her face.

I told Konstantyn Illych who I was and that the agency had received reports of how he had publicly disseminated wrongful evaluations of the leaders of the Communist Party and the Soviet society at large, and that I was here to have a conversation with him. Konstantyn Illych set his cards face down on the table and said in a level tone, 'All right, let's have a conversation.'

I had conducted dozens of these conversations before and always began from a friendly place, as if we were two regular people – pals, even – just chatting.

'Quite the flood,' I said.

'Yes,' said Konstantyn Illych, 'the flood.'

'I'll bet the children love it here.'

'No children.'

Usually there were children. I stretched my legs out in the rowboat, which upset its balance, jerked them back.

'No parents, grandparents, aunts or uncles either,' said Milena Markivna. Her upper lip curled a little – the beginning of a sneer, as if to say, But you already knew that, didn't you?

There had indeed been mention of a mass reprimand of Milena Markivna's relatives in the fifties, but amid all the other facts about all the other citizens of Kozlov – all their sordid family histories – the detail had slipped my mind. Still, the woman did not need to dampen the spirit of the conversation.

Konstantyn Illych broke the silence. 'So what's the joke?'

'I haven't made a joke,' I said.

'No, the joke I supposedly told about the Party.'

Already he was incriminating himself. 'The term I used was "wrongful evaluation", but thank you for specifying the offense, Konstantyn Illych.'

'You're welcome,' he said, unexpectedly. 'What was it?'

'I cannot repeat the joke.' I admit I had searched Konstantyn Illych's file for it, but one of the typists had already redacted the words.

'You can't repeat the joke you're accusing me of telling?'

'Correct.' Then, before I could stop myself: 'Perhaps you could repeat the joke, and I'll confirm whether or not it's the one.'

Konstantyn Illych narrowed his eyes.

'We aren't moving any closer to a solution, Konstantyn Illych.'

'Tell me the problem first,' he said.

A brown leaf, curled into the shape of a robed figurine, floated by Milena Markivna's foot. She pressed the leaf into the murky water with her thumb before turning to her husband. 'Just say sorry and be done with it.'

I thanked her for her intuition – an apology was precisely what was in order, in the form of a letter within thirty days. Milena Markivna advised me not to thank her since she hadn't done anything to help me, in fact she hated officers like me and it was because of officers like me that she had grown up alone in this world, but at least she had nothing to lose and could do anything she wanted to: she could spit in my face if she wanted to, which I did not recommend.

Konstantyn Illych was tapping his fingernails on the table. 'I'm not putting anything in writing.'

It is usually at this point in the conversation, when the written word comes up, that the perpetrator becomes most uncomfortable, begins to wriggle. Most people fail to grasp the simple logic of the situation: that once a transgression occurs and a case file opens, the case file triggers a response – in this case, a letter of apology. One document exposes the problem, the second resolves it. One cannot function without the other, just as a bolt cannot function without a nut and a nut cannot function without a bolt. And so I told Konstantyn Illych, 'I'm afraid you don't have a choice.'

He reached for the small rectangular bulge in his breast pocket. 'Ever read my poetry?'

I expected him to retrieve a booklet of poems and to read from it. Dread came over me; I had never been one to understand verse. Thankfully he produced a packet of cigarettes instead.

'Come to my next reading,' he said. 'You'll see I'm as ideologically pure as a newborn. Then we'll talk about the letter.'

Normally I'd have a letter of apology written and signed well under the thirty-day deadline and I took pride in my celerity. Even the most stubborn perpetrators succumbed under threat of loss of employment or arrest. The latter, however, was a last resort. The goal now was to re-educate without arrest because the Party was magnanimous and forgiving; moreover prisons could no longer accommodate every citizen who uttered a joke.

In Konstantyn Illych's case, next came gentle intimidation. If Konstantyn Illych stood in line for sausage, I stood five spots behind him. If Konstantyn Illych took a rest on a park bench, I sat three benches over. He pretended not to see me, but I knew he did: he walked too fast, tripping on uneven pavement; bills and coins slipped from his fingers regularly. His head jerked right and left to make sure he never found himself alone on the street. He needn't have worried – always the odd pedestrian around – and anyway I did not intend to physically harm or abduct Konstantyn Illych, though that would have been simpler for both of us. My older colleagues often lamented the simpler times.

Four days passed without a word exchanged between us.

On the fifth day I went to see Konstantyn Illych give his poetry reading at the Kozlov Cultural Club. I took a seat in the front row of the lecture hall, so close to the stage I could see the poet's toes agitate inside his leather shoes. In the dim light I was able to transcribe some of his poetry:

> Helical gears, cluster gears, rack gears,
> bevel and miter gears, worm gears, spur gears,
> ratchet and pawl gears, internal spur gears,
> grind my body
> meat grinder
> grinds
> gr gr grrr
> ah ah ah
> aah aah aah
> ah haaaaaahh

And also:

> The bear
> bares his flesh
> skinless, bears the burden
> of the air wooooooooooooooooosh

And also:

> Dewy forget-me-not
> not me forgets.
> Stomp.

I cannot guarantee I transcribed the onomatopoeic bits with accuracy; Konstantyn Illych's reading gave no indication of the number of *a*'s and *o*'s, etc.

At the end of the reading the poet placed his pages at his feet, unbuttoned his faded blue blazer, addressed the audience: 'Time for a little trivia. I'll recite a poem and one of you will guess who wrote it. Get it right and everyone here will admire you, get it wrong and you'll be eternally shamed.' A few people laughed.

Throughout the challenge poets such as Tsvetaeva, Inber, Mayakovsky, Shevchenko (this one I knew) and Tushnova were identified. The audience expressed their enjoyment by whooping and clapping between names.

Konstantyn Illych waited for the lecture hall to quiet down before he leaned into the microphone. 'Who, whom?'

This apparently was also a poem; the crowd erupted in fervid applause. I made a mental note to alert my superiors that local culture was going down the chute.

Konstantyn Illych scanned the audience until his eyes locked with mine. 'The gentleman in the front row, in the black peacoat,' he said. 'Who wrote that poem?'

Once more the hall fell silent.

I turned right and left, hoping to find another man wearing a black peacoat in my vicinity, when I saw Konstantyn Illych's wife sitting behind me. She crossed her arms, her great bulging eyes on me, beckoning me to answer. One of her hands, nestled in the crook of her arm, resembled a pale spider waiting to pounce.

Konstantyn Illych's voice boomed above me. 'The greatest poet of all time, Comrade, and you do not know? I'll give you three seconds. Three . . .'

I froze in my seat. The man to my right, whose nose looked like it had been smashed many times, nudged me in the ribs.

'Two . . .'

The man whispered, 'Grandfather Lenin!' which I found absolutely in poor taste.

'One!' Konstantyn Illych bellowed. 'Who was it, esteemed audience?' The words rose up from the crowd in a column. 'Grandfather Lenin!'

Konstantyn Illych looked down at me from the stage, tsked into the microphone. Each tsk felt sharp, hot, a lash on my skin.

It was around this time I began to suspect that, while I had been following Konstantyn Illych, his wife had been following me. I forced myself to recollect all I could of the preceding week. Milena Markivna never figured in the center of the memories – the bullseye had always, of course, been Konstantyn Illych – but I did find her in the cloudy periphery, sometimes even in the vacuous space between memories. If I stood five spots behind Konstantyn Illych in line for sausage, the hooded figure four spots behind me possessed Milena's small, narrow-shouldered frame; if I sat three benches from Konstantyn Illych, the woman two benches over had the same pale ankle peeking out from under the skirt. I began to see the task of retrieving the letter of apology in a new light.

What I suspected: It was not about the letter, rather the lengths I would go to retrieve it.

What I suspected: I was being vetted for a position of great honor.

What I knew: 'Who, whom?' had been a simple test, and I had failed it.

What I knew: My mother had been subjected to the same tests as a young woman, and had succeeded.

When I was a child, my mother was invited to join the Honor Guard. According to my father, she had always been a model student, the fiercest marcher in the Pioneers, the loudest voice in the parades. She was the champion archer of Ukraine and had even been awarded a red ribbon by the Kozlov Botanist Club for her Cactaceae collection. One evening, an officer came to our door and served my mother a letter summoning her to the Chief Officer's quarters. Within six months she was sent to Moscow for special training, as only special training would suffice for the Guard that stands at the

mausoleum of Lenin. Since our family was not a recognized unit –
my parents hadn't married because my paternal grandparents (now
deceased) didn't like my mother – my father and I could not join her
in Moscow. I was too young to remember much about this period,
but do have two recollections: one, I could not reconcile the immense
honor of the invitation with the grief that plagued the family; two,
my father assumed care of my mother's cactus collection and every
evening, when he thought I was asleep on the sofa bed beside him,
wrapped his fingers around the spines of the plants and winced and
grit his teeth but kept them there until his whole body eased into a
queer smile. For many months his hands were scabbed and swollen.
Within a year my father was gone also; he had at last been able to join
my mother in Moscow and my grandparents told me that one day
I too would join them.

When Milena Markivna entered my life, I felt I had finally been
noticed. The vetting process for the Honor Guard was still possible.
My reassignment to Moscow to see my mother and father was still
possible. I believed it was possible to make gains with hard work.

From that point on I followed Milena Markivna's husband with
greater vigilance and Milena Markivna followed me with greater
vigilance. If Konstantyn Illych riffled through his pockets for
a missing kopek for a jar of milk, Milena Markivna's voice behind me
would say, 'Surely you have an extra kopek for the man,' and surely
enough, I would. If I dropped a sunflower-seed shell on the floor
while pacing the corridor outside the couple's apartment, behind
the peephole of Suite 76 Milena Markivna's voice would say, 'It's in
the corner behind you,' and surely enough, it was. She was a master
observer, better than me.

(It should not go unsaid that, beyond mention of the reprimand of
Milena Markivna's family, her file contained little information. This
may have been because she was born in the province surrounding
Kozlov and not in the city itself, but I suspected it was a matter of
rank: if Milena Markivna were indeed my superior, tasked with the
observation of my conduct and aptitude for ceremonial duty, I would

not have access to her full history. Information is compartmentalized to mitigate leaks, much like compartments are sealed off in ships to prevent sinking.)

Konstantyn Illych, in turn, grew accustomed to my omnipresence, even seemed to warm to it. After a bulk shipment to the Gastronom, I watched him haul home a thirty-kilogram sack of sugar. By the time he reached his building, the sack had developed a small tear, which meant he could not haul the sack up to the ninth floor without losing a fair share of granules. The elevator was out of the question due to the rolling blackouts and so I offered to pinch the tear as he carried the load over his shoulder, and he did not decline. Many minutes later we stood in front of Suite 76, Konstantyn Illych breathless from the effort. Since I was there I might as well come in, he said, to help with the sack. He unlocked the steel outer door and the red upholstered inner door, then locked the doors behind us. The apartment was very small, surely smaller than the sanitary standard of nine square meters allotted per person. After we maneuvered the sack to the glassed-in balcony, I scanned the suite for a trace of Milena Markivna – a blouse thrown over a chair, the scent of an open jar of hand cream, perhaps – but saw only books upon books, bursting from shelves and boxes lining the already narrow corridor, books propping up the lame leg of an armchair, books stacked as a table for a lamp under which more books were read, books even in the bathroom, all of them poetry or on poetry, all presumably Konstantyn Illych's. A corner of the main room had been spared for a glass buffet of fencing trophies and foils, and on the top of it stood a row of dusty family portraits. I tried to find Milena Markivna in the photographs but these, too, were Konstantyn Illych's – the large head made him recognizable at any age. I wondered if she lived there, if she was even his wife.

Milena Markivna entered the apartment a few minutes after us, with a soft scratch of keys in the locks. She appraised me as I imagined she might appraise a rug her husband had fished out of a dumpster. Would the piece be useful, or would it collect dust and get in the way? Her expression suggested the latter, but her husband was leading me into the kitchen, the point of no return. Once a guest steps into the kitchen, to have them leave without being fed and beveraged is of course unconscionable.

Milena Markivna leaned her hip against the counter, watching Konstantyn Illych mete out home brew into three cloudy shot glasses. 'Lena, fetch the sprats, will you?'

Milena Markivna said she needed the stool, which I immediately vacated. She stepped on the stool to retrieve a can from the back of the uppermost cupboard and set the can down on the table, with some force, and looked at me, also with some force, as if daring me to do something about the unopened sprats. I produced the eight-layer pocketknife I always kept on my person. In an elaborate display of resourcefulness, I flicked through the screwdriver, ruler, fish scaler and hook disgorger, scissors, pharmaceutical spatula, magnifying lens, hoof cleaner, shackle opener and wood saw, before reaching the can opener. Its metal claw sank into the tin with so little resistance, I could have been cutting margarine. Milena Markivna must have noticed the surprise on my face, asked if I knew about the exploding cans.

I conceded I did not.

'It's something I heard,' she said, 'something about the tin, how they don't make it like they used to. People are getting shrapnel wounds.' After a moment she gave a dry mirthless laugh and so I laughed as well.

Before Konstantyn Illych passed around the shots, I laid a sprat on my tongue and chewed it slowly to let the bitter oil coat the inside of my mouth and throat to minimize the effects of alcohol.

Milena Markivna also chewed a sprat before the first shot, which I did not fail to notice.

Three rounds later, Konstantyn Illych spoke of the tenets of Futurist philosophy and was about to show how he employed them in his poetry when I asked about the letter of apology, due in fifteen days.

'Mikhail Igorovich,' he said. 'Misha. Can I call you Misha?'

'You may.' The home brew was softening my judgment and there was only one sprat left.

'Fuck the letter, Misha. What is this, grade school?'

I told him about the possible repercussions, about his getting fired or arrested. 'You're lucky,' I said. 'In earlier times, a political joke meant ten years.'

Konstantyn Illych set his empty shot glass upside down on his pinkie like a thimble, twirled it in languid circles. 'Once upon a time,' he began.

I wanted to shake the letter out of him.

'I got the flu,' he continued. 'Ever get the flu?'

'Sure.'

'The flu turned into pneumonia and I ended up in the hospital. Not only did I get my own room, but by the end of the week the room was filled, and I mean floor-to-ceiling filled, with flowers and cards and jars of food from people I didn't even know, people from all around the country.'

Milena Markivna placed the last sprat between her lips and sucked it in until the tip of the tail disappeared into her mouth.

Konstantyn Illych leaned in. 'Imagine, Misha, what would happen if you tried to get me fired.'

Milena Markivna smacked her lips. 'Shall I grab another can? Maybe this time we'll get lucky.'

Another week passed without success. My superior remarked that I was usually quicker at obtaining a letter, and was I not dealing with someone who specialized in the written word, who could whip up a heartfelt apology in no time? I tried what I could with the poet. I considered bribing him, but the mere thought felt unnatural, against the grain, against the direction a bribe usually slid. I began to neglect other tasks at work, but believed my persistence with Konstantyn Illych would be rewarded. I admit I thought of Milena Markivna as well, and often. She followed me into my dreams. Throughout my life, she would tell me, I was being watched over. She would award me with a certificate signaling my entry into the Honor Guard, would place on my head a special canvas cap with a golden star on its front.

I cannot say if this is true to the initiation ceremony but it was how I imagined it had happened with my mother. I would wake at night to find myself alone in my dark room but was never afraid. I knew I was being watched over.

The day before the deadline I stood at the back of the town cinema, watching Konstantyn Illych watch *Hedgehog in the Fog*. I cannot recall when I began to watch the animated film myself. I had already seen it a number of times and always found it unsettling, in the way heights are unsettling. En route to see his friend for tea, Hedgehog gets lost in the fog that descends on the forest. It isn't the fog or the forest that troubles me, as it troubles Hedgehog, it is this: Hedgehog sees a white horse and wonders if it would drown if it fell asleep in the fog. I've never understood the question. I suppose what Hedgehog means is: if the white horse stops moving, we would no longer see it in the white fog. But if we no longer see it, what is its state? Drowned or not? Dead or alive? The question is whether Hedgehog would prefer to keep the fog or have it lift to discover what is behind its thick veil. I would keep the fog. For instance, I cannot know the whereabouts of my parents because they are part of me and therefore part of my personal file and naturally no one can see their own file, just like no one can see the back of their own head. My mother is standing proud among the Honor Guard. My mother is standing elsewhere. She is sitting. She is lying down. She is cleaning an aquarium while riding an elevator. Uncertainty contains an infinite number of certainties. My mother is in all these states at once, and nothing stops me from choosing one. Many people claim they like certainty, but I do not believe this is true – it is uncertainty that gives freedom of mind. And so, while I longed to be reassigned to Moscow, the thought of it shook me to the bones with terror.

When the film ended, I felt a cold breath on the back of my neck. Milena Markivna's voice came as a whisper: 'Meet me at the dacha at midnight. I'll get you the letter.'

It was a weekday, a Wednesday, the dachas empty of people. The swamps were still flooded but this time a sleek black rowboat waited for me. It barely made a seam in the water as I rowed. Northward, the overcast sky glowed from the city. My teeth chattered from the cold or excitement or fear; it is difficult to keep still when one knows one's life is about to change. Already I could feel, like a comforting hand on my shoulder, the double gold aiguillette worn by the Guard. The tall chrome boots tight around my calves.

I tried to retrace the route I had taken the first time I visited the dacha, but found myself in the middle of a thicket of cattails. The glow of the sky switched off. Normally electricity is cut not at night but in the evening when people use it most and thus the most can be economized – this is the thought I would have had had I not been engulfed in panic. Darkness closed in on me. I circled on the spot. The cattails hissed against the edge of the boat. Willow branches snared my arms and face. A sulfurous stench stirred up from the boggy water. Milena Markivna had given me the simplest of tasks and I was about to fail her.

A horizontal slit of light appeared in the distance, faint and quivering. I lurched the boat toward it. Soon I recognized the silhouette of the shack on stilts; the light emanating from under its door. I scrambled up the stairs, knocked. The lock clicked and I waited for the door to open, and when it did not, I opened it myself.

A figure in a white uniform and mask stood before me, pointing a gleaming rapier at my chest. The figure looked like a human-sized replica of the fencing trophies I had seen inside the glass display at Suite 76.

'Close the door.' The voice behind the mask was calm, level and belonged to Milena Markivna.

I tried to keep calm as well, but my hand shook when it reached the handle. I closed the door without turning away from her, kept my eyes on the rapier. The ornate, patinated silver of its hilt suggested the weapon had been unearthed from another century.

'Down on the floor. On your knees.'

I had not imagined our meeting to be like this but did as I was told. I inquired about the utility of having my ankles bound by rope and Milena Markivna said it was to prevent me from running away before she was done. I assured her I wouldn't think to run from such an important occasion and she, in turn, assured me she would skewer my heart onto one of my floating ribs if I tried. Before she stuffed a rag inside my mouth I told her I had been waiting for this moment since I was a child and she said she had been waiting for it since she was a child as well. I told her I was ready.

She said, 'I'm ready too.'

I do not know how much time passed with me kneeling, head bowed, as Milena Markivna stood over me.

I tried to utter a word of encouragement, mention the canvas cap with the golden star on its front, but of course couldn't speak through the rag in my mouth. All I could do was breathe in the sour, pickled smell of the fabric.

At last she knelt down in front of me, one hand on the hilt of the rapier, its tip still poised at my chest. With the other hand she took off her mask. Hair clung to her forehead, moist with sweat. I searched her face for approval or disappointment but it was closed to me, as if she were wearing a mask under the one she had just removed. I wondered how this would all look if a stranger barged through the door: she almost mad and I almost murdered.

Milena Markivna stabbed the rapier into the floor, which made me cry out, and said there really was no hurry in what she was going to do. She brought over a candle that had been burning on the table and dipped my fingers into the liquid wax, one by one, as she named her relatives who had been executed, one by one, thirty years ago. The burning was sharp at first – I dared not make another sound – but soon felt like ice. Milena seemed calmer then. She took the rag out of my mouth, unlaced her boots, set her feet on them and gave me a series of instructions. As I enveloped her warm toes in my mouth, she reminded me how she hated me. I removed my lips from the mound of her ankle long enough to tell her that we were not so different, she and I; that I too had grown up alone even though that would change soon. As she brought a second candle over and began to tip it over my scalp, she asked how it would change. Barely able to speak now, I told her that it would change when she inducted me into the Honor Guard and I would go to Moscow and see my family again. She laughed as if I had told a joke. The smell that greeted me was of singed pig flesh, sickening when I realized it was my own hair. My head pulsed with pain; tears blurred my vision. Milena Markivna set the candle down and asked how I knew where my family was. I said it was what I had been told. As she slid her fingers along the blade of the rapier, she said the neighbors had told her that her family had gone to a better place too, but never specified where or why they never wrote. The darkness of the night filtered in through the cracks of the shack and into my mind and I began thinking things I did not like to think about – my mother and father and where they might be. Milena Markivna wrapped her hand around the hilt of the rapier again and told me to take off my coat and shirt and lie face down on the floor.

As I did so, one thought knocked against another, like dominoes:

There was a possibility I was not, at present, being recruited.

If not, there was no Honor Guard waiting for me.

If not, my parents' rank did not matter.

If not, my parents did not have rank.

If not, my mother was not in the Guard.

If not, they were not in Moscow.

The blade dragged from my tailbone up the thin skin of my spine, searing my mind clean. I screamed into my mouth so that no one would hear. When the blade reached between my shoulders it became warm, and from its point a sweet numbness spread through my arms. I thought of my father with his bleeding hands, understood that queer smile. My head spun and the walls began to undulate. My voice came hoarsely. 'How do you know what happened to your family?'

After a moment she said, 'They disappeared. That's how I know.'

'They could be anywhere.'

'Do you believe that?'

'Yes.' My body shook against the damp floorboards. 'No.'

It was when I welcomed the blade that it lifted from my skin. I felt a tug between my ankles, then a loosening. She had cut the rope.

'You can go.'

'You're not done.'

'No,' she said, but pushed my shirt and coat toward me with her foot. I lay limp, spent. Through the window I could see the glow of the city flicker back on. I remembered why I had come to the dacha, but could not rouse myself to bring up the letter. I found I did not care about it much myself. I would be the one who would have to issue an apology to my superior the next day, give an explanation for failing to complete my task. I would write it. My superior would read it. I would be dismissed. What next? I would go to the market for a jar of milk, search my pockets for the correct change. If I weren't to have it, a voice behind me might ask if someone has a kopek for the man. Surely enough, someone will.

Before leaving I asked Milena Markivna, 'What was the joke your husband told?'

'Oh.' She said, '█████████████████████? █████
███████████████████████████████████.'

'All this trouble for that?'

It was the first time I saw her smile. 'I know. It's not even that funny.' ■

# RADICAL SUFFICIENCY

## *Jess Row*

They kissed in the closet; they kissed in the back of the van. They kissed on an inclined plane; they kissed on a rotary turnstile. They kissed in the bleachers. They kissed on the demo lot. Their mouths a mess of rubber and tape. Their gears meshed and missed. They dripped oil. They kissed without knowing how to kiss. It wasn't in the blueprints. They kissed and ran down their battery packs. They kissed in the driveway on Sri Lankan Independence Day. And then he said, Lyle said, I want to introduce you to someone, and she said, Keerthana said, spitting out a bit of curry leaf, you've got to be fucking kidding me.

No, it's not like that. She's awesome.

Then how did I know she was a *she*.

Because, he said, coming up close, so they were parka-on-parka, breathing his stale smoke at her acne, as close as he knew how to be without robotic assistance, because you're my Sinhala queen, my ten-terabyte wet dream –

Shut up, you spectrumy son of a bitch. I wrote that for you.

His car, his mom's car, mostly rusted-out now, the Taurus wagon with the handmade bumper sticker: ROBOTS CURED MY AUTISM.

No, he said, seriously. Her name's Rachel. Don't say what you're about to say. She's not a Normal. She's hard core.

WHAT IS THIS, TEEN SODA WEDNESDAYS?

She was speaking in her mother's voice again, with the head-waggle, the chin mounted on ball bearings. He didn't know how else to describe it. The pelvic dance it made him do, thrusting the knob under his pants waistband. She flipped her controller open – it was an old flip-phone she'd customized, worth an A+ in Dr Zaganov's Reductive Design AP – and her new robot whined out of the open garage, circled around, and bit him in the leg with its rubber grips. It hurt. He was hard, he hurt. Welcome to high school, he thought.

So much as touch her breast, Keerthana said, backing up toward the house, letting the robot do the work, as always, butting his leg, so much as put your hands *under her shirt*, for any reason –

Keerthana, describing things they hadn't done themselves –

You mean her real breasts? he had to ask. You mean her real shirt?

I'm getting a new drone for my birthday, she said. You don't want to know what it can do. Go home, go home.

*And after we break up*, she texted him later that night, *you don't get to say it was all your idea. It wasn't.*

It wasn't. He would never have said otherwise. He texted back, *I would never have said otherwise. I'll put it in writing. You, Keerthana Obeysekere, and I, Lyle Chancellor, together invented RealRobotSexLive. No one's pulling a Zuckerberg here.*

Because how could it have been otherwise?

Sophomore year: after they'd built those terrible first designs, hucked them, looped back. Somehow they wound up always being last in the design lab, a retired AP Chem classroom, retired after Jonas Mikkelsen self-immolated with a few lengths of rubber hose, some duct tape, a lighter and a gas line left open. No Bunsens would burn there again. They made stupid jokes from the safety of their marble acid-scarred countertops.

Keerthana was the first one to build a unit that moved on tracks. Nothing to blow your wad over, but it had reverse clamps that when placed at a certain angle created, unintentionally, the impression of an opening. She'd put a heavy burgundy tubing over the clamp arms, because it was all they had, and it looked, you had to admit it, vulvar in nature. And so she said, joking, check it out, Lyle, I made a robot pussy.

Dr and Dr Obeysekere were not in the least fond of their daughter's potty mouth, not understanding it as what it was, a form of STEM survival. I fucking dare you, she said once to Kevin Lauermeister, who made it a practice to interrupt her every time she spoke in AP Chem: The next time you jerk off to my yearbook picture, she said, think of my cunt full of razor blades, think of the bloody hole where your tiny dick used to be. *Cave vaginum dentatum*, motherfucker. In front of his friends, at lunch, she said that.

Lyle, on the other hand, who had been through years of occupational therapy – strictly for the purpose, he sometimes thought, of being able to respond if a girl ever talked to him in tenth grade, his best chance of contributing to the gene pool – was like, that is extremely cool, Keerthana.

At that point he didn't quite have her name right.

Now I have to build a dick to stick in it.

That was basically it. That, plus a YouTube page with ten thousand subscribers. Plus a basement studio, in her house – let's face it, Lyle said, when they were installing the second set of professional lights, it's a porn set – and hundreds of willing participants, from every robotics prog in north Jersey, at least, Westchester, Lawn Guyland. The *Live* part came later, when they realized, quite abruptly, that they could film at competitions. *After* competitions, after the awards were handed out, when no one was paying attention. What else were smartphones for? Their subscribers wanted realism, they wanted amateur action, unnatural angles, newbies.

NO HUMAN BEING HAS EVER APPEARED IN A REALROBOTSEX VIDEO, said the disclaimer at the beginning of every one. ALL ROBOTS ARE OVER THE AGE OF 18.

This is what we did in high school, Lyle observed once, that can go on no transcript. Like being in a death-metal band. It's our quotient of irrational exuberance.

And that's when she put her arms around him the first time. It was two in the morning. They'd gotten their PSATs that afternoon, and Dr and Dr Obeysekere, in a mood of irrational exuberance, had had a glass of Chablis each and gone to sleep at nine thirty. She put her tongue in his mouth, and then pulled it back, and said, it's weird, isn't it, when you don't have to think about the refractive angle.

And he said, I know I could develop a mechanism for the bra catch.

Don't be a douche, she said, unbuckling his belt. Save it for your sweaty dorm cubicle at MIT, you ex-retard. After I'm long gone.

That was how he knew it was real. This is real, he said out loud. This is really happening. Not happening to robots.

Why do you have to talk and ruin everything, she wanted to scream, but instead licked the sweaty crease between his thigh and scrotum, which smelled like a sock and tasted like a penny. That was it. That, it turned out, was enough. You know, she said, a week and three bottles of Woolite later, I really liked that sweater. He grinned and said, my settings need to be adjusted. She said, we'll have to work on that.

This is teen love last Wednesday: Dr Obeysekere driving them through downtown Newark, in their white minivan, the Space Shuttle, with tinted windows and curb feelers she bought by accident, because it was the cheapest one on the lot, and now the kids try to ignore the corner-standers and 5-0 staring as they go by. Suburban Minivans from the Hood to Outer Space. This is Keerthana and Lyle sitting in the back with a parka strategically over their laps and Paul and Vanessa running interference in front of them. Half phones, half IRL. The blizzard of texts in advance of their arrival at the Robotics state semifinal.

> *heard Jeffersonville-4 is running 3 rotors #fucked*
> *never mind wheres the afterparty yo*
> *@robocall quit acting all gangsta your from Tenafly*
> *@breadandcircuses teaneck losers cant afford invisalign*

*Keerthana bringing her bae #whataloser*
*#hatersgonnahate #tenaflygrammarsquad*

This is Rachel sitting in the bleachers, with her needles, with her hand-spun yarn, her copy of *The Structure of Scientific Revolutions*, judging not judging them.

Go wash your hands, Cindy Xu whispers in Keerthana's ear. I don't want your boyfriend's jizz all over my *equipment*. But K isn't remotely listening. Staring up at her. The fawn corduroy skirt and the red Mary Janes. The thrift-shop cardigan and the grandma pearls. She wants to eat her alive.

Is that her? she asks Lyle. He gives a quick guilty look and says, yes it is. I want you to meet her. But there's no need, because Rachel trips down the stairs with her hand extended, sort of swanlike, as if auditioning for *The Age of Innocence*. It's so great to meet you, she says, as if she really means it. Lyle and I just started talking one day when we were stuck doing this boring thing in Chem, and I had no idea about any of this stuff, and it's *fascinating*. It's so illicit and post-human.

If she was anyone else, she'd want to fucking pulverize her, but instead she wants Rachel to give her a hug. Not to hug but to *be* hugged. She loves how slippery theater kids are, the exotic blooms of the literary magazine staff, rare orchids and corpse flowers, but this is more specific, she wants to feel that body against her, she senses Rachel is wearing some kind of vintage underwire if not an outright bustier. The metal of an adolescent who doesn't traffic in metal. She takes her hand, and says, yeah, Lyle mentioned you'd be coming.

I like that choker. It's very *Heathers*.

Well, brightening, she says, like the movie says, I can't really accessorize for shit.

Exactly. I can tell. You've got that thing.

A *thing*.

When you walk into a room and everyone knows who you are.

What is this flush, this prickling, the way all her pores seem to be standing at attention? Usually she hates girls. Chronically disappointed in female friendship. Ever since Michelle Dorfman slipped her a note in seventh grade: *You really need to think about hair removal products.*

I have to go, she says. SriSri needs me.

It's not as if, as *if*, she ever wanted to be some kind of *celebrity*. She tells herself that, out in the parking lot, connecting SriSri's battery pack and maneuvering it out of the van and down the skids. The thing she likes about those extra .23 ounces of lithium is the crispness of the handling, the way it rolls its radius. It's still a glorified erector set. Those are the rules. Not a hipster. But among her people: a cool nerd. A Nipster. That's a real thing. There's a Tumblr. It means, you don't wear the lime-green competition T-shirt with all the little sponsor logos on the back. A little angle in her bob and the shaved bit at the back, the black studs at the top of the ear. She knows how the little boys stare. And they're all little boys. Even the advisors. Especially the advisors.

Come on, Lyle hollers. He's stepped outside for a quick vape. You're going to miss pre-meet.

Like I give a damn about pre-meet.

Stop avoiding her.

How is she supposed to preserve her cool and still admit the truth, that it's exactly the opposite? A girl like that just makes me want to quit the rodeo. So she says, you didn't tell me she was *hot*, Lyle. You left out that crucial FYI.

Those things are all so subjective.

No, she says, they're really not. But it's okay, Lyle. I'm good with it. I'm not jealous. I'm *inspired.*

What the L does that mean?

I'll let you know when I find out.

The action all happens afterward: Rachel knows that. She stands where Lyle positioned her. After the awards are distributed, the sweaty palms wiped, tears shed, parents dispersed, sent on errands, dispatched to other pickups. The gym floor is almost empty, the remaining contestants *just fooling around*. Keerthana has her eye on this sleek little number from Summit. Fresh gears. Driver a twerpy tween, his cheeks glossy with proto-acne, in a Princess Mononoke T-shirt. She guides SriSri around its rear couplings and rubs a tentative probe up against its release arm. Mononoke stands alert, not ten feet down the bleachers, but pretending not to be. Alone. A hot target. His unit does a little double-roll, a little booty shake. Ooh, that's good, Lyle says, next to her. She ignores him. Bring it closer, he says, taking out his phone. You know my zoom's broken.

Then use mine.

You are *so bad* about clouding stuff.

Hold tight, she says, little Patel, this one is ribbed for pleasure. She thumbs the guide wheel into ADV setting, and whistles *Eine Kleine Nachtmusik* between her teeth.

Can I watch you? Rachel asks.

Just don't make it look like watching.

Rachel turns around and watches on her phone screen. Taking the world's longest selfie.

Bingo, Keerthana says. The fix is in. Watch that probe. SriSri tilts the unit over and gives it a solid thrust so hard its central screws creak and a set of Stage One lights comes loose and flaps around like a white flag.

It's like animals, Rachel says. Only not like animals.

It's really not like anything else, she says, turning inexplicably red-faced. It's its own thing. We don't use analogies, to, like, try to *justify* it. See what I mean?

I see exactly what you mean.

I don't think you do, she says. I mean, just don't assume you do. You're not machine-identified.

Oh shit. Is that a thing?

You're not writing this down, are you?

Do I look like I'm writing it down?

Mentally you do.

I'm just curious.

No such thing, Keerthana says. We don't allow it.

But she lets her keep watching anyway. Because Lyle wants it. And that makes it kind of hot. Like desire itself is looking over her shoulder, not yet quite sure what it wants. Just that it wants. There's no arguing with it.

These competitions, Lyle tells Rachel, later at Chan's, they're just so infantile, it's such lowest-common-denominator stuff. *Make the robot drop the ring in the basket. Make the robot climb a ramp.* I mean, yes, from an engineering point of view, it's not that it's not *complicated.* But what the fuck, man? Lots of things in this world are complicated and not worth doing. He gurgles Diet Pepsi through a straw. That's where it came from, he says, that's how it all began. Boredom and misdirected lust, the alchemy of so many great inventions. There's the events, the competitions, the scores, the trophies. And then afterward –

Rumor has it that the first RealRobotSexLive ever was at Massapequa High back in '08, '09, another generation back, an eon in adolescent time, when some girl, @IamKwon, strictly small potatoes, a Regional Silver, took a selfie with her Rover, an awkward spread-eagle with the grip in a sensitive place, pale flesh and razor rash and all, and some genius thought it would be better for all concerned to take the girl out of the picture altogether. Considering the major felony implications and all. In the beginning they played with latex and modeling clay and inflatable dolls ordered online, and that was funny, it YouTubed in the mid-fives, but then, nextGen, someone thought, robot sex isn't human sex, let's see metal-on-metal action! And that's when things really took off.

RealRobotSexLive: blocked in every school in the Tri-State, denounced at PTOs, featured on *Wired. I mean,* wrote the reporter, *strictly you could say it doesn't look like sex. Which raises the question: if these teenagers are turned on by this, what do* they *think sex is, anyway?*

Keerthana hangs back, picks the chilis out of her General Tso's. Watching Lyle as he holds forth. A bit of scallion clings to his bottom lip and Rachel reaches out with the napkin. It's good for him; he needs this. She should take a discreet shot and text it to Karen. They have a good but fucked-up relationship, she and Lyle's mom: especially since the divorce. Karen has never been shy in saying Keerthana is the best thing that's ever happened to him. She uses words like *lifeline* and *survival mechanism* and *eroto-therapeutic*. She's offered to buy Keerthana a car and send them to a couples resort in Cancun. Dr and Dr Obeysekere hate her almost as much as they love Lyle. But they do love him. He's just eccentric enough to be a great disrupter, her dad actually said, in front of her, barely looking up from his iPad sudoku, but he has the social skills to go out and capitalize. He could be the Black Swan of high-school boyfriends.

And none of them, none of these dear parents, otherwise wise to the ways of the teenage world, have any idea about RRSL, about the domains and the PayPal transfers and the money Keerthana and Lyle have stashed in Bitcoin and aliased bank accounts; about the sub-Reddits devoted to them; the invitations to Adult Video conventions and Comic-Con panels; the RRSL tattoos some guy does in Idaho, which Lyle wants to lawyer up and C&D.

I want you to come over to my place and listen to some records, Rachel says. And then they do. It happens just this way. Night is falling over Essex County and the house crouches back from the street, behind bushes that remind Keerthana of boulders. No one else seems to be home. They shuck their shoes at the door, and descend through an actual sunken living room with a white carpet. Where are your parents, Keerthana wants to know.

Out.

After a while, Lyle says, when they're comfortably ensconced, all three of them, draped across the futon with strategic parts touching, after a while I started to realize that Mom couldn't really let go of my diagnosis, and who can blame her? She stopped working, stopped lawyering for ten years to take care of me. Endless credit. But when it turned out, I mean when *I* turned out, when I turned the corner, got mainstreamed – there wasn't much left for her to do. Other than my laundry. So that was splitsville for them. She has purpose now, though. You wouldn't believe what it takes to succeed in the blow-drying business.

I'm telling you, Rachel says, these towns are nothing but petri dishes, and we're nothing but flowers of exotic mold. Endlessly customized achievement modules. We're the event horizon of commodified childhood.

True, Keerthana says. True, to a point. Though remember you're talking to people who make money selling robot porn. We're not exactly making the Maplewood High home page.

That's my point, she says, lighting another clove cigarette and propping her feet up on a Hegel-shaped pillow. You've done technology. I'm asking you to think about what lies *beyond* technology, like, what lies outside the grasp of a lab-based solution. And believe me I'm not talking about *art*. Art is for babies.

After a few moments, Lyle's thinking, an interpersonal silence takes on the quality of negative space, shaped by the non-moving parts of the interlocutors. He can taste the cloves.

He texts Keerthana, *is she trying to get us to sell drugs or what?*
*Or what is the part I'm worried about?*

I'm talking about radical sufficiency, Rachel says, the idea that the world is enough just as it is, that we don't need anything extra. We don't need to compete. We don't need to have a platform anymore. Or a brand. We've proven we can do that.

*We've* proven we can do that, Keerthana says. Just to be clear.

Well – she gestures at what must be a desk, under piles of cloth-bound books and LPs, at a silver sliver of a laptop perched precariously atop *Freud: The Mind of the Moralist*. If I weren't so relaxed I would get up and show you.

Show us what?

Ingénue, she says lightly, squinting with her eyes closed, as if imagining a sunny day in a dream. Ingenue.com. That was me. *Was* me, mind you –

Son of a bitch, Lyle says. You're so kidding.

So not kidding.

But no one ever found out who –

I was good at covering my tracks.

*Sold in the low seven figures,* Keerthana reads off her phone.

People loved it, Rachel says, still with the eyes closed. Something about the voice. I never wondered why. Just took the endorsements and kept switching VPNs. It was hard staying one step ahead of the bots and the Moldovans and the 4chan geeks trying to doxx me every other day. Finally it was either staff up or get out.

Tell me about it, Lyle says.

My point is: what's next? Rachel says.

For the entrepreneur who's done it all by seventeen.

You should do a TED talk.

You can get the fuck out, Rachel says, so help me. Say those initials again. I dare you.

Keerthana gets up and changes the record to *Hatful of Hollow.*

I'll tell you a secret, Rachel says. Are you ready for this? I'm an emancipated minor. My parents don't live with me most of the year. They live in Pasadena. I have them on salary. They show up for parent-teacher conferences, a few events here and there. The general understanding is that they travel *a lot* for work. The house is still in their name for tax reasons. But it's just me. Basically, financially, I peaked way early. You guys know what I mean. But I'm starting to think about my well-being over the long term, and I'm getting concerned.

I can't imagine why.

I want to get them to come back, she says. I've got six months left of high school. I want to, like, *have meals together.* I want them to give me a curfew. I'll stop using Uber and buy one of those sweet little starter cars. I want them to teach me some important life lessons. I want to *go to prom.* This is what I'm talking about. Radical sufficiency. I want to go totally normcore and see what it feels like. *De-accelerate.* I'm going to tell people I'm taking a gap year and considering my options.

Instead of what? Keerthana wants to know.

Instead of going to Stanford. She blows a cloud of smoke at the ceiling. They have this super-secret program for teen CEOs. I was admitted two years ago. Prepaid. Their lawyers wanted some kind of IP agreement but we nipped *that* nonsense in the bud. The understanding is that I'll, like, buy them a new climbing wall or endow a stem-cell line. But I'm on the verge of ditching the whole thing. Look at us. All we've done in life is chase things. All we are is a trajectory. I want to, like, *sit in a field* and do nothing for a year. While I still have my healthy self. And this amazing skin. I will never look better than this naked. I want to *enjoy my body*. I might even have a baby. I mean, why the hell not? I'm so elastic and fertile. And so are you, she says, looking directly at Keerthana. You're the only people I can admit this to.

Because we've been there, Lyle says.

You *are* there. I think this should be, like, a *movement*. A secret movement. A watchword. No hashtags, no URLs. No coverage. No PR. Just human beings and their human bodies. All face-to-face, skin-to-skin. When the apocalpyse comes this is all we'll have left anyway. We need to relearn what it means to be *here*.

*Here,* Lyle says, as if he's weighing the word for its specific gravity.

I know. It's a weird concept.

It must have really been something, Lyle says, what high school was like before the internet. He's driving K to school with one arm out the window, surfing the air with his left arm. When you didn't know what everyone else was *thinking* all the time. I don't really understand it. I guess there was the radio. And, like, *three* TV channels. It was sort of like North Korea with commercials. Also, if you wanted to make money you had to leave the house.

K puts a hand on his thigh.

Careful, he says, that circuitry makes it hard to drive.

I'm thinking maybe she's right, and we should drop it. Just drop out. No more robotics. For our own good.

Once the semester's over.

No, I mean right now.

My GPA can't absorb that, he says, feeling a pinprick of panic.

I mean, fuck it, maybe we don't *need* to go.

We're not quite in her tax bracket, Keer.

The thing is, she says, I think we can make money when we need to. I'm actually not worried about it. The thing is, I have a spectacular ass. I don't want to miss it when it's gone. I've never had a rim job from a human being.

Don't say things like that, he says, making a weird face, a baffled grimace. Don't *quote* her. It's gross.

I'm trying to be gross, she says. Admit it, Lyle, We could take this whole thing public, we could make sex robots. *Real* sex robots, not those lame fleshlight things they sell on Pornhub.

We swore we would never, ever, ever.

We swore a lot of things. I'm just wondering: do we ever really need to cross into the legit world? I mean, look at Rachel.

Your very own manic pixie dream girl.

She is *not*.

She's straight out of central casting.

That's an insult, Keerthana says, a misogynist insult, but that's okay, I'm just going to have to put it aside, because it's not really what we're talking about. Or maybe it is. I'm talking about the next level of fulfillment, of self-actualization, and maybe you don't want to go there with me. Because you're too stuck. I mean, look at me. Look at the struggles. Et cetera. The shit I have to be reminded of. What do *you* have to be reminded of? The samsaric world could actually turn out to be awesome for you. You can always go straight and douchey. I don't have that option.

So that's what this is all about, he says, you really think you've found your guru, don't you? You've had a *spiritual awakening*.

Don't put imaginary air quotes around it.

Because if you want to know something about ordinary life, he says, about actual sufficiency, meaning *that which is sufficient for survival*, assuming there is any such thing in an American context, that anything can ever be enough, you should understand that it involves jobs, and money, and working really fucking hard, like your parents do, and taking every competitive edge you can get, and silently resenting anyone who has a competitive edge you don't, even if it's not PC to say so, even if you understand your feelings of powerlessness and unfulfillment are a market-driven fantasy, and what you're calling *radical sufficiency* is just a way rich people swap one fantasy for another, whether it's *mindfulness* or *living your best life* or –

Shut the fuck up. You're the one who introduced me to her.

I thought she was interesting, he says. And hot. I didn't think she was Pema fucking Chödrön.

You just wanted a three-way.

I wanted a new friend. I like making friends. It's new to me. And you, you just want someone who *gets* you, who isn't so much *work*.

And you just want to, like, be so superior all the time, because you have a photographic memory and read in four languages, when you're just, like, dripping, *lactating* white privilege all over yourself.

Even for you that's a bizarre image, Keerthana. Think about it for a second.

I'm done thinking, she says. I'm just going to say and do whatever the fuck I feel like doing.

Finally, he says, finally! Keerthana Obeysekere, teenage rebel. My work here is done.

In study hall, third period, in her usual library carrel – earbuds in, rocking someone's YouTube playlist simply titled 'Loud', which plays Mahler symphonies slowed down to 5/6 bpm, crunk-style – she idly clicks on a folder marked 'Extinct', and without quite knowing why, opens a six-slide PowerPoint she started last April, 'Robot Sex: A Prosthetic Manifesto'.

*Promiscuity is necessary but also boring + gross. (And of course potentially dangerous.)*

*Marshall McLuhan=media as extensions of man, but extensions of man=erogenous zones, explanation for online porn, but younger generation doesn't believe in screen-genital exchange, i.e. sweaty pathetic obese guy jerking off to Reddit fapfest into Kleenex*

*Robot/genital barrier is like blood/brain barrier*

*Do people actually orgasm watching machines (I do. Not ashamed) Do boys. Are robots foreplay but not orgasm. Is orgasm necessary. Anatomical compromises.*

*Robots invested with agency, feelings, ambiguous gestures*

*Does feeling end when session ends/emotional dynamics of 'switching off'*

*? How can I get smone to pay me to research this*

You're working too hard, Rachel says next to her.

You didn't actually just say that.

I just wanted to know how it felt to say it.

As if there was any such thing.

But there *is*, Rachel says. That's what I've been trying to tell you.

You don't understand how it feels, she says. You don't know how badly I've needed someone to tell me that. You're perfect. You probably don't exist. No one is ever going to tell you that *you come off as too white on your college applications* and make you feel like shit because you hate field hockey. Another fucking Indian girl with straight APs, robotics, lab internships and oboe.

You're Sri Lankan, Rachel says, to begin with, and you need to understand the ends part of this ends versus means equation.

I have no idea what that means.

Put your hand up my skirt is what it means.

See, this is everything I'm arguing against.

Your resistance isn't the problem. You're just resisting the wrong things. The truly achieved person is a virtuoso of all things, even normalcy. Especially normalcy. We have to reverse-engineer our genius so that we can appreciate the simple things, like me going down on you in the supply closet.

And she thinks, in her heart of hearts, *I don't want an achieved person, I want an achieved robot.*

Which supply closet?

That one.

Lyle's going to be upset.

Lyle is free to come strolling in any time he likes.

He has gym, actually. Couldn't figure out a way to get out of it.

No, you see, he *should* have gym. He needs gym. He needs to remember he has a body.

And nobody is going to know about any of this, Keerthana says. No phones, right? No platforms. This is all analog. Not in English or any other language. Not on WeChat. Not on the darknet. I feel like I have to get you to sign a form.

I swear it's like fucking 1986 or something, Rachel says, and nobody knows who we are.

S he's beginning to write, and it feels weird. Her laptop, covered in stickers from R-Comps, plus bands Lyle loves, like God Bullies and Pitchshifter, has always functioned as a, well, as a machine. Not a well of feelings, not a listening ear, the way she imagines it must be for creatives and empaths. She has never in her life tried to describe an emotional state. Or for that matter even really *experience* an emotional state, rather than translate it into an assembly. All her text files are papers for English class or lab reports.

*The first time I experienced real terror in life,* she writes, *was in fifth grade, when I had Mrs Fotheringill, the strictest teacher ever, and I realized I'd lost a whole page of instructions for my poster on the digestive tract. It was while we were driving to school. I found it crumpled at the bottom of my backpack. There was nothing I could do, and I was going to get an F.*

It's so slow. The pace of it. The idea that you have to finish every sentence. *I don't know if it's worth it*, she texts Rachel.

*Stare at a plant for a while. Any plant. A ficus tree. They grow slowly, too*
*You're comparing me to a ficus*
*Now who's being slow*

Her laptop pings: Lyle messaging her through World of Warcraft. That's their hotline, the way of getting through when you can't get through. *Danger Danger*, he says.

*RADICAL SUFFICIENCY: The Post-Millenial's Guide to Life*
*by Rachel Priestly*
*Representation: Susan Greenglass Literary, susan@sgl.com*
*Publicity: Samantha Goss, OnlyConnect Communications,*
*goss@onlyconnect.com*

*Where did you get this,* she whispers him back.
*She left it open overnight, I just spidered it and took a screenshot*
*Son of a bitch she sold us out*
*You've been waiting all your life to say that*
She thumbs through the emoji menu, not knowing how to respond.
*I mean what did you expect*
*I expected the world to offer up some actual new ideas once in a while*
*Not this world.*
*???*
*They don't call it a bedroom community for nothing*
*I feel like I'm texting with the delphic oracle*
*It's time for us to blow this petri dish*
*YOU MET HER,* she says. *YOU LET HER IN.*
*I'll make it up to you somehow*
*It doesn't work that way. I feel damaged*
*Meet me in your driveway I'll be there in five*
*Also you're not damaged you're perfect*

I poured out my life to her, she says to Lyle. In his car again. In her driveway again. I believed I had a life to pour out. I felt like a character in a YA novel. I believed in romance.

Don't sell yourself short.

I believed in something that can't be engineered.

That's called charisma. Which basically amounts to the ability to fuck people over without them noticing. Until later.

I believed – she wants to say it without knowing exactly what to say. Around her, she says, I started believing in *scenes*, she says, like time can be divided into meaningful increments, edited into pithy encounters, and the rest of it conveniently discarded.

Some people, he says wearily, are always ready for their close-up. Life organizes itself around them that way. They arrive in life pre-profiled by, I don't know, *Vogue*?

We're like that too.

We are not.

We are too.

We are not.

Every part of my life, she says, folds together like a takeout box, rigid, transportable and containing nothing. Even us. *What I Learned from My Autistic Friend.*

Who's not actually autistic.

MIT doesn't fact-check admissions essays.

What would it mean to blow the whole thing up, is what I want to know, she says.

That's the wrong question, he says.

What makes you the authority on everything.

Because I have the keys, he says, flipping screens on his phone. Your parents gave it to me, you know. To prep it for the big day.

The XS-7. In the picture it crouches on a beach, clearly not wanting to be there, big as a coffee table and ugly as a giant beetle. Look at those rotors, hand-machined in Leipzig. It can fly six miles on a single charge. It has a night-vision camera, a VR headset, a speaker up to six decibels, a universal mount heavy enough to hold a firearm classed up through .225, though who would want that. It baffles her, it's always baffled her, this toddler-sized need to turn a machine into a gun, as if a machine wasn't a prosthetic self, capable of almost every other thing.

You know I'm just going to scare her, she says. I'm just going to send a message.

This conversation never happened.

Then just drop it off.

And ruin the surprise.

I don't like surprises, she says. I like identifiable outcomes. My life is a controlled explosion.

*Your life,* Lyle says, grinning. That is so Claire Danes. You love being the protagonist. Don't you.

As much as you love being my wise-beyond-your-years love interest/enabler/sidekick.

Then I should be more tragic, he says, and be suicidal, or have a heart condition, or be a vampire. As a bottomless well of attachment-object feelings I just don't stack up. I mean, I have a bottom.

I wish we were a movie, she says, and it was 1991, and we could go to Blockbuster and rent ourselves. On one of those big ugly tapes. I wish you could take me home like a useless knobby piece of plastic. And then keep me, and be stuck paying late fees for the rest of your life. Until Blockbuster goes bankrupt, and the last VHS player on Earth stops working, and I'm part of the giant trash island in the middle of the Pacific.

There's a metaphor in there somewhere, he says, but I can't quite find it.

Give me the controller, she says. Is that hard to follow?

And then this part really is like a movie of a movie of a movie. She's hovering outside Rachel's window, and Rachel is wearing some kind of getup out of *Desperately Seeking Susan,* a plaid kilt, fishnets, black lace fingerless gloves, and conducting an interview on Skype or something, speaking into the silver laptop's open clamshell, her head in the mouth of the crocodile that has swallowed us all. On a screen watching someone else on a screen through another screen, because what else is a window from the outside at night, with lights and people behind it. Keerthana thinks, *this is just a metaphor*. She means to tap the glass but she's forgotten to attach the XS-7's rubber bumpers on the upper arms, and she's miscalculated the trajectory of a forty-pound miniature German military helicopter against the surface tension of an ordinary Andersen window, which spiderwebs and disappears silently, because she hasn't taken the input mic off mute, and then she does, in time to hear Rachel scream. Papers and paperback books and all kinds of insubstant objects are flying around the room, and probably bits of glass as well.

It's okay, she says, and hears the reverb of her own voice in this very small enclosed space, and turns herself down. It's me, Rachel. I'm sorry. I fucked that up.

*Keerthana.*

She's never heard her name like that. It gives her a surge of feeling. It's as if she has never been alone with anyone. Rachel crouches fetally on the carpet with a cut under her left eye, like a hapless grown-up would. Stand up, she tells her, her voice booming through the speaker. Actually, cancel that. Lie down. Lie down on your bed.

Why the fuck should I do that?

It's easier for me to see you. And not hurt you. I can just, you know, *hover*. We can have a conversation.

I'm not having a conversation with a fucking drone.

I'm not a drone.

The light goes out with a discreet *ping*; she must have rotored the fixture right off. Through the headphones it's just the rush and whoosh of wind, but frankly, she gets it, anyone would be terrified. Look, she says, I'm going to land, and does, using the stab lock, right on the bedspread. Now everything goes silent. See, she says, no hard feelings. Now it's just me. Her voice reverbs in the room like a middle-school Wizard of Oz, though she can't tell how much of that is the mic hearing itself.

I'm calling the cops.

I just want to say that I get it. These problems are so much bigger than us. You just can't help whoring out your subjectivity to the highest bidder, and I can't help that I want you to caress me and tell me that this is what I am, that I'm a beautiful machine.

You're a beautiful machine.

No, you have to *mean* it.

Don't ever call me a whore. You're one step away from getting stuck in one of those trailers in Nevada, murdering children in Yemen.

We got those offers last year, she says. All the top robotics kids do. So help me if I ever shoot a gun in my life. Even in *Halo*. Even in a dream. I just won't do it. There's just more to life. Like, *all* of life, frankly. That's what this is, she says, saying and thinking it for the first time, making new life.

You're sick.

I am, and you still want me. Put your fingers on the curved thing on the left side.

What is that, a handle?

Never mind what it is. Touch it.

You're going to cut off my arm. Or shock me, or something.

Why the hell would I do that?

Are you sure this is okay?

For Christ's sake, she says. *Touch* it.

You can't feel it, Rachel says, scooting closer, making an *Eeewww* face. Don't pretend this is some kind of higher-level VR. You think you've made the first drone sexbot. I'd like to see your IP lawyer explain that. I have a contact in Dongguan who could get me a prototype in three weeks. Where's your non-disclosure form, Keerthana?

Now I know I'm turning you on.

Fine, Rachel says. There. Is that what you want?

And for a moment neither of them say anything.

B ut she was missing Lyle the whole time. The story returns to the past tense, as it has to, and becomes a cautionary tale. There is such a thing as joy, she was thinking, as Rachel kissed her steering arm, wrapped her tongue around the directional shaft. There is such a thing as naive joy, the thrill of finding out what our bodies are for. You may only ever find one person who wants it the way you want it. The person who knows never, ever, to use the word *robot*. She was thinking a new theory of the world: there are two kinds of people, the solids and the liquids, those who care about bodies for their own sake, and those who always want to turn a body into something else: pixels, digits. As she rotated out of the shattered window and up into the heavy, humid night over Essex County, and its liquid contours, its geography of I-don't-give-a-shit, and flicked on her GPS and entered his address, she thought, I can't wait for college. I want to turn myself into a problem that can't be solved. ∎

'We sat on the ground before our raised bone-faces, sang to them as they gleamed moonlit into the darkness. We sang of death, and it felt true.'

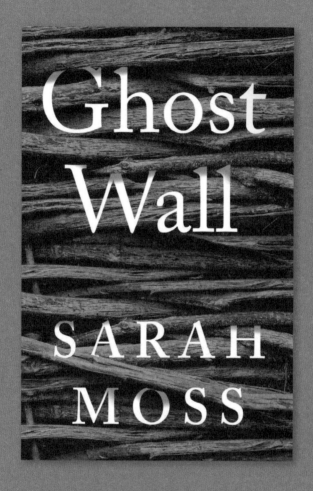

'Like nothing I have read before; its creepy atmosphere has stayed with me all summer... Moss combines exquisite nature writing, original characters and a cracking thriller plot to make a wonderful literary curiosity' – *The Times*

OUT NOW IN HARDBACK

GRANTA

# Jana Prikryl

## Bob

*i.m. Robert Silvers (1929–2017)*

I think he found relief,
a kind of carnival, only in the tunnels

he forced, as with his body, in the replies
to questions he'd shipped by overnight.

This also explains why he swam laps.
Master of the deferential, intricate

refusal, lifetime ban on anyone
once deemed faulty, whetting his wrath

on the failure to secure
a seat on the aisle for that night.

And then he says yes,
yes, with a naughty smile

accepting the lesser thing
and raving about it

because when he accepts it
it's different.

Rubs out the sub's query
and rewrites it in his hand, his pencil.

Pencils sharpened a fistful
at a time by some sub-sub.

Walks in and quietly, melodically
says to himself

Any little news or calls or things
today or no one gives a fuck?

He bares his teeth, enunciates, and bugs his eyes
to be charming—You're all moving manuscripts

around my desk and I feel like Ingrid Bergman
in that film, what was it?

*Gaslight*!—and because he's a tyrant
I dry my eyes while laughing.

It's an uncomfortable fact (for
whom?) that those who went to certain schools

sooner found ways to resist him
or stop resisting.

JANA PRIKRYL

The time it took me to see I'd never bring him
round to my view of metaphor's telling.

And then I proceeded
to pledge thirty more years to his archive.

Please understand
in tribute to him

I mean that literally.
When every man of letters was toppling

I thought this gives him
never dreaming of that kind of thing

yet another eccentricity.
Did he have material of his own, I wondered

early on, as if originality were invention, as if it weren't
some amalgam of knowledge and morality

applied to matters of substance, which among friends
we call taste.

Not that that excused my blinking
when he cut those in his vicinity:

he cut out small talk
not hearing it, convincingly deaf to its nothing,

although I suspected
he took in every word and filed it.

Romanticism too he consumed in its totality
knowing just what it was he demolished

as all the modernists did.
It being no accident his seeing what was coming

before going, did he regret his own
undoing any little thing?

Listen, he'd start
when driven once again

to issue a rebuke,
listen, I'd stiffen,

listen—

ILSE D'HOLLANDER
*Untitled*, 1996
© The Estate of Ilse D'Hollander, courtesy of the Estate of Ilse D'Hollander and Sean Kelly Gallery, New York

# ARDOR (AGHAST)

## *Anne Carson*

Who did you think they were, these young men?
Spoilsports.
Sorry?
Students.
Dressed like this?
Students are rough.
Why so many in the cafeteria?
Breakfast.
So early?
Early lecture.
On?
*Ulysses.*
Please?
On how it troubled Joyce that English has no word to distinguish *Frau*
from *Weib.*
*Frau?*
*Frau* the social feminine, *Weib* the sexual feminine.
Sexual?
Ask James Joyce not me.
We begin again. When did it appear that things are not as usual in the
cafeteria?

When they got out the ice picks.
No ice in the cafeteria?
Not at breakfast.
They spoke to you anything these young men getting out their ice picks?
Silent guys.
A translation of *Weib* could be what?
Wench.
Wench?
Bit antiquated but yes.
Young men on the hunt for a wench?
Well. Not exactly.
Why not exactly?

The investigator's small round eyeglasses gleam at her. She pauses. In the dorm room last night she'd found a copy of *The Wind in the Willows* in English. She thinks of quoting a line or two now. Just then an adjutant runs in with some papers in a folder. The investigator turns, takes the folder, waves her to the door. We resume later, he says.

~

Saturday a week ago she'd gone to six a.m. bike class at the gym. The room was cool and dark. People still blurred from sleep. She'd found a bike in the back corner, moved the bike next to it slightly further away, hoisted the handlebars to position 6.5, pushed the saddle to position 7, placed the seat post pin in the hole between 'H' and 'I'. The others were joking about carbs and watts and a heat wave expected later in the week. By then I will have left Frankfurt for Zurich, sixty degrees and rainy, she smiled to herself. Not furtive in the sense criminal but still, once you start keeping your hands under the table, who knows.

Later, looking back, the cool dark of that room, its ordinary peace, its rows of knees and whir of pedals, seem another planet. When the investigator asks her, Who did you think they were, these young men, when they came in? she will answer, Spoilsports, and he will change his tone; she is an odd one, you learn to be careful of odd ones. But this comes later, after Frankfurt, after the Danube, after jet lag and several passport controls and two hotel rooms and three lectures followed by Q&A and all the while Valerie brooding on her haemorrhoids. The day in question they wake in the town of Visp. Outside the window are Alps. Alps, she decides, are not describable. They are not *like* anything. They just *are*. Wow, says Valerie. Light floods the hotel room (actually a college dorm) but the cafeteria where they find breakfast is down some old stone stairs to the basement, low and dark. The contrast puts her in mind of the bike class. Valerie is lowering herself gingerly into a chair by a table at the wall. Get me some muesli. And a banana if you see one, V says. Bananas good for you? she asks. Valerie glares at her. She goes to line up behind some students at the food counter. The trip to Visp by train had been difficult. As they boarded in Zurich Valerie suddenly said, I hate trains. She asked why. Valerie mentioned the shabbily uniformed conductors, the garbage by the tracks and several other things. I'd no idea you felt that way, she said. They settled into silence. Green woods, green foamy rivers flashed by. You check your ticket up? said the conductor in answer to her inelegantly worded question, which was, in essence, What next? What next if we are to survive this?

~

Why did you talk to him?
He talked to me.
You knew him? Previously?
The fetter thing. Was too tight. He said.
Standard restraint.
Put fetters on people they're going to have an opinion about that.

Your talk was of wind conditions, why?

No, it's a book.

I saw no book.

Children's book.

Children? Whose children? He uses children?

No he wants to learn English. There's a book. I've read it too. As a child.

So you did know him. Previously.

I knew someone *like* him. Years ago. Never mind.

You joke but these are dangerous people. I know they are guilty, this is not my question. Where did you know him previously?

Something weird with his eyes, did you see? Blinking, looking down.

You found his murderous puberty attractive.

Probably.

When did this attraction begin? Do you rekindle now a former ardor?

'Ardor'. That's a word I never use. Another one is 'aghast'.

These jokes are your defense.

I'm sorry, yes. Let's go back.

Why not be honest.

Honest. Okay. When I was forty I had an affair with a seventeen-year-old, it was (you know) a total trainwreck, years ago, we hardly talk anymore, once in a while he phones, he's given up alcohol and drugs, goes to meetings where everyone acknowledges a higher power, So now you don't have to pretend to be good yourself, I said and he said, Typical remark by you, then he told me all excited about a rainbow he could see from his kitchen window lying flat across the driveway and I reminded him of the rainbow we saw that night at Molly's and he didn't recall it. The night we went to the stock-car races, I said and he said, Oh yes. Anyhow, Captain, I'm boring you, the thing is, when that kid came into the cafeteria I thought it was him. Him twenty years back. It looked just like him. It stabbed my heart.

The urgings of the heart can be cruel.

You really should read *The Wind in the Willows*.

Narratives hold little interest for me. What I need to establish today is that you are a recruiter for the revolutionary cell in question, or you

are not, this I tell you plainly. There will be further questions. Please do not abandon the hotel. And so to speak, I am not a Captain. You may call me Clair.
Is that your name?
More or less.

~

She swam in her dreams. Her other desire is a hotel room with a reasonable reading light somewhere near the bed. Her third desire is to be able to come up with something (anything) to say at academic dinners. She is often seated beside some radiant woman's elder husband, wild at the eyebrows, who shoots marbles in among the others' remarks and makes her laugh. During dessert she sits thinking of the long-ago affair with the person much younger, who may or may not have been homosexual, he was so patient; more than patient; watching him put on his coat and arrange his scarf she'd sometimes thought he was insane, or she was. Yet he was often in a rage, or she was. In the middle of the night she hears a [blackbird]. Decides it was a blackbird. Considers waking up Valerie then thinks not. She's been a visiting scholar in various places for a long time, too long. Growing gradually unsure she could 'teach' anyone anything, she'd lowered the bar to 'inspire' and now is content with just showing up. Just not making bestial sounds by mistake. A bit bestial themselves, the young, a bit prehistoric, they tolerate her off-colour intervals. The panting attacks come only on Friday; she hasn't taught on Fridays for years. You are now free to go, she'd said to the younger person who may or may not have been homosexual, at their final meeting. They were walking somewhere autumnal, faint mist on the path. He'd stopped to tie his shoe. She'd contained her exasperation.

~

So, Clair. What kind of name is Clair?

Approximate.

Can you –

We continue where we left off. You spoke to him a second time. And he said what?

Okay wait. Getting out my notes.

You took notes?

No. Yes. After. Basically he said he met this man called K who blah-blah-blah opened his eyes. Tender age of thirteen. Electrifying. Detroit was a test format. They were kids, no particular boundaries, experiments happened, it was four on the floor.

Slower please?

He had his ear to four on the floor when K moved it up a few gadgets, said, Time for the midnight mojo tour. First way he heard records blended on the beat. K put his rubber mask on – who believes this? a guy from nowhere, nobody, nobody dancing then K comes in, slaps down a 45 and the floor fills up like it's covered with thousand-dollar bills.

You describe a musical indoctrination?

Well, he said it was K's reggae phase, early analogue days, they started trying to replicate sounds they liked. Their mothers were away or sleeping, everything happened at once. He said something about roughhousing another DJ off to get your chance but I couldn't follow it. Then he said, Want any respect in this community, pretend to have enemies, warfarce. They didn't even know who we were.

Weaponizing?

Sort of. Making stuff in his bedroom. K had all this gear like a spaceship. Nobody could watch K work, you'd just see the end product.

Messiah complex?

Hmmm.

Radical utopian?

I don't think so. Maybe. They were looking at the world a different way, for sure. In those days, you wanted to hear a certain record you had to wait by the radio two days till it came on. They would do that. It wasn't about taking it to the next level. It was worship. K'd be

drunk, swinging on the microphone, saying, Step on this mat you can be at large in the universe.
Power mad.
Or boys in love. Of course it ended badly. He didn't elaborate on this. The old praise and blame issues, I imagine. Revenue share. He said K said to him, I taught you what *you* know, I never taught you what *I* know.
Can piracy be avoided? No. Can it be starved? Yes.
Boys too.
In your opinion none of this has power. That opinion is wrong.
I see you think so.
The great storm gathers what appears divided. Ancient text.

She wanted to mention *The Wind in the Willows*, ancient text, but his phone rang and he was gathering his papers and the moment passed. I'll send him a postcard after I get home, she thought. Find a quote. That part about unpacking the basket, however that goes.

~

What did you do with his body?
Please sit.
You look different.
We didn't. I didn't. Ah.
You interrogated him?
Not formally. Just talk. To win such thing as money I have nowhere, to win such people as kindness I have none. He says. Thinking makes me panic. There he stops. He must go back into the game. Dogs.
What game?
Yes what game.
And what dogs?
A dog is mean one way, silent another, he says.
I'm lost.
He names the chess problem set by a tenth-century Sufi. Unsolved.

Until 1980.
Cool. Or stupid. I don't know. So you play chess.
Yes.
And you saw a way to understand him.
Not in the least.
Yet he understood you.
Say anything you like just spell my name right. I quote.
Bit of a hustler.
Hmm.
People when they're young, people in their revolutionary phase, it's
never clear –
You depart soon?
Tomorrow.
There will be snow.
Is that a problem?
Not usually.
No one can solve another's desperation.
He was so small, on the slab.
Yes.
Weightless, a teacup.
Can I write to you?
No.
What time was it when he.
Four a.m.
I woke as if swept aside by.
Estimated time only.
By something.
On leaving you will close both doors. Thank you. ■

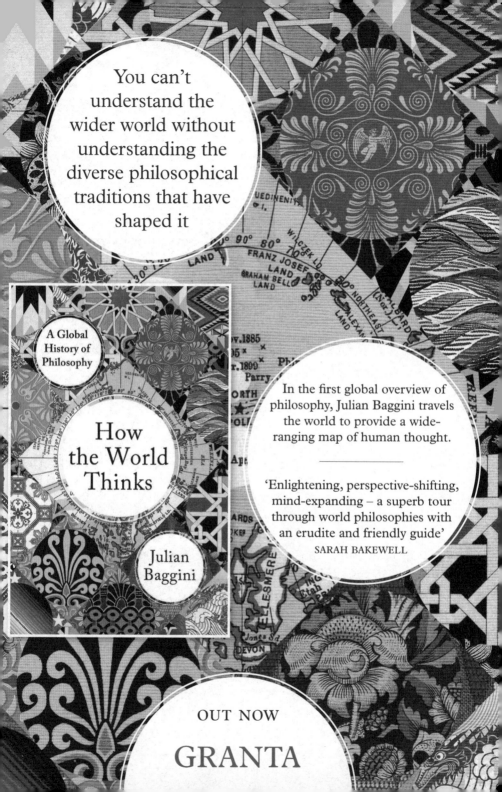

You can't understand the wider world without understanding the diverse philosophical traditions that have shaped it

A Global History of Philosophy

How the World Thinks

Julian Baggini

In the first global overview of philosophy, Julian Baggini travels the world to provide a wide-ranging map of human thought.

'Enlightening, perspective-shifting, mind-expanding – a superb tour through world philosophies with an erudite and friendly guide'
SARAH BAKEWELL

OUT NOW

GRANTA

# CONTRIBUTORS

**André Aciman** is Distinguished Professor of Comparative Literature at the Graduate Center, CUNY. He is the author of the memoir *Out of Egypt* and four novels: *Call Me by Your Name, Eight White Nights, Harvard Square* and *Enigma Variations*. He is currently working on a novel tentatively titled *Youth* and a collection of essays, *Homo Irrealis*.

**Ahmet Altan** is a Turkish novelist and political columnist. In the purge following the failed coup in July 2016, Altan was sent to prison pending trial for giving 'subliminal messages' in support of the coup. In February 2018 he was sentenced to life in prison without parole for attempting to overthrow the government. His ten novels, including *Like a Sword Wound* and *Endgame*, have been widely translated.

**Monika Bulaj** is a Polish photojournalist. Her work can be found in *Time, La Repubblica, Corriere della Sera, National Geographic*, the *New York Times* and elsewhere.

**Anne Carson** was born in Canada and teaches Ancient Greek for a living.

**Elizabeth Chandler** has worked with her husband, Robert Chandler, on translations of Alexander Pushkin, Teffi, Andrey Platonov and Vasily Grossman.

**Robert Chandler** translates from the Russian. He is the editor of three Penguin Classics anthologies: of Russian short stories, of Russian magic tales and, with Boris Dralyuk and Irina Mashinski, *The Penguin Book of Russian Poetry*.

**Cortney Lamar Charleston** is the author of *Telepathologies*, selected by D.A. Powell for the 2016 Saturnalia Books Poetry Prize. His poems have appeared in *Poetry, American*

*Poetry Review, New England Review, AGNI, TriQuarterly* and elsewhere. He works as a poetry editor at the *Rumpus*.

**Yasemin Çongar** is co-founder and general director of P24, a non-profit platform for independent journalism in Istanbul. She is also the co-founder of Turkey's online book review K24 and the Istanbul Literature House. An editor, essayist and translator, Çongar is the author of four books in Turkish.

**Bernard Cooper** is an artist and writer whose most recent books are *My Avant-Garde Education* and *The Bill from My Father*. He is the recipient of the 1991 PEN/Hemingway Award and fellowships from the Guggenheim Foundation and the National Endowment for the Arts. His visual art has been exhibited at the Miami Dade College Museum of Art and Design and the Pacific Design Center. www.bernardcooper.net

**Steven Dunn** is the author of two novels, *Potted Meat* and *water & power,* which will be published in the US by Tarpaulin Sky Press and from which 'Yokosuka Blue Line' is taken. Some of his work can be found in *Rigorous, Blink-Ink* and *Best Small Fictions 2018*. He was born and raised in West Virginia.

**Janine di Giovanni** is a Senior Fellow at Yale University's Jackson Institute for Global Affairs, a Professor of Practice in Human Rights and a member of the Council on Foreign Relations.

**Vasily Grossman** (1905–1964) was born in Berdichev, Ukraine. After training as a chemical engineer, he became a famous Soviet war correspondent. 'Stalingrad' is an excerpt from the forthcoming novel of the same title, published by the New York Review of Books in the US and Bodley Head in the UK. *Stalingrad* is a companion piece to his magnum opus, *Life and Fate.*

**Shira Hadad** completed a PhD on the works of S.Y. Agnon at Columbia University before working for eight years as editor of contemporary Hebrew fiction at Keter. She is currently co-writing a television series, *Wisdom of the Crowd*, with Dror Mishani.

**Sheila Heti** is the Canadian author of eight books, including the novels *Ticknor, How Should a Person Be?* and, most recently, *Motherhood.*

**Eugene Lim** is the author of the novels *Fog & Car, The Strangers* and *Dear Cyborgs.* His writing has appeared in *Fence*, the *Believer, Little Star, Dazed*, the *Brooklyn Rail* and elsewhere.

**Sandra Newman**'s novels include *The Country of Ice Cream Star, The Only Good Thing Anyone Has Ever Done* and *Cake.* 'The Heavens' is an extract from a novel of the same title which will be published next year by Grove Atlantic in the US and Granta Books in the UK.

**Maggie O'Farrell** is the author of seven novels, including *Instructions for a Heatwave, This Must Be the Place* and *The Hand That First Held Mine*, winner of the 2010 Costa Novel Award. Her latest book is the memoir *I Am, I Am, I Am: Seventeen Brushes with Death.* She lives in Edinburgh.

**Amos Oz** was born in Jerusalem in 1939. His books include *A Tale of Love and Darkness, Judas, Dear Zealots* and *The Same Sea.* He is the recipient of the 1992 Friedenspreis, the 1998 Israel Prize for literature, the 2005

Goethe Prize, the 2007 Prince of Asturias Award and the 2013 Franz Kafka Prize. In 1997, he was appointed Chevalier of the Légion d'honneur.

**Jana Prikryl** is the author of two books of poetry, *The After Party* and *No Matter*, forthcoming in 2019. Her essays on photography and film have appeared in the *Nation* and the *New York Review of Books*, where she works as a senior editor. She was the 2017–18 Fellow in poetry at the Radcliffe Institute for Advanced Study.

**Maria Reva**'s stories have been published in the *Atlantic*, the *New Quarterly*, the *Journey Prize Stories 29* and *The Best American Short Stories 2017.* In 2018, she won the Writers' Trust of Canada's RBC Bronwen Wallace Award.

**Jess Row** is the author of the novel *Your Face in Mine* and two collections of short stories, *The Train to Lo Wu* and *Nobody Ever Gets Lost.* His first collection of essays, *White Flights: Race, Fiction, and the American Imagination*, will be published in the US next year by Graywolf. In 2007, he was one of *Granta*'s Best of Young American Novelists.

**Sondra Silverston** is a native New Yorker who has lived in Israel since 1970. She has translated works by Amos Oz, Etgar Keret and Eshkol Nevo. Her translation of Amos Oz's *Between Friends* won the 2013 National Jewish Book Award for fiction.

**Inigo Thomas** is on the editorial board of the *London Review of Books*. He is currently writing a book about the art dealer and spy Tomás Harris.